LUCKY THIRTEEN

The Raiford Chronicles #1

Janet Taylor-Perry

ISBN-13: 978-0615884509
ISBN-10: 0615884504

Janet Taylor Perry, *Lucky Thirteen*

Disclaimer

Although initial incidents involving Larkin Sloan are drawn from actual classroom experiences—never stitches—but often taunting, insults, and several times leaving with bruises, all entities in this story are fictional. This is completely a work of vivid imagination.

Dedication

For:

Emily, Olivia, Townes, Logan, Jessica, Adam, John-Tyler, Rachel, Jennifer, Brianna, Darreous, Johnny, Meagan, Trenten, Robbie, Josh, and Barrett—my 6th grade gifted students at Florence Middle School, 2008-2009. You made this year an absolute joy. Always remember that your luck is what you make it. Your life is what you make it. So, go out and make it count.

Acknowledgements

Thanks to Lottie Brent Boggan, my friend, mentor, and editor. Those one-on-one nights where you helped me hone my craft were priceless, as you are, even if you did browbeat me into tempering the dialogue. Lottie is the author of several books: *Mr. Honeycut, Saleta's Secrets, Streams of Mercy, Redemption Ridge,* and *Return to Redemption Ridge,* her work in progress; a frequent contributor to *The Northside Sun Newspaper*; and the editor and compiler of a number of short story anthologies.

Deepest gratitude to Christina Jean Michaels, author of *Epiphany,* and Mark Cole, author of *A Child of Two Worlds,* for walking me through the process of getting this novel out.

A special tribute to my beta readers: Nidia Hernandez, who has read every word of everything I've written, and author of the *Rock Star Chronicles,* works in progress; Charles Brass, author of *The Ux Blood Trilogy (Earth Cell, Witchblood,* and *Witch Warden*—in progress), *A Child of Byne,* a novella in progress, and *Terror Cruise*—even if he did cause me great anxiety and much rewriting—Dirk Baezner, aka Norm d'Plume, author of *Into the Mind of God,* a work in progress, and Maggie Banks, author of *Siege of Jericho,* retitled *Twisted to the Right; The Children of Nineveh; Whispers at the Wall;* and *Fool's Journey,* her work in progress—though she also caused me much anxiety and rewriting.

Many thanks to my TheNextBigWriter.com family, specifically Joss Landry, author of *Mirror Deep*; John DeBoer, aka jack the knife, author of *Get the Picture, The Side Effect, State of Mind,* and a number of works in progress; Ann Everett, author of *Laid Out and Candle Lit, You're Busting My Nuptials,* and several others in progress; Cathy Jones, aka c.e. jones and Lucy Crowe, author of *Sugar Man's Daughter*; Annelie Wendeberg, aka AEKronberg, author of *The Devil's Grin* and *The Fall*; E.

M. (Emily) Havens, aka bimmy, author of *Fate War Alliance*, *Dark Night of the Soul*, and more; Susan Stec, author of *The Grateful Undead Series* (*They're So Vein*, *Blood Sweat and Demon Tears*, and *Gator Baitin'*), *Dead Girls Never Shut Up*, and *Mirror, Mirror*; Jennifer Nissley, aka JElizabeth; Patti Hauge, aka flowingpencil; Leslie Daniels, aka GrayWitch, author of *Stealing Christmas*; Robert Goswitz; Rory Noel Hawk; and lucyinthesky. If I've left anyone out, forgive me.

I owe so much to Ruth Ishee, my aunt, who let me read to her over the phone. I love you lots.

Extreme gratitude goes to Betsy Creekmore for making so much possible and for pointing me toward Lottie Boggan.

Thanks for all your moral support to my Red Dog Writers. You're the best writers' group ever.

Merci beaucoup to Chris Chambers, a former student and talented graphic designer, as evidenced by *Lucky Thirteen's* cover. He can be reached at chris@juroddesigns.com should you wish to solicit his talents.

Last a great big hug and THANK YOU, SWEETHEART, to Mary Catherine Perry, my daughter, who threw the original three chapters of *Lucky Thirteen* across the room and said she would not read another word I wrote if I made Ray the killer. So, I scrapped my first draft and now I have four books in *The Raiford Chronicles*.

Look for the next installment, *Heartless*, planned release February 14, 2014.

Come now, and let us reason together, saith the Lord: though your sins be as scarlet, they shall be as white as snow; though they be red like crimson, they shall be as wool.

Isaiah 1:18

Table of Contents

1
One Bad Day

Larkin Sloan awoke to dank, damp, decayed smell in a dark room. Confused, she tried to get up only to find her wrist shackled to the headboard of an old cast-iron bed.

"Don't hurt yourself, beautiful," a man's voice said from somewhere out of sight.

What? Where? She strained her eyes to see in the gloom.

"It would never do for you to be harmed any more than you already have been. You're supposed to be blemish free, perfect, untarnished. I already made a mistake, and you got hurt. You weren't supposed to get hurt. Latrice will be so mad at me. So, please, don't struggle. I won't hurt you. I promise."

How did I get here? What's going on? Larkin's mind swam with memories of one bad day.

The *drip-drip* of rain on the tin roof acted like a lullaby. Larkin groaned, rolled over, and wished for a moment it were Saturday so she could go back to sleep. Dreams of a faceless dark-haired man had haunted her all night after her date, Brad, dropped her off in a huff following a disagreement. She sighed deeply and opened her eyes. The young teacher hurtled from her bed when she saw the red blinking numbers of her alarm clock. Her foot tangled in the blanket. "Ow!" she cried, landing hard on her knees. "No time to be praying," she muttered, struggling to her feet.

Realizing she didn't know the correct time since the power had gone out during the night, Larkin zipped to the kitchen and snatched her cell phone from where she left it charging to check the time. She noticed a missed call, but the time threw her into frenzy.

"Darn it!"

She threw a Pop Tart into the toaster. Her cat, Cyclops, bumped her ankle. She took half a second to scratch his chin. "Sorry, no milk from my cereal today. I'm late. I've never been late. Love you." The animal purred.

She scooped her pet a cup of dry food and gave him fresh water. Snagging the Pop Tart as it sprang up from the toaster, she choked it down with half a glass of orange juice. She dashed to the bathroom and pulled her auburn hair into a ponytail. "Oh," she complained to her reflection. "No time for a shower or makeup." Larkin was glad she had dark eyes, lashes, and brows. She rationalized she had bathed before her disastrous date the night before, brushed her teeth and scooted to her bedroom.

Larkin snagged a pair of dark chocolate slacks and a bronze silk blouse from the closet. She puffed out air, thinking *I might end up alone if Brad is any example.* The men she dated didn't seem to understand her choices. She spent many nights alone with Cyclops.

The lights blinked again, plunging the already harried woman into darkness. Not one to give way to negativity, she cursed silently and jammed on her shoes that sat at the foot of the bed.

At the table in the entry she thumbed through the papers she needed to start her unit on "Things that Go Bump in the Dark." She squinted in the semi-darkness, thankful she had taught the unit before, but realized she needed extra copies of the stories since the literature books at St. Ignatius Alternative High School were old and did not contain what she used. The only one in the book was "The Cask of Amontillado."

This is one bad day on her mind, she locked the door and darted to her fuchsia VW Beetle parked at the base of the steps to the house, stopping only long enough to throw the sopping newspaper onto the porch. She glimpsed the headline: **Still No Suspects in Serial Slayings.**

Weaving through traffic she normally avoided by being early to school, she hit the play button on her cell phone to hear the message on her voicemail.

"Larkin, this is Brad. I know I'm being a coward not saying this to your face, but after what you told me last night, I just don't see us working out. Sorry."

"Phew!" She tossed the phone into her open handbag, and then laughed out loud and sang the line from the song by Queen. "'Another one bites the dust.' You spineless jerk. You have only one thought about women, and you're a coward. Not to worry. I have plenty of time. I'm only twenty-seven." Larkin set her jaw in a determined clench and gave a quick, reassuring nod. "Thank you, Lord, for showing me Brad's true colors."

She flipped on the radio half expecting the song to be on. She heard the announcer say, "Detective Reynolds informs the media that no new leads have come to light in the brutal slayings of twelve local women. Police refuse to say there is a serial killer on the loose. However, authorities urge caution to all women living and traveling alone--In other news..."

She sighed. *At least there hasn't been another victim.*

Larkin scowled when she saw an unfamiliar Nissan in her parking place. She had to take a visitor's slot, which faced the school. Looking at the building it dawned on her it was as forlorn as the day with its gray brick and long narrow windows. *It resembles a prison.* She breathed a nauseous sigh, and then grabbed her briefcase and ran, realizing she had forgotten her umbrella in her haste. Her foot splashed into a puddle. She stared down. "Sh..." She bit her tongue not to curse as she became aware she had slipped into one black pump and one brown pump in the dark.

"Morning," she said to the armed security guards at the door. Her greeting and late arrival startled the two men who

3

normally felt cheered when Larkin spoke. She flew down the hall as the bell rang to start the day. Breathlessly she slid to a stop at her door where her students already waited.

"Sorry," she wheezed as she let the teens in. "Your starting assignment is to write a paragraph about what you're most afraid of."

"Take a breath, Miss Sloan. We're all here," Terrell said, wearing a teasing grin as he slid into his desk.

"Miss Sloan, what are you afraid of?" LaKeitha asked as her backpack plopped onto the floor.

Larkin replied, "The electricity going off in the middle of the night and making me late for work."

"Is that what happened?" asked Tamara. "You're wearing two different shoes."

"Yes." Larkin looked down and groaned again. The hem of her slacks dripped water onto the floor.

Larkin taught the lesson on "The Lottery," and had a lottery of sorts to start the literature unit, her prize being a bag of M & M's. When Maya squealed she'd won, Larkin gave her the bag. Maya informed her teacher she was allergic to chocolate. "God, what did I do? Today's going from bad to worse," Larkin grumbled under her breath. To Maya she said, "I'll bring you some Skittles next time we meet." The girl nodded appreciation.

The teacher walked around the room as students worked on assignments. She realized she felt a strange sadness. *I've felt this way since I woke and my dream was interrupted.*

The bell rang for the next class. Larkin collected papers as students left. She took a breath. She had the second period of the day off and decided to use the time to gather herself. She dashed to the teachers' workroom to make copies only to find the copier broken. "Eeow!" she screeched and kicked the contraption. "Can today get any worse?"

"What's wrong?" asked the principal, Dr. Rona Fairchild, as she got a Coke from the vending machine.

"Name it."

The principal laughed. "You don't sound like yourself. The repairman's been called. Let the kids share copies until he comes." She patted Larkin's back with motherly affection.

"Teams? Good idea." Frustrated, Larkin trudged back to her room with a Dr. Pepper. Her stomach growled, reminding her she hadn't had her coffee and cereal.

Mr. Stoddard, the math teacher, caught up with her. "You get a new car?" he asked.

"No," she barked.

"Sorry. Wow. That tone. You don't normally complain. Where's that pleasant, perky person?" He grinned. "Practicing alliteration for you."

"Just a bad day." She sighed. "Sorry. No, but I want to know whose white Altima is in my parking place."

"I'm innocent. I wouldn't want that redheaded temper aimed at me." He peeled toward his room, and Larkin went to hers.

She drank her Dr. Pepper as she graded papers for her journalism class. The last one captured her attention:

Eau Bouease Gazette

January 15, 1978—Southeastern, Louisiana

Six Fraternity Brothers Slaughtered

Early this morning an unnamed assailant entered the Phi Kappa Epsilon Fraternity house with a sawed-off, twelve-gauge shotgun, killing six. Witnesses say the young woman whose name authorities refuse to release due to her age purposefully entered one particular suite. She never at any time threatened any member of the fraternity outside that one room. According to members of the fraternity present at the scene the only thing the young woman said was, "They deserved it."

5

The arresting officer remarked, "She surrendered without incident. It was as if she was waiting for us. The girl's blue eyes startled me. She looked as if she were in a trance."

Names of the victims are being withheld pending notification of next of kin.

Larkin Sloan closed the file of papers she was grading. *I told them to find an old article about something macabre.* She read the brief explanation from the journalism student who submitted the piece: *I chose this article because it was old enough. Twenty years was required, but this is thirty years old. It was interesting too because the girl got life in prison, was catatonic, still has not given a motive for killing six dudes, and is from Eau Boueuse.*

Running a petite hand through auburn hair, she wrote "100" on the explanation. *It met all the criteria.* She stood and tried to compose herself for the next class. She moaned as she remembered Dr. Fairchild telling her a new student would be coming. "Great," she muttered. "That'll give me *lucky* thirteen in this class." She pulled herself together, and finally wrote the day's assignment on the board. Sarcasm oozing, she grumbled as the bell rang, "This day just gets better and better."

Dupree Parks, the new student and an eighteen-year-old in the ninth grade, sauntered to the door just as the tardy bell rang. He was not a big guy. He barely weighed a hundred forty-five pounds and stood only five feet, eight inches. Larkin heard the girls murmuring about how cute he was. When she saw him, she had to admit he was a handsome boy with smooth milk chocolate skin and neatly braided hair, but he had been in and out of juvenile court since he was twelve. His latest charge was possession with intent to distribute. He had been arrested two days before he turned eighteen. Had he waited another forty-eight hours, he would not have been offered this last-stop opportunity. Sucking up the butterflies in her stomach, Larkin faded to the background while Miss Sloan, teacher, took over and greeted him cordially, instructing him to sit in the front desk on the far side of the room and to do the assignment on the board while she checked roll.

Dupree scowled at her and said, "You crazy? I ain't sittin' in no front desk."

She smiled and looked Dupree in the eye as she responded, "No, I'm not crazy, and that's where you'll sit. All the students have assigned seats, and that's the next available seat. Please, sit down."

Dupree did not move. "I don't want these fags and hoes starin' at me. I don't wanna sit up front."

Larkin took a step closer to Dupree and whispered so that the other students could not hear, "Mr. Parks, let's get something straight right now. You're here as a last attempt to keep you out of jail. Since you've already turned eighteen, you won't be going to reform school if you blow it here. In this room, *I* am the final authority. You *will* do as I say. You will *not* use that language in my classroom. The other students in my classes actually *learn* something. If you give it a chance, so will you. However, if you won't follow my rules, the parish holding facility is about ten miles down the road. I'm sure their rules are much harsher than mine. It's your choice."

Dupree stomped to the assigned desk and looked at the bell-ringer assignment, which read, "Write in your journal about, 'I am most afraid of...'" Having neither pen nor paper, he looked over his shoulder toward the back corner of the room where the teacher's desk was located. He growled, "I ain't afraid of nothin', bitch."

Larkin was just finishing her roll check in order to put the absentee report on her door for pick up. She crinkled the piece of paper in her fist, but walked to the door and placed the absentee report under a clip before she said, "You aren't afraid of anything, Mr. Parks? Not even snakes or rats or spiders?"

"Nothin'."

Feeling that curious melancholy she had been experiencing, Larkin remarked, "Hmmm. Well, if you use that term in my room once more toward anybody, you *will* become very afraid of the six-foot-four, three-hundred-pound, sexually-starved monster who will be your bunkmate in lockup. Until then, perhaps, you should be afraid of me."

The students stifled snickers and looked between the two. She glared at them, prompting silence.

Dupree burst out laughing. "You a scrawny little white woman. You come in here tryin' to change somethin' you don't know nothin' about. You know what these slits in my eyebrow mean?" He pointed to two shaved spaces in his eyebrow. "Maybe you should be afraid of me."

Larkin did know much of the gang liturgy and symbolism. She had learned quickly during her first year in the classroom. She had also learned not to show fear to these kids, so, although shivering inside, she calmly replied, "Mr. Parks, it appears you do *not* know who has the power in this room. Perhaps, you should leave us." She moved toward the intercom.

Dupree jumped up from his desk and shouted, "Try it, bitch!"

Larkin raised an eyebrow and pushed the button. At the same moment, the literature book from beneath Dupree's desk hit her in the face. Blood spread over her eye and down her cheek. The office responded to her call and heard screams from the three girls in the class. Within minutes, security came into the room to twelve voices telling them what had happened. One of the guards removed Dupree with an iron grip on his arm while the other escorted Larkin and the rest of the class to the office where the assistant principal took her to Catholic Charity Hospital for stitches to her right eyebrow.

At her insistence, Mr. Manning, the assistant principal, left her in the capable hands of Dr. Bixby. Larkin was surprised she was seen so quickly. The doctor put five stitches in her eyebrow and told her to go home after writing a prescription for Lorcet. Larkin laughed. "Dr. Bixby, this has been one *bad* day, but a few stitches won't keep me from my students. Besides, my car is at the school. I'll take a cab back. Thank you for your nice work."

Larkin could not believe her luck for the day was changing when she found a cab at the entrance to the ER. Sliding into the back seat, "St. Ignatius," she said.

A soft, cultured, masculine voice said, "Seatbelt."

Larkin smiled that her cab driver would worry about her safety. After the day she'd had, it made her feel good. She glanced into the rear view mirror and was startled by the bluest eyes she had ever seen looking at her. She clicked the seatbelt and the driver cranked the car. She leaned back on the seat and smelled a sweet odor on the cushion. Sleep came a moment later.

Larkin jerked her wrist. The voice, the voice from the cab, said again, "Stop. You'll hurt yourself. I'll be back."

Blue eyes! Why am I thinking about his eyes? She jerked her wrist again.

"Please stop. Relax. I'll be back."

9

2
A Real Pain

Detective Raiford Reynolds groaned, rubbed his temples, opened his desk drawer, and snatched his prescription for Amidrine. "Damn it! I don't wanna take this. I can't afford to go to sleep right now. This shit always knocks me out."

As keyed up as he was, he half expected a voice to answer him. In the last two hours, he had already taken four Advil, three aspirin, and three extra-strength Tylenol. Nothing was left but to take the Amidrine, even if it meant passing out for a few hours. The last time his head had hurt this much had been when he pulled an all-nighter studying for his last final at Louisiana State University. He had partied far too much with his fraternity brothers at Delta Tau Delta to study in a reasonable fashion. "I'm surprised I graduated," he grunted. *No, this headache is worse, but I brought both of them on myself from lack of sleep and pushing my body further than it needs to be pushed.*

These damned headaches had prevented him from playing football as much as he liked the sport and had wanted to play. He had managed baseball and golf. His body took less pounding, and his doctor would only release him to play non-contact sports in school. A stabbing ache like an ice pick through his temple shot from one side of his head to the other. The pain was becoming unbearable; the Amidrine, inevitable.

But what of my ridiculous headache? Detective Reynolds was certain his migraine, even if it was the worst one he had experienced during his three years as a detective, was nothing compared to the agony the twelve women in the pictures before him must have endured. Besides, he would be feeling a different kind of hurt, unemployment, if he didn't solve this case, and soon. The chief had personally said, "Ray, you're the best detective I have. This is an election year. Get this mess solved! I don't need this, and neither do you."

The chief's declaration had come after the seventh body was discovered. Now, there were twelve. *Oh, yes, Chief Gerard is feeling the sting of an election-year nightmare— a serial killer. The mayor is on the chief's back. And, oh, yes, misery loves company. The chief definitely intimated that if he's out, I am, too.*

But what kind of pain is that? It's not real suffering. Looking at the pictures again, a wave of nausea swept over him. He couldn't be sure whether the nausea was caused by the persistent migraine or the crime scene photos, but he determined to get his headache under control. He had no choice. He had to take the Amidrine.

Ray looked at the drink machine in the hallway. *Maybe if I take the damned pill with a Red Bull, I can get a couple of more hours before I zonk.*

He stood and stretched to his full six-foot height. He clutched the prescription bottle and chuckled as another voice came to his memory. Ray could hear his mother, "Raiford Michael Reynolds, stand up and stop slouching! You'll get a hump in your back. We might be Catholic, but I don't want you to be known as The Hunchback of Notre Dame. One of your ancestors, also called Raiford, was a knight who fought in the Crusades. Straighten that spine and show pride in the person you are."

Ray knew he always slouched when he was stressed. *What would Mom say if she could see me now? This case is more than a hunch in my back. It's enough to bend me double, maybe break my back. So what if my namesake was Sir Raiford Reynolds? It's not really my blood anyway. After all, I'm adopted. I've always known I was born in the charity ward of Catholic Charity Hospital. My birth mother was a street-walking drug addict who went by the name of Audrey—real or not, I don't know, nor do I really care. I've been blessed to have been adopted by Albert and Dorothy Reynolds. They've given me a good life.*

He looked down at his desk again and puffed out a remorseful sigh as the top picture, the second victim, burned into his brain, and a throb like a hot bullet shot through his head. He slammed his chair into his desk, stomped to the drink machine, got a Red Bull, and popped two Amidrine into his mouth, washing them down with the entire Red Bull without a breath. He tossed the can into the wastebasket and made a stop in the restroom.

Ray washed his face and wet down his short soot-black hair. He leaned on the lavatory and gasped when he saw himself in the mirror. He touched strands of gray near his temple. Although somewhat thin at hundred eight-five pounds, he was by no means skinny, but his face looked gaunt. He had an athlete's body and worked to preserve it three or four days a week at the gym, but visits lately had been few and far between. *A good workout would go a long way toward relieving this damned headache.* His two-day stubble made him look older than his thirty years. The blood-shot whites of his eyes and dark circles beneath his lower eyelids made his startlingly sapphire-blue irises look even bluer and more outstanding against his rather fair complexion and black hair. He noticed a coffee stain on his white button-down shirt. Ray grunted. "No, Mom wouldn't holler at me. She'd probably slap me." *Then, again, I can't remember having ever been slapped.*

He shook his wet hair like a dog and returned to the deserted office area. He turned the crime scene photos face down and whispered, "I can't look at you deceased right now." He then picked up the photos of the twelve dead women from when they were still alive. "Maybe living," he muttered. The detective put them in order of their deaths and stared at them as if hoping one of them would speak to him.

He reviewed in his mind: *Twelve women are dead in less than a year. The M.O. is the same. All had their throats slit. Almost all the blood was drained from their bodies. They were all obviously bound as evidenced from the bruising on their wrists. There was a different emblem painted over each ones' shaved pubic area, but there was no sexual assault. Moreover, none appeared to have been abused except for having been tied up. All were placed in the cemetery in the normal position a dead body would be laid in a coffin, and they were all wearing what could have been a white wedding dress. On the other hand, they have absolutely nothing in common.*

Serial killers usually pick a type, but my victims range from a fifty-five-year-old white nun to a sixteen-year-old black high school student, with various ages and races in between. There's no socioeconomic attachment either. Nothing makes sense.

Ray glanced at the white board against the wall where he had recorded vital information on each victim and their last known movements and whereabouts. He grabbed the badly dog-eared chart he had made and reviewed it. He had numbered the women in order and written the most important information: name, race, age, physical description, date missing and date of death, and the blasted symbols. He grunted as he looked at his chicken scratch. "Maybe it's the dates. Some are holidays. But what are the others?"

#	NAME	OCCUPATION	RACE	AGE	HAIR	EYES	DM	DOD	SYMBOL
1	Lequesha Brown	cashier	black	19	black	brown	11/1	11/22	cornucopia
2	Sister Mary Michael-Mauldin	nun	white	55	brunette/grey	hazel	11/23	12/15	crescent moon w/ face
3	Betty Kim	college student	Asian	21	black	brown	12/16	1/1	hourglass
4	Lucia Torres	waitress	Hispanic	20	black	brown	1/5	2/2	hedgehog
5	Mira Samir	pediatrician	Arabian	33	black	brown	2/3	2/20	theater masks
6	Isabeau Chanel	social worker	Creole	24	black	brown	2/22	3/21	hawk
7	Molly Jensen	receptionist	white	20	blond	blue	3/21	3/23	upside down cross
8	Charlene Winters	heiress	white	17	blond	green	4/15	5/1	May pole w/ streamers
9	Ashleigh McCall	reporter	white	21	brunette	blue	5/26	6/21	sun w/ face
10	Rochelle Waters	bank teller	black	24	black	brown	6/22	7/4	American flag
11	Destiny Whitefeather	casino dealer	Native American	25	black	brown	7/5	8/1	seven stars
12	Bianca Barnes	high school student	black	16	black	brown	9/1	9/23	lizard

"Come on!" He slammed the chart onto his desk. "Gimme a break! Speak to me!" he screamed.

Ray heard the response he had been expecting earlier. He looked up to see Special Agent Christine Milovich, the singular, but *only*, help the FBI had sent when Ray

14

requested assistance at Easter. Chris was pretty and athletically built. Ray knew she never lacked male companionship for several of the patrolmen had asked her out since she had been there. She was almost as tall as Ray and wore her dishwater blonde hair short. Her soft brown eyes stared with rebuke at Ray now. She wore black slacks, a cream-colored lightweight cashmere sweater and flat black suede Earth shoes. She crossed her arms, pursed her lips, and tapped her foot. "Ray, have you been here all night again?"

"Yes," he replied, unaffected by his temporary partner's tone or demeanor.

Agent Milovich snatched the pictures from Ray's desk. "Go! Now!" she commanded. "If you make yourself sick, you'll be of no use to anybody. I can see by the expression on your face you have another migraine. You look like shit! Get some rest, and for God's sake, shower and shave. Do that for me. I have to smell you."

Ray rubbed his head again and spoke softly. "Chris, I can't have another body turn up." He picked up the picture of the nun as it escaped her hands. "I knew her personally. Sister Mary Michael taught Sunday school when I was a boy. Who would wanna hurt this woman? Or any of them? It's just that this does make it more personal, and I don't have a clue." He finished with despair in his voice. He ran his fingers through his hair and puffed out his exasperation in one long breath.

Christine softened her tone. "Ray, get some sleep. We'll get this bastard. I promise. But right now, you need to rest."

"I know," he submitted. "I'll go to the locker room and sleep a while. And I promise to shower and shave before I come back."

She shooed him on with a little hand motion. Ray went to the back of the facility where each police officer had a locker. Several cots stood for use during disaster times.

They had been moved in after Hurricane Katrina. He plunked onto the nearest one and instantly fell asleep.

A strange, disconcerting dream floated into his subconscious as often happened. He dreamed about himself, or thought it was himself. Although the person looked just like Ray, it was someone *entirely* different.

Ray woke to the gentle shaking of Christine Milovich and her voice insisting, "Wake up."

He opened his eyes slowly and squinted against the harsh glare of the overhead florescent lights. His headache lingered. "How long have I been asleep?" he asked, a little dazed.

"Only a couple of hours," his partner replied. "I'm sorry to wake you, but another woman has disappeared."

"Fuck!" Ray rubbed his forehead and neck. "Just shoot me and put me out of my misery. This is real pain, Chris, a real pain."

3
Thirteen

Ray inhaled deeply as he stood. He still felt as if he might vomit at any second. He opened his locker and found a clean white golf shirt on the top shelf. He could not remember the last time he had actually hit a golf ball, but at least the shirt was clean. Chris's hand fell over his shoulder. It held a can of Axe and a bottle of Visine. She confided, "I commandeered the spray from Baker's locker. The eye drops are from my purse."

He smiled. "I guess I don't really have time for that shower and shave, huh?"

"Not right now. Maybe after we talk with the woman up front."

Ray and Chris walked to their shared office space after he doused his musty smell with the Axe and dropped some of the redness remover into each eye. A woman of about fifty with short salt-and-pepper hair fidgeted in a chair beside Ray's desk. Her dark eyes studied the framed documents on the wall behind the desk as she waited. Chris made the introduction, "Dr. Fairchild, this is Detective Reynolds. He's in charge of investigating this horrible ordeal. Ray, this is Dr. Rona Fairchild, the principal at St. Ignatius. She has come to report a missing teacher and is terrified the young woman might be number thirteen." Chris finished with a scowl.

Ray shook the short, stocky woman's hand. "Dr. Fairchild, why do you think this case could be related to the others?" He sat in his chair as Chris pulled another from the corner.

Dr. Fairchild gushed like a severed artery, "Because Larkin Sloan never misses school, her car is in the school parking lot, she doesn't answer her home phone or her cell

17

phone, and she didn't answer the door when I went to her house after she failed to show up for school today. Larkin has missed four days of school in five years and only because she had strep throat. She was named teacher of the year last year. She loves her job and her students. She's the most dedicated teacher I've ever had. She had a really *bad* day yesterday, but she would never neglect to call in unless something was seriously wrong. I just feel it, Detective. I'm terrified." The older woman started to cry.

Ray handed her a tissue from his desk drawer. At the same time he snatched his notepad and a small recorder. Dr. Fairchild sniffled. "Thank you." She dabbed her honey-brown eyes. "I'm sorry to fall apart on you, but Larkin Sloan is very special. I love her as if she were my own daughter. We've spent a great deal of time together in the last five years. I never told her how I feel about her."

Ray patted the distraught woman's hand. "I'll do my best," he replied, his voice sounding hollow. "You know, adults are usually not considered missing until they've been gone for forty-eight hours, but under the circumstances, I'm not taking any chances. Now, Dr. Fairchild, what happened yesterday to make things different from any other day?" He touched the recorder. "May I?"

Dr. Fairchild nodded. Ray pressed the record button as the woman began to speak. "Larkin was physically assaulted by the new student in her class. Mr. Manning, my assistant principal, took her to the emergency room at Catholic Charity Hospital for stitches after the boy threw a book at her and hit her in the face. She told him she would grab a cab back to school, so he left. I already called the ER, and Dr. Bixby, who attended her, said she left in a cab."

Ray wrote in his notepad. "What about the kid who assaulted her? Do you think he did something else?"

"No. He was in lockup and still is."

"All right. We'll need to talk to him anyway. Is he a juvenile?"

"No. He's eighteen. Dupree Parks. He's in the parish holding facility."

"At least he's easy to find. We'll also talk to the ER personnel and try to find the cabbie. What can you tell me about Miss...Mrs. Sloan?"

"Miss. She's not married, not seriously involved with anyone that I know of."

"All right. Tell me about Miss Sloan."

Dr. Fairchild smiled sadly. "She's brilliant. All her colleagues love her, as do most of her students. I already told you she was teacher of the year last year. At St. Ignatius, this is a 50/50 vote between students and teachers."

Ray smiled as he thought Dr. Fairchild's view of Larkin Sloan had to be skewed because of her obvious emotional attachment. He prompted, "Dr. Fairchild, what makes Miss Sloan so brilliant?"

"Larkin is from a small town in Mississippi, called Soso, if you can believe that. She's an only child. Her parents were killed in a car accident when she was five, and she lived with her maternal grandmother until the grandmother died when Larkin was thirteen. Then, she lived in the Mississippi Baptist Children's Home until she went to stay with a Pastor Eric Moore and his wife, Emily. They died in a house fire during her senior year in high school, and she became an emancipated minor. As far as I know, she has no family."

Ray furrowed his brow. "Sounds as if she might be a survivor. Tell me more, Dr. Fairchild."

"Rona, please."

Ray nodded.

"Although she had a rough childhood, she turned out great. She has inner strength and a deep faith. She graduated high school valedictorian. In high school she was a member of the drama club, the choir, the newspaper staff, and the soccer team. She sang the female lead in the high school production of *My Fair Lady*, was editor-in-chief of the paper, and captain of the soccer team."

Chris cut her eyes at Ray. She asked, "She was a busy kid. Isn't that a lot to take on?"

"Participation in four major extracurricular activities is a lot," Rona admitted. "I would never advise a student to do more than three, but Larkin is driven. She pushes herself to the limit."

Ray asked, "Is it possible she pushed someone too hard yesterday?"

"Not at school." Rona immediately jumped to Larkin Sloan's defense. She clutched the tissue as if she wanted to break something.

"All right, Rona," Ray said in an attempt to placate the woman's protective mode. He could sense she really did have a motherly affection for the young teacher. "You were telling me about Miss Sloan's background." *I can't imagine her singing the lead in a musical having any bearing on the case. I don't recall any of the others having a talent like that.* He said, "Continue." He made a note to check for special artistic talents for the other victims.

"She attended Mississippi College on full scholarship." The woman's voice took on an air of fantasy in Ray's mind. He and Chris exchanged looks.

Chris was tempted to tell the woman to stick to the facts of the day before, but she bit her tongue and let Dr. Fairchild ramble just in case she shared some small tidbit of importance. "She worked as youth minister at Cornerstone Church, a nondenominational church, while she was in college. She majored in education and double minored in literature and history. She graduated Summa Cum Laude."

"Summa?" Ray asked. He leaned forward and scribbled a note to himself. *Check other women's GPA. Maybe killer hates smart women.*

Chris said what Ray thought, "With all the other stuff she was involved in, she graduated Summa? She must be a genius." Her voice held a note of cynicism. "Go on."

20

"She *is* very intelligent," Dr. Fairchild reiterated, drawing her mouth into a thin line as she turned to face Chris. "Everything she endured was what swayed me to hire her in the first place. I thought if she could handle all that, she could deal with juvenile offenders. Larkin came to St. Ignatius the fall after she graduated. She has been with me five years. While here, she has taught ninth, tenth, eleventh, and twelfth grade English; journalism; social studies; creative writing; drama; music; and gifted, believe it or not, we have some gifted kids with serious behavioral or legal problems."

"All of those different subjects? How?" asked Ray.

"Not all at the same time, of course." Dr. Fairchild gave the detective a scornful look. Her tone made Ray cringe inside. He could feel the wooden ruler the nuns used smacking the palm of his hand. He felt seriously reprimanded. "She now teaches English, all four levels, journalism, and choir. She has started a newspaper and a choir. Our classes are quite small, so we don't have the population to even consider sports, or I'm sure she would've pushed at least a soccer team to coach. She coaches at the Y. Larkin believes that although these kids are in an alternative school setting, they should have opportunities to shine. Her strategies have been very successful. Most of her students have gone back to regular school and eighty percent have gone on to graduate. I told you, she's *brilliant*."

"She sounds too good to be real, Dr. Fairchild," Chris said from behind Rona.

"In some ways she is," admitted Dr. Fairchild. "She's not perfect. I've seen her throw little tantrums when she thought nobody was watching. She has a temper and is stubborn. She kicked the copier yesterday because it was broken."

Ray chuckled. "It's good to know she's human," he said. "Please, tell us whatever else you think we should know."

Chris, her eyes stretched wide, gave him a look that said—*Cut to the chase.*

He knitted his brows together and barely shook his head. Chris narrowed her eyes to slits and clenched her jaw. Ray could almost hear his partner's teeth grind.

"Very well," said Dr. Fairchild, oblivious to the silent communication. "She received her Master of Education from Belhaven College by taking courses during the summer, and we've discussed her getting her doctorate.

"I know she attends Charity Chapel, a nondenominational church where she works with the kids' Sunday school program. She lives in an antebellum house that she bought and is restoring. The house was wired for electricity in the 1950s, and nobody had lived in it for ten years before Larkin bought it." She passed Ray a piece of paper with the address on it. "Her roommate is named Cyclops. He's a scarred, one-eyed black cat she rescued from an animal shelter after Hurricane Katrina. He was scheduled to be put down, but stole her heart, just as Larkin has stolen all our hearts at St. Ignatius.

"She doesn't have a steady boyfriend although she's absolutely beautiful. I happen to know she does go out from time to time. She loves seafood, Mexican food, and margaritas."

"Can you write a description for us?" the detective asked.

"I can go you one better. I brought her picture from her ID badge that stays on file in the school system's computer data base."

Ray took the picture, and the strangest thought occurred to him. *If this woman is this pretty in a mug shot, what does she look like in person?*

Ray brought himself back to reality. "This is quite helpful. We'll get Miss Sloan's picture circulating immediately. Chris and I will start talking to people as soon as I shower and shave. I must look a fright to you, Dr.

Fairchild, but I've been working almost around the clock. I apologize for my appearance."

"Detective, I understand." With her hand that clutched the Kleenex, she pointed toward the photographs of graduations and awards, along with diplomas on the wall. "You seem to be pretty driven yourself, B.S. in Criminal Justice from LSU, Master's of Sociology from Southeastern Louisiana."

"That was online," he hastened to say.

"Still, you did the work. Plus, you got an EMT certification and a commendation for valor. Were you shot?"

"Yes, ma'am."

Chris noisily slapped her notepad on her lap.

Dr. Fairchild scowled at her. "Do whatever it takes to get Larkin back safely. If you need to speak to the other teachers, let me know the day before you come, and I'll get a floating sub so you can to talk to everybody." She wadded the tissue Ray had given her earlier and dropped it in the wastebasket by his desk. "If you need to speak to the minor students, let me know so I can have parents or guardians present. But I don't think your criminal is among us."

Chris asked, "Dr. Fairchild, honestly, what does her background have to do with her being missing now?"

"I don't know. That's your job," Rona spat. "You told me to tell you what I thought was important."

"How is what she did as a teenager important to *this* case?" Chris pressed. "Give me something current. A name. Anything that pops into your head."

Rona creased her brow. "Maybe I'm overly attached. I've never been able to have children. Larkin's the daughter I never had." She sighed. "I know you two must be grasping at straws. She's gone out several times with a guy named Brad Tisdale, but I don't think anything will come of it."

"Thank you," said Chris. "That could be a starting point."

"He's an engineer, but he works offshore. I don't even know if he's home now."

"We'll find out," Chris said.

Dr. Fairchild stood and shook hands with both Ray and Chris. Ray assured Rona as best he could, "I'll call you with any scheduling or information. Thank you."

With a nod, Dr. Fairchild left.

Ray turned to Chris. "Another paragon of virtue. Is that the connection, Chris? Are they all angels in disguise? Well, I'll be damned if I let this angel suffer the hell the others did."

Chris tapped her notes with the pen she held. "Really smart, religious, do-gooder."

Beautiful. Ray shuddered and shrugged. "We'll see. Will you, *please*, get us some breakfast while I shower?"

"Sure," said Chris as calmly as ever while grabbing her purse and heading out the door.

"Nothing sweet! Real breakfast!" Ray called after her. He picked up Larkin Sloan's picture before he headed to the showers. He looked at her soft features and glanced at the description Dr. Fairchild had written on back: *five feet, two inches, 100 pounds, auburn hair, brown eyes, double pierced ears, perfect teeth.* Ray thought again that if all he had heard and seen of Larkin Sloan were true, she was *too* perfect. He sighed.

He laid everything down and headed to the showers. As he went, he thought: *Larkin. Now, that would be an angel's name.*

4
Feeling of Futility

Ray showered and shaved quickly, which resulted in several nicks. He kept unopened packages of undershirts, boxers, and socks in his locker. The time had come to open them. He felt cleaner even in the same Levis he had been wearing. He finger-combed short black hair, used some of the communal mouthwash, looked at his reflection and grumbled, "Good enough. Now I have to make a phone call. Damn it."

At his desk, he dialed FBI headquarters...and waited. Finally off hold, he demanded assistance in what he had dubbed his "Angel Slayer" case as he'd showered.

Chris returned bearing two full southern breakfasts with juice and coffee. She caught one side of Ray's heated conversation.

"Look, it's apparent that you pompous, big-shot assholes in Washington care very little about the goings-on in a little back bayou Louisiana town like Eau Bouease you think is filled with moronic inbred Coonasses...I know I have Chris, and she's terrific, but we *cannot* do this alone." As if tapping out the number, he rhythmically drummed a pen on his desk in frustration. "We have twelve dead women, and a thirteenth is missing...Yeah, right. I would put money on the fact that you would have an entire platoon at work if these murders were taking place within the city of New Orleans...Yeah, I think I have the solution. It's time to go to the press about your lack of support. I bet they'll be *very* accommodating, seeing as how one of their own was one of the victims...What's that?....It's about fucking time!" Ray slammed the receiver down.

"Give 'em hell, Ray!" Chris shouted. "What's about time? Finally more help?"

"Yeah. They said a team of investigators including a profiler will be coming in about a week. They have to put a team together. I still want it *yesterday*."

He grinned and motioned Chris to the desk. "Let's eat. I need sustenance.

"How's the head?"

He raised his hand. "Just don't talk loudly. I think I'll feel better after I eat."

After a hearty breakfast, Ray's headache became just a throbbing nuisance. He flipped through his notes. "Fairchild said she talked to the ER doctor, but that's our first stop. There are two cab companies in town." He opened the phonebook and located both numbers. Handing them to Chris on a scrap of paper, he said, "Track the cabbie while I drive."

The FBI agent had success with the second number. One of their drivers had been assaulted and had his cab stolen. Chris got a name and address. "We'll run with this one." She waggled the scrap of paper in the air.

When they arrived at the hospital, Ray and Chris spoke with Dr. Bixby who vaguely remembered a slender dark-haired driver when Larkin got into the cab, but that was all. He said, "I didn't get a good look at the driver's face."

Ray demanded, "We need to see the security video from just before the time Larkin Sloan signed in until you saw her leave in the cab."

Dr. Bixby said, "Follow me. I'll take you to the chief of security."

They followed the doctor down several hallways. Eager to help any way he could when he heard what was needed, the security chief found the correct tape and gave it to the police.

Chris lifted an eyebrow. "VCR? Not digital?"

Ray and Chris watched the images on a VCR in the security office. Ray pointed. "Larkin arriving with Mr. Manning."

"He's being very protective," Chris muttered.

Tapping the screen, she said, "How much time? Half a minute? There's a cab."

About a minute after the cab stopped, the passenger, wearing a hooded sweat shirt and jeans, got out, opened the driver's door, pushed the apparent driver gently to the passenger side of the car, and slid into the driver's seat. The cab left.

Ray sat forward. "I can't see his face."

"He was avoiding the camera," Chris said. "He has on golfing gloves."

"Looks like it. Damn it! No prints, but those looked like expensive gloves." He glanced at Chris. "Our kook plays golf."

The hood of the cab appeared back in the frame, but they could see nothing more of the driver. When Larkin Sloan left, she went directly to the cab. It backed up and left the area.

"That was too damned strange," groaned Ray. "Chris, do you have the same feeling of futility as I do?"

"It's frustrating Ray, but we'll get there. There's something off about a man who's a killer. Did you notice how gently he moved the driver?"

"Yeah, but he wasn't after him."

"Maybe," said the FBI agent not in total agreement with the detective.

Ray held up the tape. "We have to take this one."

"Of course," the security officer agreed. "Just sign the proper form." The hospital employee pulled out a form for the detective to sign. Ray slipped the tape into a manila envelope and labeled it.

"Next stop?" Chris asked in the parking lot.

Ray held up a finger. He walked to where the cab had been parked and looked around carefully. "Nothing. I was hoping for a cigarette butt or gum wrapper."

He turned to his partner. "Larkin's house, just in case the cab took her home and she passed out from the pain killers or had an allergic reaction."

"Right." Chris nodded with pursed lips. "If nothing else, we might learn something more about the too-perfect Larkin Sloan."

"Then, Dupree," Ray said, getting into his car. "My gut tells me he knows something."

Ray and Chris drove to the antebellum house owned by Larkin Sloan. Located in an historical part of town and set rather far from the nearest neighbor, the house, surrounded by a picket fence, looked like a picture postcard. The grass was neatly clipped. Chrysanthemums lined the walkway. The snow-white paint with charcoal shutters and trim was fresh. The wide, inviting veranda above steep stone steps supported a porch swing at one end and two old-fashioned rocking chairs with a wicker table between them at the other. All along the porch eve hung wind chimes in a multitude of sizes of varying materials. The gentle breeze created a relaxing, soothing symphony. The high-pitched tinkle of the seashells combined with the hollow, discordant bump of bamboo and the low metallic clank of copper pipe produced a calm, which Ray inhaled, surveying the front porch. Chris looked at him as he breathed deeply with his eyes closed. *It's so peaceful here. I haven't felt this connected and serene in almost a year.*

"Ray?" Chris nudged him with her elbow.

"Sorry."

Ray tried the front door while Chris tried the back door and a side door. All were locked, as were all the windows.

28

There was no response to resounding knocks and several pulls on the velvet bell cord.

Lifting the edge of the welcome mat, "Not that obvious," he remarked. "Now, where would this woman hide a spare key?"

"Nowhere," Chris grunted with a scowl. "Not safe."

"This is the South where we still want to believe in the goodness of our fellow man." Cynicism oozed. He looked around and laughed. "In plain sight, of course." One of the wind chimes consisted of a dozen keys jingling together. Ray cupped the keys in his hand. "Which one is it, Chris?"

The agent examined the keys before choosing an antique brass key. "This one. It looks like the easiest one to get off."

Ray slipped the key off its small hook. It fit the front door lock perfectly. Ray and Chris stepped through the door into a foyer that made them feel as if they had entered a time warp and were in the 1860s before war had torn the country apart and devastated the South. Nothing in the vestibule would have made them believe they were in 2008. The floors, the furniture, even the rug seemed to be in mint antebellum condition. Stepping into the living room let the two know they were still in the twenty-first century and the owner's adventure in the restoration of the old house was far from complete. A mixture of a few antiques with many modern conveniences, including a computer, returned the pair to reality. The only thing in perfect antique condition was the polished hardwood flooring.

Ray was suddenly startled by a bump against his leg and a gravely meow. He bent down and picked up the animal. "Hi there, Cyclops." The cat's one eye was bright blue, almost like his own. "Appropriate name. She's not here, is she?"

Cyclops let out a loud meow.

"No, and you feel scared, too. You don't know what will become of you without her. I tell you what: You can go home with me until we find her."

Chris stared. "Ray, have you lost your mind?"

"No. This animal would be dead without his mistress. I'll keep him safe for her until she comes home." *Rona's suspicions are right on target. She really does know Larkin.*

"What if..."

The detective shook his head vehemently. "Don't even say it."

"Ray."

"I mean it, Chris. This one gets saved. Let's look around, but I think it's pointless. There's nothing here to tell us where she is."

Ray and Chris discovered only two bedrooms were furnished, one clearly an unused guest room. The other, which showed signs of use and had its own private bath, had to be the one Larkin used. In an otherwise pristine house, the bed was unmade. Ray looked down and saw a brown pump and a black pump. He pointed. "She left in a hurry." He dipped his head toward the still-blinking alarm clock. "I bet she overslept and got dressed in the dark. Remember that round of severe thunderstorms?" His cheeks dimpled as he pictured Larkin frantically getting ready for work.

Brow furrowed, Chris remarked, "Dr. Fairchild said she had a bad day. I'd say the worst if she's been abducted by our killer." She searched the closet and commented, "She has a conservative wardrobe."

"Really?" Ray asked holding, up a couple of dangling pieces of jewelry. "These aren't earrings, Chris. What are they?"

"Belly button rings," she answered. "So, Miss Sloan has her navel pierced." Short dark blonde hair touched the base of the agent's neck as she shrugged. "No big deal, Ray. Lots of people have body piercings."

"I bet Dr. Fairchild doesn't know." Ray sniggered. "Maybe Miss Sloan has a really wild side."

30

Chris cocked one eyebrow. "Maybe it just makes her feel pretty. Most of the men I know think belly button rings are sexy. Don't you?"

He puckered his lips. "Yeah, on perfectly tight abs."

"She's an athlete according to Dr. Fairchild. I bet her abs *are* perfectly tight. I'm checking the bathroom."

Chris came out to find Ray banging the side of Larkin's computer. "What's wrong?" she asked.

"It's password protected," he growled. "I wonder what she's hiding on here. I don't know enough about her to guess her password."

"Well, bring it along. We'll get our techno geeks to get in. There was nothing significant in the bathroom. She has no prescription drugs, not even the pill. Of course, she could be like me and carry that in her purse. She had some acetaminophen and some ibuprofen, nothing stronger, and some Benadryl and Neosporin and Band-Aids. She's not a drug addict."

"Not an alcoholic either. There's a bottle of white wine and some margarita mix in the refrigerator and a bottle of Cuervo Gold above the stove. Dr. Fairchild said she liked margaritas."

"Yes. One thing is for certain, though. She's not here."

"Yeah." Ray gusted a sigh. "That was too much to hope for. *Allons.*" He waved his hand forward.

She gave him a half frown at his use of French.

"Let's go," he clarified.

After thoroughly searching Larkin Sloan's house, which included taking her computer, Ray bagged the cat's food, but decided to get a new litter box and litter.

Chris questioned, "Are you seriously taking the cat with you?"

"Somebody has to take care of him."

"Then why don't you just come by and feed him?"

"No, he needs to feel secure."

"Ray, it's a cat."

31

"He's special to Larkin!" Ray said defensively. "He was a lost cause until she came along. I will *not* let her be a lost cause."

Chris gave Ray a puzzled look, dipping one eyebrow. "You've finally lost it," she said.

"Lost what? My mind?"

"Your objectivity. You're obsessed."

Stubbornly, he picked up Cyclops. "Maybe. But look at this animal. God forbid, but if Larkin Sloan *is* dead, nobody else will want him."

Chris sighed. "I guess you're cat sitting."

The strange trio drove to the parish lockup. On the rather cool, damp day, Ray left the cat in the car with a scratch under his chin and instructions not to tear up the seats. As if he understood, the animal curled up on the back seat.

Dupree Parks had nothing to do but think about the mess he was in. For the moment he was alone without a cellmate. "I tried to be a gang banger, but that didn't work. What now? What am I? A smart kid criminal?" He smiled ruefully at the thought. "That's not really funny."

I'm a criminal, but I'm a man of my word and fiercely loyal to and protective of those I love. Dupree shook his head. *There're just very few people I love. Mostly, I'm a loner. I don't fit into any group—not even a gang. I ain't as street-wise as they are. I don't like to hurt people.*

"I'm sorry, Momma. You're a tigress who never gives up and fights for my survival. You threatened some of my brothers with a loaded shotgun. You filed assault charges on that asshole ex-husband, Dwight." *Oh shit! If I get sent to the big house, he'll be there. I'm a dead man.* He sighed and fought back tears. "I blew my last chance and broke your heart."

Dupree kicked the wall at the thought. "I wanna be somebody—and get outta this place."

Is that dream truly like a raisin in the sun, shriveled and dried up by my own hand. He murmured, "I'm so sorry, Momma. I need Divine Intervention." *Poverty is a quagmire and already holds my foot fast. The quicksand will just suck me under. I won't be like Walter Lee Younger and rise above shattered dreams.* "Damn it." *I can't even admit to my friends I actually read* A Raisin in the Sun *and liked it and understood it. I did this to myself and that makes me angrier than anything else.* "God, why am I so bad?"

His mood grew surlier by the minute. By the time the guard came to get him, Dupree sat at the bottom of his self-imposed pit.

"Couple of cops here to see you, boy. Straighten up."

Dupree curled his lips in a snarl as the guard slapped cuffs on him.

The prison guard escorted him to an interrogation room devoid of all color except the clothing worn by visitors or inmates. Chris sat in one gray folding metal chair at a table, and Ray leaned against the wall. Dupree plopped into the other chair and promptly announced, "I ain't talking to y'all without my lawyer."

"Really? I'm Detective Reynolds. Do you have something to hide?" snapped Ray.

"Like what? I ain't done nothin'."

"Like the whereabouts of Miss Sloan."

"Whatcha talkin' 'bout?"

Reynolds stopped slouching. "Miss Sloan, the teacher you assaulted yesterday, is missing. Where is she?"

Missing? He shook his head. "I don't know," Dupree practically screamed. "I didn't do nothin' to that bitch! The last time I seen her, a guard was takin' her to the office. They brung me here 'bout twenty minutes later, and I been here ever since. Now, I ain't talkin' no more without a lawyer. You gotta give me one, and you gotta pay for it

33

'cause I'm too poor. I ain't stupid. I know my rights." He brought his cuffed hands against his chest.

"You think you're smart, don't you?" The detective leaned on the table, his eyes two inches from the young man's face. "Like what? *Fooyay!* I think you've graduated to the big time. Agent Milovich, how does aiding and abetting a kidnapping and murder sound to you?"

"Serious. This is Louisiana. Could get the death penalty."

Agent? FBI? Dupree turned his head to break eye contact. He began to fidget, but said nothing. *That man's got the crazy eyes.* Dupree shivered perceptibly. *He looks familiar.*

Ray stuck his head out the door and spoke to the guard. He came back in and leaned against the wall in complete silence. He stared at Dupree. The tension resulted in a Mexican standoff between Ray and Dupree. Chris watched curiously. After fifteen minutes of utter quiet and Ray's gaze never faltering from Dupree, the boy slammed his fists onto the table and screamed, "Fuck you, man! Don't look at me like that! Look...that man...he gave me a crisp Benjamin to do something to upset her so bad she'd leave school. I didn't mean to hurt her, just upset her!"

"What man?" Ray jumped on the little tidbit. "What did he look like?" He pushed himself from the wall.

"I don't know." He shrugged. "He was white. 'Bout your size and..." *No. It can't be.* Dupree stopped as a look of horror spread across his face.

"And what?" Ray prompted, leaning on the table with both fists resting on the cold metal.

Oh, shit! Dupree scooted the chair away from the madman so near him. "Man, it was *you!*"

"What?" The detective jerked up straight.

"Man, it was raining at the bus stop. This white guy same size as you, wearing a hoodie, gave me a hundred dollar bill to get Miss Sloan so upset she'd go home. Said he'd meet me today to give me another hundred if I

34

succeeded. I'm tellin' you, it was you! Where's my hundred?"

"Why on Earth do you think it was me?"

"'Cause, man. I ain't never seen nobody with eyes that blue. Man, them was yo eyes!"

"Bullshit!"

Chris looked back and forth between the men, her expression total shock. "Oh, hell, no!" said Ray.

His shoulders slouched. Ray walked out of the room, hunched in dejection. He bumped the shoulder of the public defender as he came in.

Dupree reiterated, "I ain't lyin'. That man looked like Detective Reynolds, 'cept he was real scruffy."

"I believe you," said Agent Milovich.

The attorney that entered said, "I believe my client asked for a lawyer."

Dupree looked surprised at the turn of circumstances. Chris continued, "Dupree, are you aware that twelve women have been murdered?"

"Yeah. I seen it on the news." He laced his fingers together on top of the table. "Do you think this guy done it? Is he gonna kill Miss Sloan?"

"Maybe."

That ain't good. His heart raced. Dupree knitted his eyebrow together. "I'm real sorry I helped him. But a hundred"—He waved a hand in the air—"Two hundred could feed me and my momma a while. Miss Sloan—she cool. She a feisty l'il ole thang. I like her. I'm real sorry, but I ain't lyin'. Hey, do you think you could get me a pencil and some paper? I think I'll write about what Miss Sloan wanted us to and give it to her when you find her. She be real spunky. I bet she'll find a way out, and I'll tell her I'm sorry. But I ain't lyin." More relaxed, he leaned back in the chair.

35

"One more question," said the FBI agent.

"No," the lawyer objected.

Dupree said, "It's okay."

Chris nodded. "Where's the hundred dollar bill?"

"Cashed it in at the store for smaller bills. Lotsa places won't take big bills."

The agent cringed. *Damn it. No chance for fingerprints.*

Chris got a pencil and some notebook paper for Dupree before she left. Dupree did write, but nobody would ever know Dupree Parks was most afraid of having his dreams wither and die like a raisin in the sun. He hid the essay under his mattress, and, with his own feeling of futility, prayed he would get one more chance and Larkin Sloan would be found alive.

Outside the rain had returned, but Ray welcomed the refreshing drops on his face because they would hide the tears he could not stop. He heard steps behind him and his partner's voice, "Ray?"

Chris withered under the gaze Ray gave her. All the pain in the world seemed to show in his crystal blue eyes, and it pricked her to the core. *Oh, my friend.* She swallowed hard.

He whispered against the distant roll of thunder, "For almost a year I've looked at pictures of dead women and felt sick. I take a prescription acid reducer every day to keep an ulcer at bay. I throw up at least once a week from either my stomach or a migraine. I take migraine medication two or three times a week. I take Ambien just to sleep without nightmares. But *nothing* I've experienced hurts as much as that one accusation I read in your eyes. *You* of all people."

"Ray," she said in an apologetic tone, "for the record, where were you?"

36

"Talking to number twelve's boyfriend with his mother and the school counselor present."

"I knew that. I just wanted to hear the words."

Nonplussed, he looked at Chris. "I don't understand. This was just another exercise in futility."

Chris argued, "No, it wasn't. I believe the kid. We now at least have something to start with. We have a white man about six feet tall with blue eyes. You said he knew something. You were right."

They got into the car. Cyclops mewed a greeting. Ray thought his feeling of futility might pass. This was a clue, the first that would add to Ray's stress level.

Late in the afternoon, Ray and Chris drove into the cheap apartment complex where Maurice Lambert lived. The cab driver had been rendered unconscious and left at the back door of the very hospital where his fare was last seen.

A man of about sixty admitted the police officers and answered their questions to the best of his ability.

Holding up a recorder, Ray asked, "How did you come to be at the hospital?"

"I took a guy there," Lambert replied with a nod.

"Where did you pick him up?" Ray continued.

"Near St. Ignatius." The cabbie shrugged. "He seemed a little odd, but I thought that was why he was going to the hospital."

"Odd how?" Ray frowned.

Lambert scratched his head. "He seemed a little out of it, but he had on expensive clothes."

"Describe him, please," Chris requested.

"About six feet, in need of a shave, blue eyes." The cabbie scowled toward Ray. "He looked a lot like you, Detective."

"Oh, my God," grunted Ray. "Go on."

"He had on a hooded sweat shirt, the kind lots of serious runners wear, not cheap, and blue jeans. I took him to the hospital and suddenly felt his hand over my face. There was a sweet smell. I woke up at the back door of the hospital."

Ray nodded. "Did you at any time see a petite red-haired woman?"

"No. I went on into the emergency room and got examined. The doctor said I'd been drugged. I called the dispatcher and another driver picked me up. My cab was around the corner from the taxi office."

Examination of the cab turned up a few long red hairs, but there were hundreds of fingerprints as would be expected in a taxicab. Ray figured the assailant had used chloroform. He knew from the video, the man had worn gloves at least part of the time.

Ray and Chris made one more interviewing stop that evening. Chris had found an address for Bradley Tisdale. They knocked on the door of a small, well-kept house not far from St. Ignatius. They heard a man's and a woman's laughter inside. An attractive man with dark hair and strange lavender eyes opened the door. "Yes?"

Both investigators showed their badges. An unexplainable feeling of annoyance with this man made Chris begin the questions. "Bradley Tisdale?"

"Yes." Brad nodded.

Trying to keep her tone even, Chris asked, "The one who's dating Larkin Sloan?"

Brad grimaced. "Not as of night before last. Why?"

"Miss Sloan is missing." Chris whipped out a small notepad. "We're questioning anyone who might have information."

"Do I need a lawyer?" Brad came onto the small porch and closed the door behind him.

"Do you?" asked Ray, giving the man a once over and finishing with a half snarl on his lips.

Eye twitching, Brad answered, "I haven't seen her since I took her home. We had an argument. She's miss goody-two-shoes. We don't click. I broke up with her."

"How did she react to that?" Chris asked.

A cocky shrug preceded, "I haven't heard from her."

"Excuse me?" said Chris. "You broke up with her and she didn't react?"

Brad shifted from foot to foot. "I left her a voicemail. Now, if there's nothing else, I have company. If you have any more questions, I'll come see you with a lawyer." He stepped inside and closed the door on the law enforcement.

"What a prick!" Chris exclaimed.

"Yeah," Ray agreed, "but he doesn't know a thing. And his eyes aren't blue. Let's call it a night." As they walked back to the car, Ray dialed Dr. Fairchild's number and told her they would be at the school the next day.

Interviewing thirty-five teachers and staff at St. Ignatius proved frustrating. Ray had secretly hoped one of them would resemble him. None did.

Mr. Manning was the last interview of the day. The man with blond hair and hazel eyes looked worn out. It appeared the assistant principal was feeling guilty for having left Larkin Sloan to take a taxi.

Ray sighed and began, "Mr. Manning, you didn't do anything wrong, so relax. There was no way you could've anticipated Miss Sloan's abduction. However, did you see a cab and driver at the ER?"

"A taxi pulled in shortly after us. Why?" Manning asked.

"Did you get a look at the driver?" Ray asked for clarification.

The assistant principal nodded. "Old guy."

"How about the passenger?" Chris interrupted.

"No. I was focusing on getting Miss Sloan inside." Manning twisted his hands together.

Chris asked again, "Was the cab still there when you left?"

"Um"—Manning squinted his eyes as he thought—"I don't recall seeing it."

Ray rubbed his head. He could feel another migraine, or it might be the same one that had never completely stopped. He puffed out his cheeks. "Thank you, Mr. Manning. I think that's all for now."

Mr. Manning nodded sadly. "Let me know if I can do anything to help. If I had just stayed with her…"

"Don't blame yourself," said Chris with a compassionate pat to the man's shoulder. The assistant principal left the authorities to move to the next phase of their investigation.

Ray's irritation escalated as reporters bombarded him with questions at the station the next morning. "I hate these assholes," he muttered to no one. When one of them clutched his arm to get his attention, he snapped, "I will make a statement in half an hour on the front steps. Until then, I have nothing to say." He glared at the young man. "Let go of me." The reporter lifted both hands as the cop's tone and bright blue eyes burned into him.

Half an hour later, Police Chief Gerard, Agent Milovich, and Detective Reynolds appeared as a united front on the front steps of the police station. Since Ray had promised to make a statement, he took the microphone.

"As you are aware by now, day before yesterday, a thirteenth woman was reported missing. Miss Larkin Sloan, a teacher at St. Ignatius, remains unaccounted for, her whereabouts unknown." Ray displayed a photograph enlargement of Larkin.

"We are questioning a number of individuals regarding Miss Sloan's disappearance. Any information the public can provide would be greatly appreciated." He provided an anonymous tips phone number.

A reporter shouted, "Detective Reynolds, do you have a suspect?"

"Not at this moment. Any information that can be made available to the public will be made available. I have nothing else at this time."

Ray left the podium.

The reporter shouted, "Is this a serial killer?"

Ray stopped. Chris touched his shoulder. The chief discreetly nodded. Ray could feel his persistent migraine, and he knew the people of Eau Bouease had a distressing sentiment of senselessness. The detective returned to the microphone. "I think it's safe to assume we're looking at one killer, but that's all I can give you."

I'm looking like the prime suspect did not leave his mouth. However disconcerted he felt about the fact that the one lead they had pointed to him, he knew they were on to something. His mood of ineffectiveness ebbed.

5
Alone in the Dark

"Wait! Don't leave." Larkin Sloan's voice rang into the gloominess.

"I'll be back. I have to take care of you for a while. There's a sandwich, an apple, and a soda on the table beside the bed. There's also a bottle of Advil if your head hurts. The chain attached to your wrist is long enough to reach the toilet directly to your left, but not this door. Please, don't do anything to hurt yourself. I have to let Latrice know you're all right."

"Please." Her plea fell on deaf ears as she heard the door close. She knew she was alone.

Her heart prayed, *God, what do I do? What does this man want?*

After sitting quietly for some time, her answer came. *Play along. Don't upset him. Talk to him. He's reasonable, and he's not acting of his own accord. Someone is controlling him.*

Larkin's eyes adjusted somewhat to the gloom. There was a small horizontal sliver of a window high in the wall, just enough that she could see it was almost dark outside. *Dr. Fairchild will notice I'm missing. She won't take that lightly. She'll find me. Dr. Bixby saw me leave in the cab. Maybe he saw the driver. Cyclops! Oh, please, God, let someone take care of Cyclops.*

The captive looked around in the gathering shadows. She could make out the plate and soft drink can on the table just as the man had said. She could see the outline of a doorway. *That must be the bathroom.* She stood carefully and felt woozy. *Of course, I was hit in the head with a book and apparently drugged somehow.* She made it to the little

42

cubicle, which contained a commode and a lavatory. After she relieved herself, she splashed water on her face.

Back at the bed, Larkin became aware of the gnawing in her stomach. She had not eaten since six that morning, and only a Pop Tart at that. *I was rather preoccupied at lunch time.* Pressing a hand to her stomach, she eyed the meal prepared for her and wondered if it was safe to eat. *Somehow, I think it is.* A voice wafted on the air repeating a line from the movie, *The Last of the Mohicans,* "Whatever occurs, stay alive. I *will* find you." She looked around to see who was speaking, but she was alone.

Determined to survive, Larkin took a bite of the sandwich. It was tuna made with dill pickles, onion, and mustard, on whole wheat, the way she liked it. The apple was a tart Granny Smith, her favorite. She picked up the soda can. *If this is Dr. Pepper, my captor knows me very well.* It was.

As she finished her meal, such as it was, she heard a scratching sound. She pulled the pillow on the bed in front of her and cringed, envisioning massive rats scurrying across the room. She was not the squeamish type, and she did not fear the creatures. Still, her skin crawled as she thought about one scampering over her in her sleep. *I wish Cyclops was here to eat the varmint.*

Larkin found herself taking shallow breaths hoping to stop offending her nostrils. The place smelled of mold, mildew, and decay. She absentmindedly scratched, wondering if the mattress might have bedbugs.

The room began to rattle. Larkin clutched the edges of the bed. The room shook so hard she feared she would be tossed to the floor. Several minutes of violent vibrating told her she was near the railroad tracks. Feeling the wall indicated this was not a warehouse and she was underground. She could feel the dampness, and the grittiness left on her fingers had to be nitrate residue. *This place is a basement. Where am I? What kinds of places have basements when they're already below sea level—if*

I'm still in the same parish, and I think I am? She racked her brain. *I should be preparing my lesson and PowerPoint of Edgar Allan Poe, not trying to figure out a way to escape some lunatic. Poe*—the thought hit—*"The Cask of Amontillado!" Of course! This could be a place that would have had a wine cellar.* Larkin thought and thought—*a place with a wine cellar near the railroad tracks. When I get out, I have to know where to go, and I will get out!*

She was no stranger to events in the news. The smell of decay, possibly blood, made her wonder if this soft spoken, almost apologetic, man who had brought her here was behind the disappearances and deaths of twelve women. *With his mannerisms, it just doesn't add up. Then again, Ted Bundy was a charmer. Nonetheless, I don't think the man will harm me, but I'm sure I'm still in danger—just not from the man who seems nice; but, perhaps, from whomever this Latrice person is. It's someone who knows me, or has at least gone to the trouble to spy on me to be able to know things about me such as the foods I like.*

With darkness upon her, Larkin had nothing to do but think. The atmosphere felt oppressive. She could almost feel drops of condensation in the humid, stagnant air. She let her mind drift. She wondered if the police had figured out the link she had noticed in the murders the past year. *Do they realize all the women have been killed on some form of holiday, whether Christian, pagan, or national? Probably not because nobody thinks about days like Ground Hog Day, the equinoxes, or the solstices being special holidays unless they're familiar with Celtic beliefs.*

She felt compelled to share her theory with that detective from the news. She never really watched the news, but halfway listened as she graded papers or wrote. If something interesting caught her attention, she listened more closely. *What is that detective's name? He usually holds the press conferences. He has a pleasant voice.*

She shivered. *My captor has a pleasant voice.*

44

Reynolds. Yes, that's it. The newscaster said it this morning on the radio. I'll call him when I get out. The worst he can do is laugh at me. And if I'm right, I have a whole month to get through to the voice at the door. Nobody else will die until Halloween.

Maybe I'm a witch and can work some magic on this guy. She laughed. *I do have a black cat.*

Larkin's thoughts turned to her students. *What will become of them? Why was Dupree so belligerent? Is he truly a lost cause? Does he have something to do with my being here?*

Lightning flashed in the small window, and in its wake, she saw the silhouette of a cross. *Yes! I know where I am. This is the old abandoned monastery. It's in the worst possible part of town, and nobody will care if they see someone going in and out. Homeless people often sleep in the courtyard and portico. It's as historical as my house. It once had a wine cellar before the Civil War. The monks imported and sold the finest wine. The train track was laid in the 1870s and runs right behind it. About a year ago, the "For Sale" sign disappeared. I had hoped a religious group had purchased it and planned to restore it and use it to minister to the community.* "Oh, my God!" she said out loud. "What if some strange whacked-out satanic group bought the place?" She paused as if expecting the rats to reply. "What if all these killings have some crazy religious motive behind them?"

Larkin rubbed her eyes and tried to shake the cobwebs from her brain. Fatigue weighed on her. She became conscious that her right eye was no longer numb and was beginning to throb. Realizing there was nothing she could do alone in the dark to free herself, she took two of the Advil and rested on the pillow. She tried to pray, but her thoughts flew in a hundred directions. She felt a connection to her best pal, Cyclops, and instructed him to send her some help. *Silly thought I know, but any haven in a storm.* As she drifted into a fitful slumber, she dreamed of blue eyes, the bluest she had ever seen. The eyes seemed to be in pain and darted to and fro as if frantically searching for something. An irritated, frustrated voice, the voice she had heard earlier in the evening, a familiar voice, accompanied the eyes. "I have to find Larkin. I won't let her die." The eyes seemed to stare directly at her, and she could not break their gaze; neither did she want to. She found solace in those eyes.

6
Compassionate Captive

Larkin started awake as the door to her prison creaked. "Hello?" she ventured into the darkness. The sliver of window told her another gray dawn was approaching.

"I brought you some breakfast," said the voice from the night before. "Are you all right? Do you need anything?"

"I need to go home."

"Sorry. I can't grant that wish." The man came closer. "I hope you like sausage biscuits. I brought coffee and orange juice. Cream and sugar?"

"Just cream—three."

"Want some coffee with your milk?" The man's voice sounded light, almost laughing. He offered her a Styrofoam cup.

She pretended not to be able to reach the cup. "I can't reach it. Can you come closer?"

"Really? Why? Do you want to see my face? Latrice wouldn't like that."

"Who's Latrice?"

"She tells me what to do. She told me how to get you here and what to do to keep you here and how to take care of you. She told me what to make you for dinner last night. Was it done right?"

"It was delicious. Thank you *so* much." She didn't try to keep the sarcasm out of her voice. "Do you always listen to Latrice?"

"I just started hearing her a couple of weeks ago."

"I see," Larkin said, realizing she might be dealing with a mentally unstable person. She walked as far as her leash would allow. "I really can't reach it. See?"

Larkin heard relief in the man's voice as he said, "I guess your chain is a little short."

"It does reach the bathroom though," she said, trying to draw him into a conversation. "But it's not really a bathroom. How am I supposed to bathe?"

"I...I don't know. Latrice didn't say."

The man took a couple of steps closer, but kept his face averted as he handed her a sausage biscuit and a cup of coffee.

"I appreciate it," she said honestly.

"Can you carry your juice, too?"

"Um." She balanced the biscuit on top of the cup. "Sure."

The man turned to leave. Larkin said, "Please don't go. Stay and talk to me for a little while. Have breakfast with me. I don't like to eat alone."

"But you live alone."

"Ah, but my cat always has breakfast with me." Larkin could not help but feel the lonely melancholy as she thought of breakfasting only with Cyclops and the last time she had been with him, she hadn't even been able to do that.

"I had a dog when I was a kid," the man said guardedly. "He was a golden retriever. His name was Dawg, D-A-W-G. I named him Dog, you know like in *Big Jake*. John Wayne's dog was just Dog, but I spelled it D-A-W-G because he was a Southern dog."

"What happened to him?"

"He was in the back of my dad's truck when my dad and my little sister, Ronnie—Rhonda—hit a deer. Dad lost control, and they were all killed. I was thirteen." He paused. "Sometimes Dawg still comes to show me the way to go."

"I'm sorry. You know, my parents were killed in a wreck when I was five. We have something in common." She had a fleeting thought, *Another Son of Sam? Oh, my God, he's listening to a dead dog.* "Cyclops is all alone. He might *starve* without me," she said, hoping to gain sympathy for her pet as leverage.

48

"I have to go. I'm not supposed to talk to you." The man stopped slouching and headed for the door again.

Larkin surmised he was about six feet tall. He wore jeans and a hooded sweatshirt, utilizing the hood over his head to shield his face. It was hard to gauge his weight with the shirt on, but he seemed thin, not skinny, but perhaps buff.

"Why can't you talk to me?" she asked, desperate to keep her captor talking.

"Latrice says your voice is strong, and you'll only confuse me."

"I don't want to confuse you. I just want to know why someone as nice as you has me chained to a bed. Are you going to rape me or kill me?"

"Neither! I would never do that," the man said in a frightened voice. "I don't want to do anything to you. Latrice wants you."

"What does Latrice say she wants with me?"

"She says you're the last. You're supposed to purify this country and bring forth a leader to stop the chaos."

"How am I supposed to do that?" Her stomach roiled.

"I don't know. Latrice didn't say." A well manicured hand massaged the man's temple area as if he were getting a headache.

"Let me ask you something. How can a person do anything if she doesn't even know Latrice? When will she be coming to meet me?"

"On your special day." He dropped his hand to his side.

"The day I'm to die like twelve other women? You said you wouldn't hurt me."

"No! No!" the man said. Clearly agitated, he clenched his fists against his thighs.

"Latrice wants to hurt me, but you don't. Don't listen to her. Listen to me."

"Stop!" the man screamed as he put his hands over his ears. "Too many voices. I am getting a headache."

49

Larkin spoke softly. "I'm sorry. If you can't listen to me, listen to Dawg. Where would he lead you?"

The man said pathetically, "You don't understand. There are so many voices. It's a cacophony. Latrice said if I listen to her, the voices will stop."

"How many voices were there before Latrice?"

"Do you really care?"

"Yes."

"A lot before I started taking pills. Then, not so many."

"Are you taking your pills?"

"No." He shook his head. "Latrice said she could make the voices stop without them."

"She lied. Don't listen to her anymore."

"I would do anything to stop the voices."

"Anything?"

"Yes."

"Would you take your pills even though Latrice says not to?"

"I have to get some more."

"Get some and come back and talk to me. I can't promise the voices will leave, but I *will* try to help you. I swear it."

A strained silence lingered several moments. "Why would you want to help me if you think I want to hurt you?" he asked barely above a whisper.

"You don't want to hurt me. Latrice does. She wants to hurt you, too. She *is* hurting you right now by not giving you your medication. You need it."

"I can't go back to the health department to get the pills."

Larkin could tell she was getting through to the man. "Why?"

"Latrice is there."

"Is Latrice's voice there?"

"No, she's there."

"Is Latrice here?"

"No!" The man's agitation elevated. "Latrice is *not* a voice, Larkin. She's real. She'll be so mad I talked to you."

"Don't tell her. Do you know where the free clinic run by Charity Chapel is located?"

"Yes."

"They'll take care of you. Tell them Larkin sent you."

The man began to pace. "I have to get out of here. I have to stop the voices." He headed for the door.

"Please!" Larkin shouted.

"Please what? Listen to *your* voice? Let *you* help?" The peculiar man came into the small patch of light very close to her, and she looked into the bluest eyes she had ever seen—the same eyes she had seen in her dream, yet not the same. These eyes were lost, begging to be found. Though they had deep dark circles, this man's eyes were breathtaking.

Without thinking, she reached out and touched his cheek. She whispered, "No, follow Dawg. I'm sure he'll lead you to safety. If you don't think you can trust me, trust him. Maybe he's your guardian angel."

Blue eyes backed away and left Larkin alone.

She put her hand to her mouth and closed her eyes. She prayed. *Oh, God, is he crazy? Please, God, send an angel to guide him. He's in so much pain, so much trouble. Please, protect him. Show me how to help him.*

Something about the man made her feel deep compassion for him. Larkin could not help but think something about this man just did not add up. *He looks and smells like a street urchin, but the clothes he has on, although dirty, are top-line.* She had recognized the Diadora logo on the sweatshirt. *Only serious athletes wear that. The jeans are American Eagle, top-line mall apparel. His speech patterns are educated and cultured; his vocabulary, amazing. And he also looks vaguely familiar. Where have I seen him?*

She rubbed her own temple. She lay back and gave into sleep once more. Again she dreamed of blue eyes, but this

51

time Cyclops was with the blue eyes. The eyes seemed more focused, more determined.

7
Confused Captor

Though almost closing time, the free clinic remained packed with people. A nurse walked into the center of the waiting room. "Ladies and gentlemen, we have to close for today. I have the sign-in sheet. Dr. Grant will be here tomorrow at eight, and we'll start where we left off."

The indigent sick moaned, but started shuffling out the door. Against the tide, a hooded figure approached the nurse. He touched her arm with some force and spoke hoarsely, "Please, I can't wait until tomorrow. I need to see a doctor today."

"I'm sorry, sir," the nurse replied calmly. "Come back tomorrow."

The man covered his ears and looked around furtively before he shouted, "Shut up!"

The nurse jumped at the outburst. Blue eyes pleaded at the woman again and he whispered, "Please? Larkin. Larkin said you would help. Larkin sent me."

The nurse asked quickly, "When did you see Larkin?"

The man shook his head. "Recently. Please, make the voices stop. Larkin said to tell you she sent me. Her voice is very soothing. I don't want it to stop—just the others." The man fumbled in his jacket pocket and handed the nurse two prescription bottles. "I need these. Please, help me."

The nurse took the bottles and read the labels. "Haldol and Abilify?" she questioned.

The man nodded. The caregiver looked concerned. "These are very strong meds. I'm not sure we have samples here. I'll see if Dr. Lucas will write you a prescription. I'll do it only because Larkin sent you."

The man nodded again and plunged his hands into the pockets of the sweatshirt, his shoulders hunched. The nurse

53

went into the back of the clinic and spoke with Dr. Lucas, a member of Charity Chapel who dedicated one day a week to the free clinic, as did two other doctors and three nurses from the church. The clinic was only open three days a week. Those who could pay a nominal fee did, but medical care was available to all.

Dr. Lucas wrote down the name, address, and phone number on the bottles. He asked, "Does he appear to need these, Sybil?"

"Oh, yeah. He was telling voices to shut up, but he seems to be seeking help—And *Larkin* sent him."

"Yeah, but when?" Dr. Lucas unlocked the pharmaceutical cabinet. He put three of each pill into its bottle and wrote the prescriptions. "Give him these, but ask him to come back on my day next week. Make sure you get his name to see if it's the same as on the bottles, and I'm calling the police. He might know where Larkin is. Try to keep him talking until the police get here."

Sybil came back into the now empty waiting room except for the figure who sat holding his head. She gently touched the man's shoulder. When he raised deep-set, hollow, bloodshot blue eyes to the nurse, her heart went out to him. The caregiver went to the water cooler and filled a paper cup. Then she handed the man one of each pill and the water. "Take 'em," the nurse's gentle voice encouraged.

He shakily took the two pills and swallowed them. Sybil asked, "How long have you been off?"

"A few weeks. Thank you." The patient looked around and scowled at the government-issue green paint and cheap aluminum chairs. "I could make this place look more inviting."

She took the cup from his hand. "Is this really your name?"

He nodded. "Yes. I have to go. I have to take care of her. She'll be hungry, and she wants a bath."

"Who? Larkin?"

The man looked around, agitated. "I have to go. She's going to be so mad if she finds out. Thank you." The man snatched the bottles and the prescriptions from Sybil's hand and flew out the door.

Ten minutes later, Raiford Reynolds and Christine Milovich walked through the door. Dr. Lucas and Sybil met them, and Sybil pointed at Ray. "Good, Lord! You just grabbed prescriptions for Haldol and Abilify from me and ran out the door."

"What?" Ray asked in confusion.

Sybil repeated, "You could be the guy who was just in here except he needs to shave badly."

"Tell us *everything*," the police detective demanded.

A short time later in the car, Ray said to Chris, "Three people would identify me in a line up. This is crazy!" He handed the name and information to Chris. "And *that* is crazier."

The hooded vagabond handed the prescriptions to the pharmacist who looked at the customer in disgust. She asked, "These are pretty expensive. Do you have the money for them or insurance, by chance?"

The man reached into the pocket of his jeans and pulled out a roll of money. "Yeah, I can pay you. Haven't you ever heard the adage, 'Don't judge a book by its cover'?"

The woman frowned, but filled the prescriptions and took his money. He walked to the door, followed by the pharmacist. Immediately as he stepped out, the woman locked the door, flipped over the closed sign, and lowered the blinds. The sign on the door read, "Hours: 9:00 A.M. to 6:00 P.M., Monday – Saturday. Closed Sunday."

The man muttered to himself, "Must be closing time." It was almost dark as he darted away like a long-distance track runner. After nearly forty-five minutes of hard running, he stopped and leaned on a park bench, winded. In the darkness only a handful of people jogged or walked their dogs in the park. He collapsed onto the bench and breathed deep gulps of air. Seemingly unable to help himself, he fell asleep.

Larkin was so hungry she felt sick. All she had ingested for two days was water from the tap in the lavatory. *Have I scared the poor man completely away and doomed myself to die of starvation?* Lying on the bed, she bolted upright when the door flung open and her breathless captor came in. He sank to the floor right beside the bed.

"What happened? Where have you been?" Larkin asked frantically.

In answer, the man held up two full bottles of pills. Through gulps of air, he said triumphantly, "I got my meds, and ran all the way back. I only stopped a minute."

Larkin sank back on the bed. It dawned on her that this man had no concept of time. She asked gently, "Do you know how long you've been gone?"

Blue eyes looked at her, questioning and confused. "A couple of hours."

Larkin shook her head.

"How long?" he asked.

"Two days," she answered matter-of-factly.

"I left you alone for two days? *Mo chagren*; I'm sorry." The man began to pace. "Oh, you must be starving." Wringing his hands he added, "Latrice gave me money to take care of you. I used some of it for the meds. Was that wrong? Never mind. It doesn't matter." He gestured for Larkin to wait. "I'll be back in a few minutes."

Larkin was beside herself. She tried fruitlessly to force her hand through the cuff. *If he's gone a few more days, I'll be skin and bone, and my hand will slip right through.*

She didn't have to wait long. Her captor returned within an hour. "Latrice told me you like Mexican." He sounded almost happy. "I didn't know exactly what, so I got a lot of different things." He set two bags from Taco Bell on the bed. He lit several candles and illuminated the room, barren except for the bed and two rotting wine casks, on which the man set the candles. Larkin watched in dismay.

Her captor slid the hood from his head and sat at the foot of the bed. He was no longer trying to hide from her. She didn't know whether that was good or bad, but she couldn't help but notice the man was very good looking in spite of the fact that he needed to shave. His short raven-black hair had a few flecks of gray at the temples. He looked at Larkin; cheeks dimpled slightly, deeper on the right side than the left; and shrugged. "I'm sorry. I lost all track of time, but I should've realized how long it had been. I took the two samples of meds the nurse handed me. I ran from the clinic and straight to a pharmacy before I stopped on a park bench to rest a minute. I fell asleep. I thought it was only a little cat nap. I haven't slept much lately. The voices were too loud. That's where I woke up and ran back here. That was two days ago? I thought it was the same day." He ran a smooth hand except for a callus on the middle finger near the nail through his hair and laughed a little bitterly. "It's too weird that I slept so long in the park, and nobody noticed or cared."

The guy opened the two bags and began spreading out the food. He handed Larkin a large cup of Dr. Pepper and pulled out a second cup into which he plunged a straw and took a long draught to wash down two pills he had in his hand. He held up his cup at her stare. "Coke. I got something for me, too. Is that all right?"

She nodded and sipped her drink. At the sight of the food, she pointed, "Taco. Chalupa. Do they have sour cream? I love sour cream."

Prolonged exposure had dulled her senses to the putrid smell of her surroundings. Larkin bit into a crunchy taco and thought food had never tasted so good. She had devoured two crunchy tacos and a chalupa before she realized her captor was laughing at her.

"What's so funny?" she asked. "I was starving."

"So I see." Larkin's captor sobered. "I really am sorry. And I've been thinking. You might be right. Latrice might be the crazy one. I'm not so confused any more. You see, I've been on meds for a long time, since my senior year in college. My mom made sure I took them. She would call me every morning and say, 'Ray, did you take your pills?' She died, and I sort of forgot to take my pills every day. Then the prescription ran out. Now, I'm taking them again, and I'm hearing Mom's voice. But that's okay." He held up both hands and pushed gently on the air. "She always gives me good advice. She's telling me I shouldn't listen to Latrice anymore."

"And turns into a chatterbox?" Larkin asked with a grin. "So, your name is Ray?"

He nodded. "My name is really Raiford. My folks called me Ray for short. It's not what I've always wanted to be called, but that's okay. You may call me Ray. Will you talk to me for a while? Latrice was right about one thing. Your voice is strong."

Larkin argued, "Only because deep inside you wanted to hear the voice of reason. Ray, is Latrice a real person?"

Ray nodded again. "Yes. I told you she wasn't a voice. The voices have never made any sense. They were just intangible voices, like I could hear other people's thoughts—the more people, the more voices. Yeah, Latrice is real, very real. I went to the health department to get my meds. It's easier to go there than to drive into New Orleans

58

where my shrink is. She was new. I thought she actually liked me—me a whacko who hears voices. Yeah, right!"

"You're not a whacko, Ray. You have an illness, and you need your medicine. Ray, don't leave again."

"I have to get us something to eat."

"Yeah. Well, go to the store. Bring an ice chest and something we can make. We need to talk a lot."

"All right, but may I do it in the morning? I'm tired. Although I apparently slept for two days, I am really tired."

"It's your body trying to heal itself the way God intended. All right," she conceded, "we'll sleep, but where will you sleep?"

Ray shook his head. "I'm not going to hurt you, Larkin. I would never force myself on you. I've never been *that* crazy. I'll sleep right here on the floor if you'll share one of your blankets."

She handed him a blanket, and he lay on the floor by the bed and fell asleep instantly.

8
Determined Detective

Ray and Chris arrived back at the police station. At his desk, Ray reached in the drawer and pulled out his Amidrine. At his partner's frown he quipped, "I need my meds!"

She laughed. He took a pill with a swig from the bottled water on his desk. Looking at Chris, he winked and joked, "At least, I don't hear voices."

"True. But you do have another headache, huh?"

"One's trying to come on, but I'm determined to stop it before it starts." He guzzled more water. "That's beside the point. This case just gets more bizarre by the day. We really need to find this guy. Apparently, he's some lunatic who's heard God tell him to do it."

"I don't think so," Chris argued. "I'm not at all sure this guy has hurt anybody." They heard footsteps. "There's Baker with the search warrant. You gonna fall asleep on me?"

"No way! Somebody with my face is making me look really bad. *Allons.*"

Chris shook her head with a wry smile as she was beginning to pick up some of Ray's Cajun French. He laughed lightly at her expression, his dimples showing, the right one a bit deeper than the left. "Let's go. I wanna know what makes this guy tick."

After a short drive, Ray and Chris arrived at a modest, but classy, neighborhood of relatively new townhouses. Inside the suspect's home, it was apparent he probably had not been there in a while. They walked through just looking

60

around at first. Molding dishes sat in the sink. Chris opened the refrigerator. "Oh!" she gasped, closing it fast. "The stench. It smells like sour milk and rotten bologna."

Ray sighed. "The rest of the house is spotless except for a thin layer of dust." The living room contained a sofa, a recliner, and a fine entertainment center with tables that matched. Two barstools stood at the bar which separated the kitchen from the dining area. A glass and black wrought iron dinette set with four chairs filled the dining room. The only decorations in the house were a pen and ink drawing of a medieval castle hung over the fireplace and an oil painting of a Victorian village on the wall between the two windows in the dining room. Ray continued his observation. "Orderly. Not cramped."

Chris agreed with a nod. "Yes, he seems to be uncomplicated. It makes me wonder about his mindset."

"How?"

"Getting his meds the way he did. He seems to be coming to his senses."

They walked through the rest of the house. The bed in what appeared to be the master bedroom was made. Chris opened the closet. "His clothes are hung neatly. Suits and silk ties. He's a professional."

Ray opened the drawers of the dresser and chest of drawers. "These things are sorted by color. Boxer briefs, just like me." He laughed. "There's a drawer of socks missing a mate. I keep mine in a clothes basket." He opened the valet on top of the dresser. "Must make *real good* money. Onyx and diamond cuff links and tie tack. Money clip with about fifty bucks." He picked up a watch. "It's a Rolex!"

Chris agreed. "Yeah, he must make *good* money. Nice suits—nothing off the rack. One's an *Armani*."

Ray whistled his appreciation. The FBI agent crossed the hall while Ray checked the bathroom. The second bedroom appeared to serve as an office and home gym. It contained a desk with state-of-the art computer equipment, a drafting table, a treadmill, and a Bowflex. Several finished and unfinished blueprints lay on the table. All were initialed "R. G."

The downstairs half-bath appeared never to be touched while the upstairs bathroom, which could be entered from either bedroom, had everything in compulsive order; toiletries were arranged methodically.

"He's been here," Ray said.

Chris stuck her head in the door. "How do you know?"

The cop pointed to two small clean circles in the dusty countertop of the upstairs bathroom. "But he didn't stay. He came long enough to get his medication bottles. That's where they sat. Where has he been staying?"

"I don't know," Chris said. "I think we need to get a description of him to all the local pharmacies."

"Yeah." Ray nodded. "I can just walk in and say, 'Hey, I look just like a mass murderer. Take my picture.'"

Chris snickered in spite of the seriousness of the situation. "We still need to get it out there."

"I know."

"Then," Chris continued, motioning Ray into the office/gym, "we need to go to Bertram and Associates. That's the name on the blueprints." She fingered one of them. "It appears our whacko is a brilliant architect. I would give my right arm to live in this house."

"It *is* nice," agreed Ray, looking over Chris's shoulder. Returning to the bathroom, he bagged the toiletries to obtain fingerprints and DNA and confiscated the computer from the office.

As they left the house, the next door neighbor and her daughter arrived home. The little girl squealed in delight, "Mr. Ray!" and flung her arms around Ray's legs. The mother seemed pleased, too, to see the man she thought was her neighbor.

"Mr. Gautier, it's nice to have you home again. You've been gone such a long time that I thought you had moved." The woman eyed Ray's holster and gun strangely.

Ray looked at Chris and shook his head in disbelief. Juggling the computer, he reached into his pocket and took out his badge. He extended his hand and politely introduced himself. "Hello, ma'am. I'm Detective Raiford Reynolds, and this is my partner, Agent Christine Milovich. It's come to my attention in the last few days that I resemble your neighbor."

"No," the woman countered. "You look *just* like him. I'm Carol Johnson, and this is my daughter, Sheena."

Ray patted the little girl on the head. "Hi. I'm sorry I'm not your friend." He turned back to Carol. "We are, however, looking for Mr. Gautier. What can you tell us about him?"

"Is he in some kind of trouble?" asked Mrs. Johnson with a dubious expression.

"We're not sure yet. We need to talk to him though."

"I find it hard to believe Ray Gautier could be in any kind of trouble." Mrs. Johnson shook her head. "He's a very nice man. He lives alone and is very quiet."

Ray asked, "Are you familiar with his friends or family?"

"Not really. I never met his family. Some Fridays he goes out, but he never has company unless a courier delivers something to his house. He's an architect."

"Would you call him a loner?"

"He's not antisocial, just quiet. Last C-H-R-I-S-T-M-A-S he built a D-O-L-L-H-O-U-S-E for S-A-N-T-A." She glanced down at her daughter who looked about three. "My husband's in Iraq, and Ray has been great helping with Sheena."

"What about his background?" Chris asked.

"He had a rough Christmas season himself. His mother who lived in Lake Charles died unexpectedly shortly after Christmas. He took it pretty hard."

"Of course," Chris said. "How did that affect his demeanor?"

"He acted a little strange sometimes after that, but I didn't think much of it, considering his loss. He mentioned she was the only family he had."

"Right." Ray noted Chris writing in a notepad when he couldn't since he was holding the computer.

"So he has no family?" Ray asked for confirmation.

"He had a sister. He said Sheena reminded him of his little sister who had been killed in a car accident many years ago."

"Did you visit with him frequently?"

"Our conversations usually took place out here. I've only been in his house once to see the blueprints for"— Carol stretched her eyes wide so as not to give away a secret to the child who looked back and forth among the adults—"He was very respectful about my being a married woman, almost old-fashioned. The only time he ever came into my house was to put together you-know-what. I offered him some eggnog, but he declined. He said he took medication that didn't mix well with alcohol."

"When did you last see him?"

"About two weeks ago. He left one morning, and I haven't seen him since. When he left, it was strange that he wasn't dressed nice like he usually dresses. He had on jeans and a sweatshirt. He usually wears suits and ties when he goes to work unless he's going to a construction site; then, he wears jeans and a sport shirt. The only time he wears sweats or warm-ups is cool evenings when he jogs."

"So, would you say he's in good physical shape?" Chris questioned.

"Great shape. I know he's run in a couple of charity marathons."

"Did you ever hear him talking to himself or overhear any conversations with someone else?" asked Chris.

Sheena piped up, "Mr. Ray told me sometimes he hears things other people don't hear. He said it was his music to create. I miss Mr. Ray. He brings me treats home from work."

"Yes, he does, Reese's bars," confirmed Carol.

"Well, thank you," Ray said as he fumbled to hand Mrs. Johnson his card. "If you think of anything that might help us find him or if he comes home, please, call me."

Carol called after them, "Officers, should I keep my L-O-A-D-E-D G-U-N handy?"

"Can't hurt," Ray said with a curt nod.

Ray and Chris took the bagged items and Ray Gautier's computer to the police lab, and Ray started back out the door rather than heading for his office. Chris asked, "Where are you going?"

"To Bertram and Associates."

"Ray, it's after eight o'clock." She chortled. "Nobody will be there. We'll have to go in the morning."

"Of course," he said. "It's just that this is the first real lead we've had."

"I know," Chris agreed. "I have an idea. Let's have dinner together, get a real night's sleep, and I'll meet you here at seven A.M. And I swear if you don't go home, I'm gonna lock you up for your lunacy."

"You would try." Ray agreed to Chris's suggestion. Before he left he typed in the information he had on Raiford Gautier for the Office of Motor Vehicles. "I'll have a printout in the morning." He grinned, but being determined to learn more about his look-alike, Ray called his mother after he got home rather late.

"Raiford Reynolds!" Dorothy Reynolds answered cheerfully. "What are you doing calling your old folks so late?"

Ray's father piped from the background, "Speak for yourself."

His mother continued, "Is something wrong?"

"I'm not sure, Mom. I have to ask you something very personal."

"Of course, honey. What do you need?"

"Mom, did Audrey by any chance have twins?"

"Why would you ask that?"

Ray explained what was going on.

Dorothy answered, "Honey, honestly, I really don't know. Father Dawler only told us your mother was named Audrey and that she had been a prostitute. He said he thought she might have been on drugs and you might have some problems because of the drugs and the fact you were premature." Her voice took on a nostalgic twang. "But you were the most beautiful baby. You looked just like a little toy, and the only problem you've ever had is migraines." She sighed. "Adoptions thirty years ago were still very private, almost secretive. You know if Dad and I had known there were two of you, we would've taken both. You should've been together if that's what happened. Of course, the agency may have thought they were helping two couples who desperately wanted a baby. Ray, I would never suggest you abuse your powers as a detective, but you can get information civilians can't. Look into it.

"Ray, not to change the subject, but will you be able to come this weekend?"

"I don't know, Mom. I think Ronnie would understand my trying to keep someone alive."

"I'm sure she would, honey." She took a long breath and sighed. "I'll call you if you can't get away."

"Thanks—for everything. I love you, Mom. Tell Dad I love him, too. Good night."

Ray sat for a while thinking about his life. The cat he had brought home with him jumped onto his lap. He rubbed Cyclops's head absentmindedly as he thought. It had been good for the most part. He had been spoiled rotten. As his mother had said, the only physical problem he had ever had was migraines. Now, he wondered. *Is there another just*

66

like me, and maybe he has real problems stemming from poor prenatal care?

Ray made a note in his notebook:

> Visit Bertram and Associates
> Visit Hall of Records
> Question nuns at Catholic Charity Hospital

He was more determined than ever to find Larkin Sloan alive and, now, to find and know the other Raiford. He fell asleep with the cat beside him, but he had disturbing dreams all night.

9

Patient Partner

"You're late," Ray said as Chris drove into the parking lot. He waited leaning against his antique Mustang.

"It's seven-oh-two. I brought breakfast. Coffee does not breakfast make. I know you haven't eaten."

"We have a lot to do."

"They won't even open until nine."

"The Hall of Records opens at eight."

"Why the Hall of Records?"

"I have a twin." He plunged his hands into the pockets of his slacks.

"Ray?"

"I'm certain of it."

"Well, shut up and have breakfast. Knowing you, we'll miss lunch, but I love you anyway. At least you obviously went home last night." She nodded approval. "Black is your color."

Ray dressed in gray dress trousers with a black button-down shirt and a silver silk tie. "I wanted to make a better impression at Bertram and Associates than I did with Dr. Fairchild."

"The navy slacks with a light blue oxford shirt and blue striped tie you wore to conduct interviews at the school were fine." Chris patted his cheek, and asked, "But how on Earth do two sets of adoptive parents name their kid *Raiford*? It's not exactly the most common name, now is it?"

"Just luck I guess." He shrugged.

They walked into the station together. He held the door open for her. His first stop was the printer. "Fuck me!" he blurted, holding up a document.

"What?" asked Chris taking the printout from Ray. "Shit!" She looked up at her temporary partner, eyes wide. "Maybe you *do* have a twin. Blue Escort. That's a lead."

She grabbed a second fax. "Prints show nothing. No record, not even a traffic violation."

Ray nodded and they sat down. He gratefully ate the ham and cheese croissants. Stifling a burp, he commented, "If you stay around, Mom can quit harping on me about needing to gain weight. I'll get fat."

"Are you saying I'm fat?" Chris teased.

"No way!" Ray raised his hands as if in surrender, nodding his head toward her navy-blue pin-striped pantsuit with a simple white silk blouse and blue loafers. "You're beautiful." He pointed his finger at her. "That is *not* sexual harassment."

"I never thought it was. Thanks for the compliment."

"Chris, may I ask you something?"

"Sure."

"Why aren't you married with a houseful of kids? You love mothering people."

"I'm the eldest of seven. My mother died when I was twelve. I mothered six siblings. I still have time. I'm the same age as you, Ray. I could ask you the same basic question."

"I never met Miss Right, someone who could actually deal with being a cop's wife. I *was* engaged. When I got shot during a domestic disturbance call—that ended that." He spread his hands out in front of him in a sharp, flattening motion. "She went running to the arms of my so-called best friend."

"Marry me, Ray." Chris laughed. "I understand."

Ray laughed loudly, dimples etching deeply. "No. You'd strangle me on our wedding night. My best friend you might be, but we're too much alike to be lovers."

"True," she agreed, "but at least I'm patient enough to put up with your bullshit."

"Well, will you go with me to the Hall of Records?"

"Yes, but *after* we go to Bertram and Associates, just in case we get bogged down going through hundreds of old records. You know the case is more important than your personal needs."

"What if they're connected? What if I have an identical twin"—He picked up the printout of Raiford Gautier's driver's license—"who's killed twelve women?"

"You'll deal with it. You can come to work for the FBI. We're all screwed up in the head."

"Thanks, Chris. I'm glad to know you think I'm screwed up in the head, just not as badly as my twin."

"Ray, somehow, I don't think our guy is a killer. Maybe he's just someone who needs a little mothering. Hey! He looks as good as you. Maybe I'll take him home with me since I can't have you."

Ray laughed as he dropped his Styrofoam cup into the trash. "Well, move your butt, Mom. Let's get to work."

Roughly two hours later, Ray and Chris walked into the opulent lobby of Bertram and Associates where the patterned flooring reflected the light from the crystal chandelier. The receptionist greeted them with enthusiasm. "Mr. Gautier! How nice to see you."

"Here we go again," Ray muttered. He introduced himself and Chris and asked to speak to anyone who could give them information that might help them find Mr. Gautier.

After a brief trip down the hall, the receptionist escorted them to the owner, Walter Bertram, himself. When they walked into the office, Mr. Bertram exclaimed, "My goodness! Janice said you looked like Ray, but this is unbelievable."

"More unbelievable is that we have the same name," Ray said.

"True," agreed Mr. Bertram, shaking hands with both officials. "Please sit down, detectives. Have you finally come to investigate my missing person's report?"

"You filed a missing person's report?" Ray asked.

"Yep. And I haven't heard a word." Bertram moved to stand behind his chair.

"No, sir," Ray admitted. "That's not why we came, but I'll look into it. We need to find Mr. Gautier because it's possible he's involved in the disappearance of Larkin Sloan."

"No way!"

"Tell us everything you can about Raiford Gautier," said Chris as she and Ray sat in chairs on the opposite side of Bertram's desk.

"Wow!" Bertram exclaimed. "It could take a while." He sat down in his executive chair.

"We're patient," assured Chris with a genuine smile.

"Ray's a wonderful man and a gifted architect. He's like a son to me."

Here we go again. Ray shook his head. *Another surrogate child.*

Walter Bertram looked fatherly to Chris with his glistening bald pate encircled by a blue-gray ring from ear to ear around the back of his head. He was a tad on the heavy side, but his soft gray eyes defined by deep crow's feet made him look gentle and made her think of her own father. His statement penetrated her thoughts. "As a matter of fact, I've been contemplating making him my partner. He's just that good. Since I'm in the middle of a divorce, Ray's the closest thing I'll ever have to a son because my daughter has no interest in the business. He designed the entire community where he lives. You've seen it, I assume, so you know how good he really is." Bertram laced his fingers together on top of his desk.

"He does have talent," Ray agreed. "How did he come to be a part of your company?"

"Ray applied for an internship here when he was in college. I'm a Tulane alum, so I offer an internship to architectural majors. His drawings were excellent, his grades outstanding. He came to work for nothing; he was on scholarship, no real income. He was here on Mondays, Wednesdays, and Fridays and drove back to Tulane on Tuesdays and Thursdays for his classes."

"And he's been with you since?" Ray prompted.

"Not quite. He was a very likeable young man. I'm a sucker for a hard-luck case. So, I invited Ray to stay in our garage apartment. He ate all his meals with us. My wife did his laundry. We fell in love with him, but, more importantly, our nineteen-year-old daughter did, too. Yes, Ray loved her, too, *more* than she loved him."

"So, he's involved with your daughter?" Chris asked.

Bertram frowned deeply at the memory. "Not anymore. They went to New Orleans for Mardi Gras at my daughter's—Abigail's—insistence. Ray isn't a big-crowd type. His idea of a crowd was a fraternity bash." He chuckled slightly. "He was a Delt at Tulane, just like me."

A Delt? Ray could not believe this man who looked like him was in the same fraternity on a different campus.

"Thousands of drunks just didn't appeal to him, but he loved the girl. While they were there, some drunks mugged them. Ray took the worst of it. He defended Abbey. He ended up in the hospital with severe head trauma. After that, Ray started hearing voices. His doctors said he was probably schizophrenic and the brain injury aggravated the problem. *Bullshit* is what I say." He slapped the top of his desk to emphasize his irritation. "Trauma caused it."

Chris waited a moment for Ray to speak. When he didn't she asked, "So, you're saying Mr. Gautier has a mental condition?"

The older man sighed and re-laced his fingers across his slightly protruding middle. "He started taking medication and got better. Nonetheless, my very immature child couldn't cope with a boyfriend with a serious psychological

72

condition. After being physically and mentally damaged, Ray had to deal with emotional damage—Abbey's rejection. He went home, but still managed to graduate with high honors. Ray is very intelligent and compulsively diligent." Bertram folded his arms as if to protect his memory of Ray Gautier.

Chris took over the questions, uncertain of what had come over her partner. "He left your company. When and how did he come back?"

"Abbey moved to New York. I found out Ray couldn't get a job, as brilliant as he was, because of his condition. I called him and offered him a job. When he asked about Abbey, I told her she had moved. He came back to work for me about four years ago. I'm the only one here who knows about his condition."

"How has he behaved?"

"Until his mother's death at Christmas, Ray hadn't had any symptoms. After her death, I think he stopped taking his meds. He started missing work, coming in late. Then, he stopped showing up. He wasn't at home either."

Bertram glowered at the two law enforcement officers. "I filed a missing person's report, but in light of all the brutal murders, one missing schizophrenic was insignificant. I'm angry, detectives, but that's how I feel. And if you think Ray has killed anybody, you're the crazy ones." He pointed a decisive finger at the two younger people to drive his point home. "When you find him, treat him right. Bring him back. He needs somebody to watch after him. I owe him that. He probably saved my daughter's life and lost a great part of himself in doing so."

Speechless, Ray mumbled a hasty good-bye and thanks. Chris thanked Mr. Bertram for his time and promised to call him when his Ray was found.

Visibly shaken, Ray left the office with his shoulders slouched, but Chris held back a moment to speak to the owner of the company. "Mr. Bertram, my partner was adopted. He thinks your Ray is his twin. What you've shared with us has made a world of difference to *my* Ray." She looked toward the door with worry etched on her face. "I promise you no harm will come to yours from us, but if he does contact you, get him to come to us. That way we can ensure his safety and both their sanities."

She left her card and found her partner in the lobby. He started to speak, but she put her finger to her lips. "Shh. Let's go. It's time for a long patient afternoon in the Hall of Records."

"You don't understand. I know who beat him up. It's been seven and a half years, but I was at the same Mardi Gras celebration. If I had gone with my fraternity brothers rather than staying with Rob to get a tattoo, I would've met him then, and none of this would be happening."

"Don't be silly. None of this is your fault. Now, let's go see what we can find out at the Hall of Records." Ray's revelation weighed on her, but she refused to voice her thoughts.

Usually a magpie, Chris was quiet all the way to the Hall of Records. Ray studied her facial expression. It was obvious she was deep in thought about something that brought a crease to her brow.

"What's wrong, Chris?" he asked. "You look as if you're ready to cry."

"I'm fine. I was just remembering some unpleasant things. Don't worry about me. My life experiences are where I get the patience to deal with you. We're here."

"Something's bothering you."

"I *don't* wanna talk about it." Her tone felt like a slap in the face. Ray had never seen her in such a mood.

"Okay," he said with reluctance. "For now."

Chris scowled at him. She knew he would eventually get her to talk and she dreaded it.

74

10
Vital Information

The clerk at the Hall of Records balked at Ray's request for all the birth and adoption records from thirty years earlier. Chris pulled FBI identification. "These records might be linked to a serial killer."

The woman hit a few keys on her computer and grinned crookedly as if she had won a battle. She informed the two waiting law enforcement officers, "The records are too old to be on a disc or microfiche, but you're welcome to search the paper records in the warehouse. They are located in Building M, row thirteen." She rifled through a drawer and handed them a key.

Chris snatched the key and glowered at the clerk. She leaned across the counter and whispered, "We have twelve dead women, and you want to be a bitch about some records? Vital info—info, *honey*—that a *decent* person would be going through every scrap of paper with us to find if she thought it might help catch a killer. Guess you're not *decent* people. So you'll know, impeding a federal investigation is a felony. How would you like to be locked up in the cell next to this whacko?" She straightened up and smoothed her slacks. "I guess you wouldn't be in any danger though. All the dead women seem to have been *decent*, unlike *you*."

The clerk stared at Chris, slack-jawed, too afraid to say a word in her own defense. When the door closed behind the law enforcement, she sank into her chair. Ray bumped shoulders with the county tax assessor as he entered and said loudly enough to carry into the hallway, "Your phone call can wait. I have a list of surveys to be pulled immediately."

In the car, Ray said, "I can't believe what you just did. That's my style, not yours."

"Little you know." She leaned her head against the glass in the passenger-side door. "You said we were alike. And I didn't like her. I don't appreciate being talked down to. I'm probably ten times smarter than she is."

"Hands down," he agreed.

Chris lifted her head. "Ray, this is why we haven't caught the guy. People don't care."

"*We* care."

"Yeah. Before you ask, I really don't think the other Ray is a killer, especially after our visit with Bertram."

"Maybe. What if he's acting out against the girl who rejected him? Or what if he found out about our *wonderful* birth mother and that made him snap?"

"Did you ever wonder if your birth mother was all bad?"

"Huh?"

"Never mind." She put her head back on the cool glass. "What if we find out he *is* your twin? How does that affect what you do?"

"If he's a murderer, I'll arrest him."

"If you don't, you know I will."

"Yeah. We make a good team. Chris, rather than my working for the feds, maybe you should stay here when all this is over."

"That's a thought," the agent said as they pulled in front of the warehouse.

Ray sighed. "The buildings seem to have survived Katrina, but I hope the records weren't damaged or eaten by rats."

They walked expectantly to the door. Chris turned the key in the lock. The door creaked on its hinges, and although the weather was cool, the warehouse was stuffy and dusty.

"Oh, gag! The foul odor." Chris slapped a hand over her nose.

"The smell of mildew means paper should still be intact, at least," Ray said, wrinkling his nose.

Chris insisted, "Leave the door open."

Very little light filtered through the grimy windows. Ray fumbled with a light switch by the door. Half a dozen lights hanging from chains mounted to the beams in the ceiling cast shadows up and down the rows.

"Lead the way," Chris said with a look of disgust on her face. "If one silverfish crawls on me…" She shook a fist at the man beside her.

They walked to row thirteen. "There must be a hundred boxes here," Ray lamented.

"Pick box thirteen," Chris said.

"Why?"

"Let's see," she said, oozing sarcasm. "Building M, the thirteenth letter of the alphabet; row thirteen; you were born on January 13th."

"Friday," interjected Ray, with a mischievous grin.

"The thirteenth woman is missing," Chris continued, undaunted by Ray's smart-aleck comment. "Do we have a recurring theme here?"

He shrugged. "It's as good a logic as any." Ray wiggled the box labeled M-13-13 from its place and sat down in the middle of the dirty floor.

Her look of disgust deepening, Chris sat beside him and used the key to cut the tape. "Ugh!" she grunted. "And you can pay my dry cleaning bill."

He waved her comment off with a slight flick of his fingers. "Should I try the thirteenth folder?" Ray asked, a wry smirk playing around his mouth.

"Why not?"

He pulled the thirteenth folder out. It was labeled "*Birth Records— '78*." He spread the contents on the floor.

Halfway through the mound of papers, Chris uttered, "Jeez!"

"What?"

She handed Ray a certificate that read: *Live birth; 13 January 1978; monozygotic twins; male; 2'8"; 13:00; 2'4"; 13:13; race—Caucasian; mother—Audrey van Zandt, age 13; father—unknown.*

"Oh, my God! Audrey." Ray scanned the file. His hand shook as he read. "She was just a baby, and she wasn't a whore or a drug addict. She was just a baby having a baby. The damned priest lied." He choked out the words.

"Yes, but even I, a Yankee, know the name from case studies."

"It *can't* be the same Audrey van Zandt."

"You know damned well it is. That name is too uncommon in southeastern Louisiana, and the dates match. She has never given a reason for going into that fraternity house with her daddy's shotgun; just, 'They deserved it.' Ray, I would put money on the fact that those six boys raped her. She was Catholic. She couldn't have an abortion. Birth size indicates you were very premature, not unusual for a girl so young and twins." Chris hesitated before she suggested, "Ray, she's in the state penitentiary. Talk to her. Drive up tomorrow. The name of the biological father is unknown. You might be able to determine which one was your father."

"My father is Albert Reynolds, and my mother is Dorothy Reynolds. I love them very much." Ray walked out the door, shoulders slouched.

With a sigh, Chris slid the box against the others, but took the file with her. *You seem to always walk away from personal issues that hurt.* She called, "Ray!"

He turned toward her, nostrils flared, eyes flashing. "Why would I want to know which one of those assholes sired me? God! If your theory's correct, she should get a medal, not a prison cell. So what if she had time to think about it? It drove her mad. Maybe that's why one of us is killing people and the other verges on lunacy when his head is about to burst!" he shouted.

Chris hollered back, "Maybe that's why you're both good men who were raised by great parents! The girl had the guts to give you to somebody that could love you and take care of you. That takes guts! That takes more guts than you'll *ever* know!" Hot tears smarted her eyes.

Ray looked at the woman who never lost control as reality dawned on him. He asked calmly, "Was it boy or a girl? How old were you?"

"Girl. Fourteen. Enough said. Let's go." She pushed the lock on the door, slammed it, and walked briskly toward the car.

He dogged her steps. "No, it's not," argued Ray. "What happened, Chris? Tell me. Talk to me."

"Now is *not* the time."

"Yes, it is. Were you raped? Is that why you're so angry?"

"No." She shook her head and stared at the ground. "Maybe if I had been my father would've been more understanding. No, I was just young, lonely, and careless. I had so much responsibility after my mother died. I wasn't allowed to be a child any more. I was *so* lonely."

She poured out a story she had never talked about. "I got involved with Ted Metz. He was the same age I was. We were each other's first. Oh, we thought we were in love." She released a long, sad sigh. "Wow! When I got pregnant, you would've thought the world had ended. His parents accused me of doing it deliberately, and I was suddenly the biggest slut on Earth. They prohibited him from ever seeing me again. They were so desperate to make sure he accepted no responsibility for his actions they sent him to military school. And they refused to have anything to do with 'that little bastard child that most likely didn't belong to their son anyway.'"

She made a slight rocking motion and clutched the file she held to her chest. "My dad said he couldn't afford another mouth to feed. And he really couldn't. He struggled to take care of us. Single fathers don't get help like single mothers. Dad insisted I give the baby up for adoption. He said he wanted me to have a *real* life and assured me someday I'd have a family with a man that *really* loved me." She pressed her eyes with her thumb and middle finger, index finger resting in the center of her forehead. "It broke my heart, but I knew he was right. Well, I haven't found that love yet, and, *trust* me—I've looked in *all* the wrong places. I just hope my little girl has had a good life." She moved her hand to her cheek as she felt flushed even in the cool air. "I hope she doesn't say things like, 'My *wonderful* birth mother,' with the disdain you do." Her lip trembled. *And I pray that my little girl doesn't hate me.*

Ray shook his head. "I'm sorry. I didn't..."

She waved her hand in front of her. "Now, I've told you my deepest, darkest secret. Searching through those records put me in a funk. However, the adoption records aren't here. Let's talk to the nuns. You know what happened to you. You need to know what happened to your brother."

"And you need to know what happened to your daughter."

"Now is *not* the time, Ray. Let's go." With her hand raised into the air, she tried to lighten the moment. "*Allons!*"

The truth slapped Ray as he acknowledged, "My brother. My God! I have a brother."

At the hospital, the investigators learned that thirty years before Catholic Charity Hospital had run an adoption service. Ray argued for over an hour before he convinced Mother Superior Mary Alex Samuels she would be helping save lives by giving him the records. She finally conceded when Chris mentioned a court order, which Ray had been hesitant to do against a church supported organization.

While the old nun retrieved the documents, he whispered, "Separation of church and state would make that order hard to get."

Chris shrugged. "Not impossible, and she bought it."

"I think she just wants to do the right thing."

After the mother superior gave him the files, Ray scanned his own but saw nothing he did not already know except he was adopted second. He was the younger of the two and had been in incubation longer. The rest he already knew because the Reynolds family did not keep secrets from one another.

He read thoroughly the other baby's file. He had been adopted by Louis and Maria Gautier of Lake Charles. Maria was a bookkeeper, and Louis was a farmer.

Ray asked the mother superior, "Why didn't you keep us together?"

"I actually argued for that, but Father Dawler overruled me and forbad me to tell either couple they were getting a twin. I know the Reynoldses would have taken both. Being a banker and a nurse, they could afford it. The Gautiers would probably have taken both, but they were less financially stable. They adopted a little girl six years later, the last adoption we did."

"Well, one vital piece of information is still missing. Who was our father?"

"I don't know, Detective. I really don't know. Audrey left without a word within hours of your birth. She shouldn't have been moving. She was so weak. I remember she hemorrhaged badly. She could've bled to death. Two days later, she killed those boys in the fraternity house."

Chris shared her theory with the older woman. Mother Mary Alex nodded. "It makes sense. Maybe you should talk to Audrey. Let her know she did the best thing for you."

"Did she?" Ray said doubtfully, but only for a split second before he hastily added, "Yes, I know she did. But, well, I think we need to see her together, show her that we found each other. First, I have to find him."

11
Dream Sequence

Darkness shrouded the city, and slumber overtook even those who would fight sleep. The need to rest and to dream became paramount.

Raiford Reynolds took the files he had found regarding his birth and adoption to his home and read every word as he sat on his sofa with Cyclops purring beside him. He had often had strange dreams about someone who looked like him. Now, he understood why. He yawned and put his head back.

"The nightmares, Cyclops. Some nights I dread falling asleep." He rubbed the cat's head. "I frequently keep long hours, which usually gives me a migraine. Now, I'm on meds—Ambien to sleep undisturbed."

However, on this night he did not take a sleeping pill. Neither did he hear the folder slip from his lap onto the floor. The dreams that came to him both disturbed and calmed his exhausted mind.

Time rewound...*He was an early teen, plowing furrows; and he smelled the new-turned earth, at first a pleasant aroma. Then, the same scent sickened him as he stood between two graves, freshly dug.*

Time went further back...*He was a boy framing a house with a deeply bronzed older man. The man referred to drawings and remarked in heavy Cajun, "These are perfect, Ray. How did you do this so well? You have to do this for a living. I don't want you to dig in the dirt like me."*

Time fast forwarded...*He was in college. He felt a searing pain in his head from a brutal blow. A disharmony of voices floated around him, and a woman's voice saying good-bye left him in a heap upon the floor.*

Once more, time flew forward....*As a grown man, he placed a kiss on the forehead of a gray-haired woman in a coffin. He instantly floated into the presence of an auburn-haired angel who slept peacefully above him.*

Ray woke himself when he mumbled, "I'd like to be there." Sitting up, he said, "That wasn't *my* life—it was my brother's." The weird connection he had felt as a child in his dreams solidified. He released a long puff of air, picked up the cat, and went to bed. "I know that place in my dream, Cyclops. Where is it?" the detective asked his feline friend as he stroked the animal and drifted to sleep again.

Larkin Sloan watched the man who held her captive sleep. Strangely, she felt his presence in her life would keep her safe. She had no fear of the man and lay back easily. She wondered if her captor could be the man of her dreams as she drifted off to sleep.

In spite of being a captive, Larkin slept peacefully in her new surroundings. For years, she had dreamed about a faceless man, always with dark hair. Lately, she had dreamed of blue eyes. At all times, the presence of this man gave her a feeling of security. She loved this faceless creature, whoever he was.

The man with dark hair and beautiful blue eyes who slept on the floor left his body and the place where they were. She left her body and followed. She felt the need to keep him from walking into grave danger, a danger she thought she knew.

She watched the man walk aimlessly around the city. As they turned a corner, she lost sight of him. He vanished. Fear overtook her, and the only recourse she had was to go back to where she had left the body.

When she walked in, the man sat on the bed. He remarked in a familiar voice, "I've been looking for you and him." He pointed to the body of her captor still asleep on the floor.

"What do you mean?" she asked. *"That's you."*

The man on the bed shook his head. "That's not me. I'm right here. Where is he? I need to find the two of you so I can take care of you."

She started awake. Her captor, a captive within himself, slept on the floor. Nonetheless, she knew that for her at this moment in time, she was in the safest place she could be. She reached down and gently stroked the ebony hair of a man who had captured her heart.

Chris Milovich slipped under the covers in her hotel room. Usually she tossed and turned quite some time before she fell asleep. This night she drifted into another world immediately.

Her normal dreams of a faceless child that she was always chasing were replaced with another disturbing dream. *She walked into the police station to find her friend and temporary partner in pieces like a jigsaw puzzle on the floor. As hard as she tired, she could not put him together. There was a big piece missing.*

Behind her, she heard, "Ahem." She turned to see the man whole and complete standing behind her. He said, "I think you're missing this piece." He pulled out his own heart and handed it to her.

She placed the beating heart in the puzzle and it fused into a perfect man in peaceful slumber. Chris turned to the man behind her. "Now, you're incomplete," she said, feeling tightness in her own chest.

The man shrugged. "I'm sure mine is around here somewhere. Will you help me find it?"

Chris nodded. "Yes, I'd like that." She took the man's hand.

85

Eyes popped open. "Shit," Chris said to the darkness in her room. "What was that all about? When I tell Ray about this dream, he's gonna tell me to get some meds." She turned over and tried to go back to sleep.

♣♣♣

Ray Gautier slept curled into a ball on the floor of the old monastery. After resuming his medication, he had no trouble sleeping. He had peaceful dreams of playing with a boy so much like him as he had dreamed his whole life. There was joy in those dreams. The voices ceased to torment him. Tonight something was different.

A million voices swirled around him as if in a whirlwind of sound before a voice, a very strong voice, called him. "Ray, let me help you."

Ray found the source of the voice. The cyclone stopped swirling, and the only voices he heard were his own and the one before him. He stood face-to-face with himself. He questioned, "How can you help me?"

"Trust me."

"But you're me."

"No, I'm not."

Ray screamed in his sleep and sat up. He felt a gentle hand on his shoulder as Larkin asked, "Ray, are you all right?"

He shook his head. His voice strained, he said, "I really am insane. I really am."

12
The Voice of Insanity

"You are *not* insane!" Larkin snapped as her patience began to wear thin.

"Yes, I am," he argued. "Now I'm dreaming I'm two people." Ray shivered and pulled the thin blanket more tightly about him.

"Did you take your meds?"

"You know I did. You saw me. Larkin, all the voices didn't disturb me as much as feeling torn apart."

"Ray, listen to me. You have to go for help."

"I have to call Latrice."

"Why would you get in touch with that maniac?"

"You're right. I can't call her. She thinks I'm some derelict who sleeps in street gutters." Ray Gautier looked around him and laughed sardonically. "I almost do. I'll have to see her face to face."

"No!" Larkin shrieked. "She might realize you're not under her influence anymore."

"I have to. If I don't make contact with her, she might come here to see what's wrong. I'll be fine. I look like crap. I smell like crap. It's a good time to go see her. I'll go this afternoon."

She could not convince Ray to stay. All she could do was pray he would pull off his deception.

As the public health facility closed, Ray Gautier loitered on the street, hood shielding his face, but eyes alert. He waited until the tall, muscular woman with short dark hair came out. She saw him and vigorously walked over. "What's wrong?" she demanded. "What are you doing here?"

"She wants a bath," Ray babbled. "She won't stop bugging me for a bath. She's giving me such a headache."

"A bath?" The woman held her hands in the air and shook her head. "I don't want her grimy, moron. She has to be spotless, clean, *pure*. You haven't touched her or anything, have you?"

He knitted his eyebrows together. "What do you mean?"

"You're a man, a pitiful excuse, but a man. You know what I mean."

"Oh." Ray shook his head. "Momma's voice wouldn't allow me to do that."

"Be a good boy." A half smile crossed her face. "Listen to your momma."

"Oh, I do."

"I hope so. Mommas give good advice. Let me clarify one thing. When's your birthday?"

"January 13th."

Latrice shook her head. "Not a Gemini. Mommas usually give good advice, just like me. You didn't listen to me very well with the Dupree kid. He's crazier than you. You should've picked someone less volatile."

"Are you still mad at me?" Ray looked at the ground and shuffled his feet.

"No, you got me what I wanted. In addition, the little thug is off the streets. How's Larkin's cut?"

"Healed, and only a tiny scar. I snipped the stitches just like you said to. I'm sorry." He bit his lip like a little boy. "Don't be mad at me. You're the only person who cares about me."

"I'm not mad. Do you need more money?"

"Yeah. She really likes Mexican food. Oh, did I tell you she wants a bath?"

"Yes," she hissed. She took out her wallet and handed Ray three crisp one hundred dollar bills. "I only have three hundred on me. Go get a big washtub and some bath gel that smells really good. Connect a hose to the faucet in the bathroom. And pick her up something clean, but cheap, to wear. I have a special garment for her day. And take a bath yourself. You stink." The woman started to turn away.

"When?"

"Huh?" She whipped back toward the hooded vagrant.

"When is her day? Why is it so special?"

"I already told you why. She'll culminate the purification process. She'll bring forth *he who will stop the chaos.*"

"And the voices?"

"Yes, Ray. I promise your voices will stop."

"When?"

"Halloween."

"How? Will you give me some new medicine?"

"Something even better. Trust in me, Ray." For a moment Ray thought he could see a forked tongue and he envisioned Kaa, the snake from *The Jungle Book.*

Latrice's voice went on in its hissing fashion. "The voices will stop forever. I promise. I'll take care of you just as soon as Larkin has fulfilled her purpose." Latrice, her dark maroon scrubs swishing, stalked away.

The vapors from her voice hung like ice shards in the fall air. Ray shivered.

He crumpled the money in his fist as he realized the voice of insanity had just spoken to him. He did not want anything Latrice had touched. As he walked down the street, he handed the cash to a homeless bum who wondered why someone as bad off as he was would give him three hundred dollars.

Ray bumped and rattled through the door carrying a large washtub.

"What in the world?" Larkin asked.

"A bath for the lady and a few other surprises."

"Well, the first surprise is you. You look like a million bucks."

Ray had bathed, shaved, and wore clean jeans and a royal blue Polo sport shirt. In clothes that fit properly, it was easy to tell the man was in excellent physical condition from the muscle tone in his arms alone. He obviously worked out. "Yeah?" he asked with a genuine smile and deep dimples. "Thank you. I went by my house. I couldn't stand the sight or scent of myself for another second."

"Are you crazy?"

"Why?"

"What if the police had found you?"

"Now, who sounds crazy? What if they had?" He pushed the heavy wooden door shut with his foot. "You'd be free and safe, and I'd be in jail. As a matter of fact, I've been thinking about that. We'll talk after your bath."

He put the tub by the bathroom door and gathered several packages out of it.

"How did you get that stuff here?" asked Larkin.

"My car. It's not spectacular, but I like it. I have a white Nissan Altima." He gave a one-shoulder shrug. "I know. The voice of insanity is taunting me, but I refuse to give in."

Her jaw dropped. "You're the one who was in my parking place."

"Oops. Sorry."

"I got soaked."

Ray chuckled as he attached the hose to the faucet and started the water into the tub. "Come on. Time to get soaked again. I don't know how hot you like it." He handed Larkin a bag from Bath and Body Works. It contained bath gel, shampoo, and conditioner, all in cucumber-melon scent. "It smelled nice," he explained.

He handed her a bag from Wal-Mart. It contained washcloths, towels, a package of disposable razors, shaving cream, deodorant, a brush, two toothbrushes, toothpaste,

90

deodorant soap for him, and undergarments in surprisingly the right size. "I guessed," he said.

The last bag, from Victoria's Secret, Ray put on the bed. "For when you get out."

Larkin placed her untethered hand in the warm water. It felt marvelous. She felt Ray's touch on her other wrist, and her shackle slipped off.

"I'll wait outside. Knock when you're done," he said to her unspoken question. "I won't hurt you. I told you that. You remind me so much of Rhonda. She would've looked a lot like you if she'd grown up. I loved my little sister very much." He left Larkin to her bath and brought several more items in from his car, including a heater, more blankets, and more clothes for both him and Larkin.

Every instinct inside Larkin told her to run as fast as she could the second Ray left the room. With one hand on the doorknob, a still, small voice whispered to her, "No. Stay. You *are* the one who will end this."

Startled, she looked around her. "God, is that you?"

13
The Voice of Reason

Raiford Reynolds jumped when his phone rang. He answered quickly, "Reynolds."

"Ray, it's Mom. Sorry to bother you at work, but I didn't ask when we talked earlier. I called to see if you'll be able to come tomorrow. It's the anniversary of Ronnie's death."

"I know, but I just can't leave. The Sloan woman is still missing, and I haven't found the other Ray yet. Mom, he *is* my twin brother." He rubbed his forehead as if a migraine was coming on. "Am I crazy to want to find him and to prove he's not a killer?"

"No, honey. It's the right thing to do. When you find him, bring him home. You said he has no family. We can be his family. We'll get him the help he needs."

"How sweet. That's why I love you. You're always understanding and reasonable."

"So, listen to the voice of reason. You're doing the right thing, and I love you all the more for it. Keep me up to date. 'Bye for now."

"'Bye, Mom." He hung up and smiled.

From the other desk, Chris asked, "And Mom said?"

"I'm doing the right thing."

"I told you so. Did you tell her about my dream?"

"Yep."

"What did she say about that?"

"When the time comes, you should follow your heart."

A frown creased Chris's brow. "That doesn't sound too reasonable to me. I only know this man from my research with you."

Ray shrugged. "If you don't wanna hear the answer, don't ask the question."

Chris scowled and went back to running pictures of the different drawings that had been on each of the victims through the computer. Without looking at her partner, she said, "Take the Amidrine before you're sick."

Larkin knocked on the heavy wooden door. She wore the pink pajamas with matching silver pin-striped pink tank top, soft velour pink robe, and fuzzy pink slippers that had been in the other bag. Her wet hair hung in copper ringlets over her shoulders.

Ray came back into the room. She asked candidly, "What's going on in your head?"

"What do you mean? I'm finally listening to the voice of reason. You told me I need to go for help. I think you're correct. I've begun to act." He swept a hand on each side of his body. "As you can see, I've cleaned myself up. You look a whole lot better, too. I didn't buy you any makeup. I think you look just fine without it."

"Thanks." She smirked. "Do you buy clothes, or um, lingerie, for women often?"

"I don't consider that *lingerie*." Ray laughed. "I call that *comfortable*. I've bought lingerie. Believe me, it was *not* cotton, and it did *not* cover that much." He arched an eyebrow. "Do you think *that's* lingerie?"

She blushed and changed the topic. "Where did you get money for all of this? Did Latrice give you money?"

"She gave me three hundred bucks and told me to get you something clean and cheap. Larkin Sloan, you don't deserve cheap." Ray proceeded to bring in several more packages, including a crumpled brown grocery sack.

The clothes he had purchased for her were not cheap. It was hard for her to believe they were exactly the right size and colors she would have chosen for herself. *This man has good taste in women's clothing,* she thought.

"How did you get these things?"

"I used my credit card."

"Ray!" Larkin screeched. "They track those things."

"I don't care." He shrugged. "Now that I'm back on my medication, I'm thinking very rationally. I'm not a homeless bum who holds a sign on a street corner that reads, 'Will work for food,' although I gave Latrice's three hundred dollars to one. No, I am a college graduate and an architect at Bertram and Associates. You asked me once if I had anyone. Yeah, I do—my friend, Walter. I just lost track for a while. It won't happen again."

"Okay," she relented, and then pointed at the grocery sack. "What's that?"

"That nasty outfit. I'm going to burn it when this is over, but I thought I'd better hang on to it in case I have to see Latrice again."

He pulled out a cell phone. Larkin listened to the one-sided conversation. "Walter, this is Ray...I'm fine...Really, I'm fine...I'd love to come back, but I have a little problem...I need your advice...How did you know...He did? So, you think I should go to him? I will first thing tomorrow...Walter...Walter... Damn! I lost him. My battery's dead." He looked at the phone and stuck it in his pocket. Sheepishly, he said, "Well, maybe I didn't remember everything. I wish I had. He was saying there was something I needed to know about this Detective Reynolds. Oh, well." He shrugged and gave a little dip with one corner of his mouth. "Walter says I should definitely go to him though.

"Larkin, I'm not going to chain you up, but I think you should stay here. You'll be safe. Latrice doesn't want anything to do with you until Halloween, but if she should discover you're free, she might do something. Will you stay here and wait for me to bring Detective Reynolds?"

Still hearing the voice from earlier, she sighed, "Yeah. I trust you to do what's right."

"Well, then." He smacked his hands together in one sharp clap. "I hope you like Chinese. It's my favorite, and

94

since this will most likely be our farewell dinner, I was selfish."

"I love Chinese, and there's not a selfish bone in your body."

Raiford Reynolds reluctantly answered his cell phone as he drove home in his black, fully restored, 1967 Mustang Shelby GT. "Reynolds."

"Detective, this is Carol Johnson, Mr. Gautier's neighbor. His car is gone from where he always parks it."

"The Escort?"

"No, his new one."

"What kind of car does he have?"

"A white Nissan Altima."

"Do you know the license plate?"

"No, sorry. I just thought you'd want to know."

"Yes, thanks." He hung up, annoyed that the Office of Motor Vehicles had a blue Escort registered to Raiford Gautier. They were so far behind since Hurricane Katrina, they didn't have his new car registered to him yet. "And I've been looking for the damned Escort. White Altima—it was sitting in front of the townhouse, and one of the teachers at St. Ignatius mentioned Larkin being aggravated that a white Nissan had been parked in her parking place." He slapped his forehead. "Shit!"

He still had his phone in his hand when it rang again. "Reynolds," he said shortly.

"Detective Reynolds, Walter Bertram here."

Gautier's neighbor and boss calling back to back? Something is afoot

"I've spoken with Ray," Bertram said. "He said he's coming to see you tomorrow. I tried to tell him about your relationship, but the phone died."

"Do you think he'll really come?"

"He sounded coherent. If he's taking his meds, he'll be there. Please, keep your word. Don't hurt him."

"I have no intention of hurting my twin brother. I discovered we have the same birth mother, and we were adopted by two different families. That's our *real* relationship, not just look-alikes. I know it sounds like a fairytale. Maybe like all fairytales, there'll be a happy ending. Thanks for calling."

14
Coincidence or Connection

Ray Reynolds arrived at the station early. The first thing he found was a fax showing that Raiford Gautier had been on a shopping spree with his platinum Visa. Ray scowled. "Is he really nuts?" he mumbled to himself.

When Chris arrived, he pounced to open the door as the knob rattled. "Oh, it's you," he said disappointedly.

"Nice to see you, too, Ray," jabbed Chris sarcastically. "Did you sleep last night? You look like hell."

Dark circles shadowed his blue eyes. "Not much." He looked at his khakis, a pale yellow button-down shirt, and brown loafers. "At least I'm clean, but I neglected to shave."

"I kind of like the shadow. Gives you that bad-boy image."

"Thanks." He smirked. "Bertram called. He talked to my brother—my *brother* is supposed to be coming in this morning. I'm a nervous wreck."

"Chill, dude!" Chris quipped. "Seriously, relax, Ray. I'll be right here with you. Let's work."

The two of them sat down to reread the files they had compiled on the victims, hoping that some thread would finally unravel and give them a real clue.

A couple of hours passed when the dispatcher buzzed Ray. "Detective Reynolds, you have visitors."

"Send 'em back," Ray said exultantly, thinking Gautier had gone to Walter Bertram first and Bertram was coming with him. *Better yet, Larkin Sloan.*

Three fairly young men walked into the office that housed Ray and Chris. Chris put her head in her hands. "It's only Curly, Larry, and Moe." She grinned at the three FBI agents. "Ray, let me introduce you. Agent Lawrence Dantzler, Agent Patrick Swift, and Agent, Profiler, Steve Journey."

As Chris introduced the men, Ray's analytical detective's mind assessed them. *Bet Dantzler's team leader;* he was. They shook hands. *Germanic heritage; big man, two hundred thirty pounds on six and half feet. Looks like a Viking, platinum blond hair and bright blue eyes.* The detective vaguely caught a quick discourse between Dantzler and Chris.

"Lawrence, are you still fighting in the mixed martial arts circuit?"

"Yeah, why?"

"It looks as if your nose has been broken recently. It's misaligned."

"You should see the other guy. I won the bout."

Ray noted *Dantzler could be a force to be reckoned with. Swift could vanish in a crowd. He's so ordinary looking in that gray suit. Bet it came off the rack at J. C. Penney. Five-ten and one sixty, average. Caramel hair in a tight curl matches his eyes exactly. Looks like a faded tint-type photograph.* The two men shook hands. *Callouses. What does he do besides push papers? Orange discoloration on his fingers—yard work?*

Ray tried not to stare at the profiler, Steve Journey. *Poor guy; everybody's definition of geek.* He pushed his black rimmed glasses up on his rather beaky nose to hide big dark brown eyes. *Yep, dork. Might help if he'd cut that hair. Looks like straw, but limp as spaghetti. Style it at least. That stringy mess shouts dweeb. Ph. D. Gotta be intelligent.* Journey's firm handshake gave Ray second thoughts about his character.

Ray's summation of the FBI men took thirty seconds. With some relief, the detective said, "Good to have you fellows. Maybe now we can get a little more work done."

He reached the credenza behind his desk and distributed a stack of files among the three. "Get busy." he said dryly. "The table in the room across the hall is available." He stood and rolled the portable white board with all the victims' information on it toward the door so he could transfer it to the other room. He was tired of looking at it.

"That's all the space we get?" asked Agent Dantzler.

Ray explained, "We're not set up for what we've been given, gentlemen. There was only one other detective here before Chris came. Baker is handling *all* the other cases and running gofer for us. That's why I asked for you. We don't have the space or the manpower. At least you get the coffee pot," he finished.

Chris put in, "We'll leave both doors open so we can holler and run back and forth."

"I see your situation." Dantzler nodded his understanding. "We'll make do. Is the coffee fit to drink?"

"It is if Chris made it," replied Ray.

"Guilty!" She raised her hand.

The three agents retreated to their assigned area, but the traffic and voices between the two rooms became frenzied. Even with all the activity, Ray kept a constant watch on the clock. At eleven, he leaned on Chris's desk and whined, "He's still not here."

"Relax, Ray," she bit, irritation with her partner showing. "He'll come. Something might've happened to delay him."

To take his mind off his brother, the detective ordered pizza delivered on the department's tab. As the pizza arrived, Brian Baker stuck his balding, sandy-haired head in Ray's office. Baker, a little older and a little heavier than Ray at thirty-five, five-eleven, and hundred ninety pounds had been Ray's original partner as a rookie patrolman. "Y'all got a sec?" he asked, his hazel eyes looking askance.

Ray almost choked. He stammered, "What is it? Is there a guy out there that looks like me?"

"No," Baker replied. "I hate to bother you, but my gut tells me you need to know this."

Gusting a sigh, Ray said, "Please, tell me Larkin Sloan's body hasn't been found."

"No, that's not it, but I have *twelve* cases that are really strange. I don't know if this is coincidence or connection to your case, but you need to know."

"Hold up. If this is connected, you might as well tell it once. Let's step next door, and you can meet the FBI boys."

Grabbing a few folding chairs, Ray, Chris, and Baker joined Dantzler, Swift, and Journey. Ray introduced his former partner as Baker brought a stack of files with him and snagged a slice of pizza and a Coke.

After choking down some food, he leaned back and commented, "Keep eating guys and gals while I unfold a tale of the macabre for you. You can decide whether it's connected to your own horror story."

He took a swig of Coke and began. "The first thing that arouses my suspicion is the dates of death: November 22nd, December 15th, January 1st, February 2nd, February 20th, March 21st, March 23rd, May 1st, June 21st, July 4th, August 1st, and September 23rd."

"What the hell?" Ray shouted. "Why didn't you come to me sooner with this? Those are the *exact* same dates my victims died."

"Yeah, I know. Man, you've been pulling your hair out over these women. My vics are all nobodies, drug addicts, homeless guys, or mentally unstable. They're all different and insignificant, but it's been plaguing me. It's just too coincidental to be coincidence."

Ray whispered, "Walter Bertram's one insignificant schizophrenic," and shot Chris a knowing look.

Chris prompted, "Baker, tell us more."

"Okay. All my guys were found within five miles of your vics. It's just that they all died differently." He spread out folders.

"Victim number one was a homeless John Doe who was bludgeoned to death. One blow tells us somebody strong hit him and also knew exactly where to bash him to kill with one whack. Frontal lobe might not have been instantly fatal, but behind the ear—Doc said he was dead in seconds. A mass transit bus driver discovered the body under a bridge one mile from the cemetery where your vic was found.

"Victim number two was a known bipolar named Chase Perineau. He was discovered shot in the head with the gun in his hand by his sister at his home, four miles from your vic number two. The M.E. ruled him a suicide." Baker shrugged.

"Vic number three is Bob Jones, a known heroin addict. He was found at home by his neighbor. His apartment is five miles from the cemetery. He has been ruled an accidental overdose."

Agent Journey abandoned his pizza and leaned forward in undivided attention.

Baker continued, "Number four is Benton Campbell, a homeless man who frequented the missions and soup kitchens. He was found in the street gutter two miles from the cemetery by the street sweeper. His throat had been slit by a very sharp instrument, probably a scalpel.

"My fifth victim is another homeless John Doe. He was suffocated with a garbage bag and left propped against the dumpster at the mortuary next door to the cemetery to be found like trash by the trash collector.

"Six is a known meth addict and dealer, George "Baby" Bates. He was found by a group of kids in the driveway of a crack house three miles from the cemetery. He was shot in the back of the head execution style. Could it be drug or gang related? Sure. Still, the timing intrigues me."

101

By this time, even the skeptical Lawrence Dantzler had stopped eating and hung on Baker's every word.

"Seven is probably the most senseless in the group. He's Dwayne Jolly, a mentally challenged man who lived in a group home half a mile from the cemetery. They always put these poor less-fortunates, who really try to be as normal as possible, in the worst locations because we *normal* folks are scared of them. Don't get me started on that. My younger brother has Down's, and it pisses me off when people treat him badly." He waved a hand. "Anyway, the other residents of the home witnessed Dwayne being run over in a hit-and-run by a stolen black SUV with tinted windows. Of course, none of them could identify the driver, and the car had been reported stolen at least twelve hours before the incident. Moreover, there was not a speck of evidence in the vehicle when it was discovered. As a matter of fact, it appeared to have been detailed, and parked around the corner from where it was stolen." Baker took a gulp of Coke.

"Eight is John Weems, another homeless victim. He was found in his cardboard dwelling on the main homeless drag three miles from the cemetery. Routine patrol of the area found him with an ice pick through his temple.

"Number nine is another homeless John Doe. He was strangled with a wire and found on a park bench across the street from the cemetery by a morning jogger. He was just a kid. The coroner guesses sixteen or seventeen since all his wisdom teeth hadn't erupted. Hispanic, maybe illegal.

"Frank Dozier is number ten. A veteran of the Gulf War, he was a homeless drunk. He was found in the parking lot of a liquor store four miles away. He had drunk a cocktail of booze and antifreeze."

"Homeless veterans piss me off," Chris muttered and received affirming nods all around. "You're on a roll, Baker. Don't let me stop you."

"Tim Bourbon, a known schizophrenic, is the eleventh victim. He lived in the same apartment building as Bob

102

Jones. Another resident found him hanging in the laundry room. Of course, he has been ruled a suicide. Scratch marks on his neck from his own nails, make me think otherwise. The M.E. says maybe he changed his mind, but it was too late. *Could* be, I guess." He squinted his eyes in skepticism.

"Last, is one more homeless John Doe. He was stabbed multiple times and found near Catholic Charity Hospital, which is only two and half miles from the cemetery. It appears he was trying to get to the hospital. A woman walking her dog found him. There was a trail of blood leading from the cemetery gate. You did touch on this one, Ray. You thought he might've witnessed something."

"Yeah, I remember that one." Ray nodded.

Baker passed around his files. "As you can see, there's no racial discrimination or age discrimination. I've marked on this map where all the bodies were found."

Ray reviewed the evidence along with the FBI. The detective looked up. "I would say my killer has recruited multiple accomplices and then gotten rid of the witnesses. I'll be damned if the next one dies." Ray looked at Chris and pure rage showed in his face. "Baker, you're my original partner, and now, I believe, you're our new partner. You're a part of *this* team now. There is definitely a connection here."

15
Profiling a Killer

"I agree," commented Agent Journey. "Let's look back at your victims, Ray. All of them had their throats cut by a very sharp instrument, maybe the same scalpel as Baker's number four. Access to a scalpel indicates someone in the medical or scientific community." He grimaced. "Every woman had her blood drained. We could be looking at a blood sacrifice of some kind."

"Sacrifice?" asked Ray.

"Yeah. Don't interrupt."Journey held up his hand. His assertive response was the second step in proving to the cynical detective he was not a nerd. "All of them were dressed in a white dress that could be used as a wedding dress. None of them were married, and none of them were sexually assaulted.

"Each one was placed reverently in the cemetery. That indicates a respect for the victims."

Ray snorted. "Respect?"

"Reverence even," the profiler asserted. "The bizarre aspect is the painting on the shaved pubic area. The drawings are strange. Chris, I saw you with one of these on your computer screen when we arrived. What have you found out about these drawings?"

"Well, some of them have an obvious relationship to the date of death: Thanksgiving—a cornucopia; New Year's—an hour glass; Groundhog Day—a hedgehog; Easter—an up-side-down cross, although it was early this year and fell in March; May Day—a maypole; Independence Day—a flag. I don't have a clue what the others are," she responded.

"Obviously," continued Journey, "the dates are significant." He tapped the documents in front of him with the pen he held, and then chewed the end of his pen, grating Ray's nerves. The detective let out a long impatient sigh.

Journey looked up. Ray spread his hands in question.

"Oh, sorry," Journey said as he realized all eyes were on him. "Holidays?" The word sounded like a question.

"I had that thought, too," said Ray. "What holiday is celebrated on August 1st?"

"Ask Jeeves," quipped Baker.

"What?" asked Ray.

"My kids use the computer to find answers like that," replied Baker. "Go to askjeeves.com and type in your question."

Ray jumped from his chair and ran to his computer. He was redirected to ask.com. He zipped back across the hall fifteen minutes later with a printout. "*Fooyay*! August 1st is called Lammas. It's a Wiccan sabbat as are all the others we didn't know. February 2nd and May 1st are also Wiccan sabbats, Imbolc and Beltane. We have the spring and fall equinoxes and the summer and winter solstices. I would never have realized the significance of these dates." The detective gripped the papers and shook them slightly as he looked around the room. "December 15th is Yule. It's the pagan holiday for which the Catholic Church more or less established Christmas so pagans would convert."

"Great!" Journey's cry sounded like a cheer. "Now we have something to work with. Some of the other dates are significant, too. April 15th is tax day." He snorted slightly. "Warped sense of humor to take the little rich girl on tax day, and September 1st was Labor Day this year as well as Easter falling on March 23rd. You've got a real sicko on your hands, Ray." He leaned back and steepled his fingers, putting the tips of his index fingers to his lips. "I'm going to say the first part because it's the norm. Your killer is *probably* a white male between twenty-five and forty-five. That's the profile of most serial killers, but it is *not* written in stone."

The agent leaned forward onto his elbows resting on his thighs. "Your guy is way above average intelligence, probably well educated. He's very religious and was most likely raised Catholic. Somewhere along the line he became disillusioned with the church and explored alternative religion. He apparently appreciates Wiccan beliefs and probably dabbles in the occult—maybe *more* than dabbles. He's very patriotic. There's a good chance he's former military." He lowered his hands. "I say that because of the choice of weapons on his accomplices, a garrote and an ice pick, as well as a high-powered hand gun on the drug dealer. Has the slug been traced to any particular gun?"

Baker shook his head negatively.

Journey pushed against his thighs, bringing himself up straight. "He's very strong. He has moved bodies alone and delivered a death blow with one lick. And he's charismatic. He can get these men to help him." Journey's thin eyebrows disappeared behind his glasses as he thought. "Hmmm?"

"What does 'hmmm' mean?'" asked Ray.

"I had a fleeting thought this case could involve a woman."

"Why?" Ray asked, pinching his temples with a finger and thumb. *No headache, please.*

"Well, to get these men to follow..." Journey began.

"The promise of drugs, healing," Ray argued.

"Could be, but let's not rule out a woman as unusual as that is. Remember that there was no sexual assault. Whatever is going on here, it's not about power. Rape is about power. The way the bodies were treated after death shows great respect, even admiration, for the female victims. On the other hand, your killer hates men. Their corpses were treated with disdain." Journey sat up very straight. "The lack of sexual assault could indicate a woman or a homosexual or somebody that just can't get it up. Too, Wicca is what modern day witches are called. It's a recognized religion and actually celebrates Nature.

106

However, most of the people I've met that really hold to Wiccan beliefs are female." He held up one hand to preclude Ray's argument. "There are some men, but it really seems to appeal to women, maybe because they see Nature as a goddess. Nonetheless, the killings of the women are ritualistic, a religious sacrifice. So, this person has totally perverted *all* the religions involved. Your killer is a Wiccan wannabe because if he or *she* really was serious about the craft, he or she wouldn't be killing anybody." He let out a low whistle.

"My biggest dilemma is determining how the female victims were chosen." He scratched his head. "All the males had a need or illness that could be used and manipulated. The promise of healing or a home, as you said, Ray, is a big incentive. Your killer chose men that society holds in low esteem, men nobody would miss."

Journey scrunched his face in thought. He reached into his coat pocket, pulled out a black ponytail holder, and gathered his long hair into a ponytail at the nape of his neck.

Okay. So he's brilliant. Ray raised an eyebrow. "What else is on your mind, Steve?"

"I'm thinking." He rubbed his hand across his lips several times. "There's some correlation in having suffered or sacrificed something. Several of the women worked in a service-related capacity. Look here."

The profiler pointed to several names. "The first woman must have suffered greatly after the car accident that left her scarred. The nun's heart must have been broken after being jilted at the altar."

He wagged his head. "The Waters woman sacrificed for her country. The social worker helped people. Even your latest victim, the missing woman, had a really rough childhood, and she's a teacher, which is service oriented." He emitted a low growl. "Damn! It's so disconnected."

Ray grunted, "That's what I've been saying for months."

Journey shrugged. "Your notes indicate some of the women weren't very hospitable, like your reporter. I don't know, Ray." The profiler grimaced. "The good news is that your Larkin Sloan has until Halloween." He closed the file with authority. "That's the biggest Wiccan holiday of all. It's the Celtic New Year. If this has some link to the occult, your killer might have figured she has a gift that might make connecting with the spirit world more profound."

"She sings," Ray said. "But I couldn't find a 'talent' for any of the others."

"Not that kind of gift," Journey clarified. "Something that would make her 'spiritually' special. Wiccans believe this holiday coming up is when the veil between this world and the other world is thin. Your missing woman has until Halloween."

"Eleven days," mused Ray. "God, I hope we find her before that, and I have a good idea who the other male victim will be." He looked at Chris again. She gave him an encouraging nod.

He nodded back and said, "Gentlemen, I have another unbelievable story to tell you."

16
The Man in the Mirror

Larkin stretched and yawned as her eyes opened slowly. She actually felt rested. Looking around briefly, she realized it must be afternoon as the shadows were already long. She sat up. "Ray!"

"Huh?" he asked groggily

"Wake up!" she said frantically.

"What's wrong?" Blue eyes stretched open, wide awake.

"What time is it?" she asked.

"Oh, my God!" Ray shouted as he looked at his watch he had taken when he went home. "How could I have slept so long?"

Larkin calmed down. "It's all right." She looked at her wrist. "I'll make us some coffee."

Ray had run an extension cord to the basement from an outdoor outlet and attached a multi-plug to which were hooked a lamp, a coffee pot, a toaster, and a small refrigerator. Last night he had added a small space heater for the wine cellar was quite chilly. Except for the refrigerator and the lamp, they plugged in the appliances as needed since the wiring in the building was antiquated and potentially hazardous.

Larkin chatted as she made coffee. "No offense, Ray, but your coffee is too strong. I'll make it from now on. Take your meds and come butter some toast."

Ray was already putting his pills in his mouth. "I don't have time to eat. I was supposed to go to Detective Reynolds this morning. It's already past noon."

"You'll go after breakfast. Sit."

He joked, "You've gotten bossy without your bracelet."

"I can be worse." She wrinkled her nose at him. "Butter the toast." Larkin poured two bowls of Rice Krispies and cut strawberries into them. She noticed Ray obediently buttering the toast.

She touched his shoulder. "Everything will be all right. After we eat, you'll go to the police just like we discussed. I promise I'll be right here when you bring Detective Reynolds back with you. We'll tell him everything we know, and hopefully it'll be enough for him to put the lunatic away."

"What if he puts me away, too?" he asked quietly. It was the first time he had voiced his fear. "I don't want to go to jail. Or to the nuthouse."

"I won't let that happen. I promise."

"Latrice made promises, too." The architect's normally steady hands shook as he buttered the toast.

Larkin took the knife from him and laid it on the folding card table by the door. "I'm not Latrice," she said as she slipped her arms around her strange captor. He leaned his head on her shoulder, and she could feel his body shake.

Ray whispered, "I'm scared."

"Me, too," she said. "Look at me." She took his face in her hands and noticed the dark circles under his eyes again. *Stress related.* "You can do this," she encouraged. "I believe in you. God won't let you down in this. We prayed about it last night. You have to have faith."

He stood up straight and nodded. "Don't pour milk on my cereal. I can't eat right now. I need to go ahead and go. You really won't leave, will you?"

She shook her head. "As God is my witness, I'll be right here when you get back."

He changed into a pair of khakis, a soft yellow button-down shirt, and brown loafers, but he did not take time to shave, leaving himself with a heavy shadow. After a look back at Larkin for assurance, he left.

The local reporter who had grabbed the detective's arm and finally gotten an admission of a serial killer sat in his car across the street from the police station as he did every day waiting for a break in the biggest story of his career. He had seen three strange men earlier. He glanced up from texting to his employer and wondered how he had missed Detective Reynolds leaving the building, but he was entering again. "Strange," the man said to himself.

Ray Gautier nervously approached the dispatcher's desk. The chubby bottled-blonde woman looked up. He said, "I need to see Detective Reynolds."

"Very funny," replied the woman.

"Why is that funny?"

The woman cackled. "I'll play along. All the way down the hall. Turn right. Last door on the right."

"Thank you." He waited a moment for the woman to buzz the door open.

Raiford Gautier heard voices in the room on the left, and he smelled the pizza. It was past lunch time, so it was logical people were eating. Ray heard, "Eleven days. God, I hope we find her before that, and I have a good idea who the other male victim will be." There was a brief paused before he heard the same voice, which sounded like the voice from his dream, say, "Gentlemen, I have another unbelievable story to tell you."

He knocked on the door frame to a room where five men and a woman sat with open pizza boxes and stacks of files. The three men facing the open door stared at him, mouths agape. Chris Milovich glanced over her shoulder and tapped the dark haired man, who also had on a soft yellow button-down shirt and khaki pants, beside her just as the man in the doorway said, "I'm looking for Detective Reynolds."

Detective Raiford Reynolds stood and turned around.

Raiford Gautier gripped both sides of the doorway as the room began to spin.

Detective Reynolds sprang across the room to support the other man who was on the verge of losing consciousness. With Ray Gautier's arm draped over his shoulder, Ray Reynolds whispered, "Everything will be fine. There's a lot to explain, but everything will be fine." He led the man he had been looking for all morning across the hall to his office and shut the door. Excited voices next door became muffled. Chris's voice took charge, and the detective knew his partner had the situation under control. *She'll offer Baker and the FBI sufficient explanation until I get back to them.*

Detective Reynolds steered his charge to the chair beside his desk. He grabbed a bottle of water from the small refrigerator on the other side of his desk, opened it, and handed it to his mirror image. "Are you all right?" he asked.

Ray Gautier stammered, "I...I...I have finally...gone completely...insane."

"No, you haven't. I thought the same thing a week ago. Take a swig and try to stay calm. There's much to tell. Let's start this way. Hello, Raiford Gautier. I'm Raiford Reynolds, your twin brother."

The look on the unsuspecting twin's face said it all.

"Something stronger, maybe?" suggested the detective as he opened his drawer and retrieved a bottle of tequila.

"I don't drink," replied Ray Gautier.

"Of course...your medication. I do sometimes. Right now, I need a shot." Detective Reynolds poured a shot into a glass he pulled from the drawer and knocked it back. "Where would you like me to start?"

"Your name and my face?"

The detective laughed. "I knew I'd like you. Sit right back and I'll tell you a tale." He leaned back in his chair and began a discourse.

"Thirty years ago our birth mother, Audrey van Zandt, had a pair of twins. We were adopted by two different sets of parents who by some *ironic* stoke of fortune named us both Raiford. Are you following me so far? You did know you were adopted, didn't you?"

Gautier nodded. "Go on."

"All right. I didn't know about you either until a few days ago. You apparently had something to do with the disappearance of Miss Larkin Sloan, although I, personally, don't think you were acting of your own volition at the time."

"She's fine," Gautier rushed to say. "That's why I came—to take you to her so we can figure out what to do." He made as if to stand.

"I gathered that," remarked Detective Reynolds, indicating the man should stay seated with a hand wave.

Gautier ventured, "Are you going to arrest me?"

"No, I think you're as much a victim as Larkin."

A sigh of relief was followed by, "I thought for certain I'd be behind bars about now."

"Then, why did you come in person? Why didn't you just call? It took a great deal of courage to come in here, especially not knowing a thing about me." Matching blue eyes connected in an unexplainable bond.

"Walter tried to tell me last night."

"Yes, he told me. He called and told me to expect you. He's a good friend. You can rely on him."

"I know." Gautier took a long draught of water. "Well, where do we go from here? It'll be difficult to have two Rays. Do your friends call you Ray?"

"Yes, they do. Would you believe we both had sisters we called Ronnie? Yours was actually Rhonda and mine was Veronica. This is the anniversary of both their deaths. My sister was older and not adopted. Yours, younger and

113

adopted, but it's still strange. It gets stranger. We are both Delts—you at Tulane while I was at LSU. You graduated Magna Cum Laude while I barely scraped Cum Laude. I thought briefly that you might be a little smarter than I am, but then I decided not." A smirk played about the detective's lips. "You probably did better because you studied while I played. Now, let's talk strange." He leaned forward and pointed from himself to his brother. "Look at what we're wearing."

Ray Gautier still seemed a little confused as he stared at his reflection. "I've dreamed about you, and I thought I was crazy," he said.

"And I've dreamed about you. Neither of us is crazy, but you're right. We need to do something about our names, or it'll be just like somebody yelling 'Momma' in a mall."

Gautier found himself laughing. "You know, I've always wanted to be called Raif. Raif Gautier sounds like an architect's name, doesn't it? It's a little more exotic than Ray. Now that I have no family to offend, I could do that."

"If you want, have at it," said Ray.

"Yes, I want." He bumped both arm rests on the chair with the palms of his hands. "From this moment on, I am Raif Gautier, architect. We still have a lot to talk about though. Our first priority is Larkin."

"Agreed," affirmed Ray.

17
Face to Face with an Angel

Ray frowned. He sat back in his chair, formed a fist, and rested his chin on it with his elbow against the arm of the chair. "Before we go anywhere, why don't you at least tell me how you became involved in all of this?" he suggested.

"I got off my meds."

"Can you be a little more specific? Walter Bertram told us what happened to you. He seemed to think your problems really started with the death of your mother."

"I guess he's right. Mom would call everyday to make sure I had taken my meds because she knew that when I get busy working, I forget to even eat."

Ray sniggered. "And they call me a workaholic."

Raif scowled. "I'm not a workaholic. I just get involved with my designs."

Ray leaned forward and waved a hand. "I'm not judging you." *I know how involved I can become in a case, especially one like this one.* "Please, go on."

His brother nodded. "I realized I had run out of my medication and the prescription had expired when I started hearing voices, so I went to the health department for a quick fix so to speak. There was this new nurse, Latrice. She has a hypnotic voice when your mind is already playing tricks on you. Somehow she convinced me she would be able to make the voices stop. All I had to do was bring her Larkin. Actually"—He paused—"I took Larkin to the old monastery. I'm supposed to take care of her until Halloween."

Raif shifted his position. "She talked about Larkin being the one who will purify the country and unleash somebody to run things. When I wasn't lucid, I was desperate for the voices to stop. I would've done anything." He stopped and waited for some form of reply.

"I'm listening," Ray assured.

"I guess you know I paid that kid to upset Larkin, but she wasn't supposed to get hurt. Latrice was livid. Larkin is supposed to be pure and unblemished. However, Latrice didn't count on Larkin's persuasive personality. She got me back on my meds, and now I think Latrice is planning to hurt her."

"Kill her," interrupted Ray. "Sacrifice her for some whacked-out religious thought. Then, she plans to kill *you*. Journey said he thought there might be a woman's hand at work here. Well, I'll be damned if I let that bitch hurt anyone else, most of all, my newfound brother." The detective glanced at his watch. "We've already wasted twenty minutes talking. Let's get this show on the road." They stood. "Okay, Raif, lead the way. I'd like to meet this paragon of virtue or angel or whatever she is. Chris needs to come with us. You'll like her. She's pretty much an angel, too."

Ray took a pair of handcuffs from his desk drawer and sighed. "I'm not going to use these unless I have to. I want to believe you, but my first priority is the victim here. I have to make sure you're on the up-and-up, so don't forget there will be two guns pointing at you, okay?"

Raif nodded. "You're being more than fair."

A quick stop across the hall resulted in introductions, a nutshell story, and the beginning of an investigation into a nurse named Latrice at the health department.

Chris stopped in the door of the station. "Ray, there's a reporter across the street."

"Damn it! Distract him while I get Raif into the car."

"How?"

"Flirt with him." He splayed fingers in the air. "Whatever it takes."

"I despise that jerk." Chris's eyebrows creased.

"Do it anyway." He gave her a cheesy grin and pretended to bat coquettish lashes.

"Oh, you owe me big time." Chris glared at Ray, but walked to the reporter's car. "Trying to catch a byline?" she asked with a grin.

"Agent Milovich, nice to see you again," the reporter replied. "Got anything for me?"

"Yeah. We got three FBI boys today. That should be a lot of help."

"That *is* good news. Names?"

"Lawrence Dantzler is the team leader. Then, we have Patrick Swift, and Steve Journey, the profiler. In a day or two, we'll have a profile to release. I'll call you when it's ready." She dipped her head closer to the open window and heard a car pull up.

With Raif lying in the back seat of the car, Ray called through to open passenger window, "You ready to go, partner?"

"Yeah." She stood straight and half turned.

"You really gonna call?" asked the reporter.

"As soon as the profile's ready to be released," assured Chris over her shoulder. She slid into the passenger seat.

Ray peeled away. "One more minute won't make a difference." Chris snapped her seatbelt and looked over her shoulder. "You can get up, Mr. Gautier."

"Raif."

She dipped her head. "I'm Chris. Where's your Altima?"

"Left it in the parking lot," Ray informed. "Is Clark Kent salivating over the tidbit you gave him or you?"

"Shut up," she retorted. "All I told him is that we got the FBI team today. Now, just drive."

♣♣♣

At dusk, the black Mustang parked in the alley behind the old monastery.

Larkin had put on a jade green sweater and jeans from the outfits Ray had bought for her. When she heard voices outside the door, she flung it open with one word, "Ray?"

The stunned captive stood face to face with two men whose faces she could not tell apart. *Detective Reynolds from the news. That's where I saw the face.*

Raif went into the room, calming a confused woman. "It's all right, Larkin. Neither of us is crazy. Sit down, and I'll explain."

She complied as Raif continued. "First, this is Detective Raiford Reynolds and his partner Christine Milovich."

"Raiford?" asked Larkin. "How is that possible?" She placed both hands to her temples and shook her head vigorously as if the action would clear her thoughts.

"Long story," he went on. "Suffice it to say twins placed for adoption to two different families who ironically chose the same name. However, from now on, he's Ray, and I'm *Raif*."

"Why?"

"Do you remember I told you Ray wasn't what I had wanted to be called?"

She nodded.

"Well, Raif is the short name I always wanted, but it wasn't what my folks called me. It would've been too uppity for them, and I didn't want to upset them."

"Are you sure?"

"Yep. Now, I'm turning you over to my brother so we can decide what to do next."

"If you say so." Larkin turned her gaze to another face. "Well, Detective, what do we do to get this crazy woman and protect Ray...Raif at the same time?"

"You really are an angel, aren't you?" said Ray, mesmerized.

"What?" Larkin barked. *What does he mean by that?*

118

"I'm sorry," the detective said. "That was inappropriate. First of all, what are you doing here? Why weren't you out that door and gone the second Raif turned his back?" He pointed toward the exit.

No angel here, she thought. *I refuse to tell him a voice told me to stay. He'll think I'm nuts.* She said, "I gave him my word. I'm not a liar. I don't deceive people, Detective. I promised...*Raif* I'd be here when he brought you."

"What if he hadn't?"

"I had faith in him. He's not the same man who brought me here. I almost ran the day he took off my shackle, but something told me to stay." Larkin wanted to bite her tongue. *Dang it! I just told him.*

Ray looked at his brother. *Does she hear voices too?* "Is she always like this—angelic?" the detective asked.

Raif nodded.

"Don't talk about me as if I weren't here," said Larkin in a tone that was anything but saintly.

Raif smiled. "Oh, Ray, she can be very assertive."

"So I see," the detective acknowledged. "Why don't you tell us what you know?"

"I think I know your connection among the victims."

Ray looked taken aback. "How?"

"I'm smarter than you think." Larkin laughed. "Tell me about your twelve victims and what else you've figured out, especially some little something you *didn't* release to the press. Then, I'll know for sure."

"I'm grasping at straws. I'll give you every detail, if you can give me a connection."

18
The Deadly Virtue

"Oh, by the way, it's twenty-four victims," corrected Ray.

"What?" Larkin asked, dipping her head to the side.

"If this Latrice woman *is* our killer, she has also killed the other twelve men she coerced or tricked into helping her."

"But of course. She didn't use Raif for anyone but me," said Larkin. "Then maybe both of us should consider ourselves lucky thirteen." She gave Raif a significant look. "Tell me everything, Ray. May I call you Ray?"

He nodded and pointed from himself to his partner. "Ray and Chris."

"Good," she said with a sharp downward thrust of her chin. "Now, tell me everything. Don't leave out details the way you do for the press. I'm a big girl. I can handle the disgusting."

"If you insist. It's not pretty." *I'm already so knee-deep in shit, I don't guess telling her can hurt.* He cleared his throat. "I'll start at the beginning with all the things they had in common and then, I'll be specific to each victim. Is that all right?"

"Sure."

Ray looked for a place to sit.

Larkin smirked. "Floor or bed?"

Ray sat at the foot of the bed and began. "Each victim had her throat cut with a sharp blade and most of her blood was drained from her body. Each was dressed posthumously in a white wedding dress. It had to have been post mortem because there was very little blood on the dresses. Either that or the killer is extremely exacting and meticulous. I can't imagine they didn't struggle. The only evidence of any abuse was bruising around one wrist. The victims were carried to the cemetery and arranged as if lying in a coffin. This is the part we didn't release to the press." He looked up at the ceiling as if he needed help to go on with this grisly tale. After his unuttered prayer he delved in. "All of them had their pubic area shaved, but none were sexually assaulted. However, we did divulge that each one had a different drawing painstakingly painted on them. We just left out that they were painted across their pubic area."

Larkin involuntarily rubbed her bruised wrist.

"I'm so sorry," whispered Raif.

"Oh, no." She shook her wavy auburn hair negatively. "I've already forgiven you. I was just thinking I really am lucky thirteen. I won't die and neither will you. Please, go on, Ray."

Raif folded himself onto the floor to listen. Chris grimaced as she looked at the packed dirt floor. "Hold up," said Raif. He got his blanket and partially unfolded it for Chris to sit on. She smiled at his chivalry and sat down as he offered her his hand. He sank down beside her. He whispered, "What's wrong?" to the grimace on her face.

"It stinks to high heaven in here."

"I guess we're used to it. Would you like some water? There's some in the fridge."

"Sure. Thanks."

Raif got a sealed bottle for each person and sat back down.

Ray began, "I've gone over this so many times, it's seared into my memory. The first victim was LaQuesha Brown, a nineteen-year-old African American cashier at Wal-Mart." He scowled. "You know, it might be easier if you read my notes." He pulled a notepad from his back pocket. His scowl deepened. "You might have a hard time with my writing."

121

Larkin held out her hand. "I'm a teacher," she reminded. "Your handwriting can't be any worse than some I have to read on a daily basis."

As she opened the notepad, Ray's folded and frayed chart fell out. She scanned it and found his corresponding notes in the notepad. He interrupted her reading. *I won't mention blonde for a female should have an E at the end.* "Um, my notes about the male victims are toward the back. I copied information from Baker's files."

"Thanks," she said. "Who's Baker?"

"Another detective. He's been investigating the deaths of the men. He brought his investigation to my attention when he noticed the matching dates."

"Ah." Larkin read for a moment. "Hmmm."

"What?" Ray asked eagerly.

"I have a hunch, but let me finish reading. Raif, come sit by me. Read with me."

Larkin sat cross-legged on the bed. Raif sat beside her, his legs stretched straight and crossed at the ankles, and looked over her shoulder. He laughed lightly. "Well, I see one difference in us, my brother."

"What's that?" asked Ray.

"I have meticulous handwriting. Some of my teachers used to say I wrote like a girl."

"I just write fast when taking notes," Ray grumped.

"Hush." Larkin snickered. "Let me look at this." She read quietly for a time, pointing occasionally to an item for Raif to consider. She asked, "Ray, have you connected any dots?"

"Only that they were all killed on some form of holiday. Other than the obvious ones, some are Wiccan sabbats."

"Yes, I see that. The drawings have to do with moon phases and seasons for some of the dates. The men"—She looked at Raif and patted his leg—"The men were all someone with a need. Raif, even you had the need for your medication. Latrice lied to you to get you to help her. I know now, having gotten to know the real you, that under normal circumstances you wouldn't have listened to her at all."

"I apologize *again*."

"No need." She smiled at Raif and turned her attention to Ray. "Tell me about this little note about the reporter. You seem to think you're somehow responsible for her murder."

"What?" Chris said, her voice higher than normal.

Ray rubbed his head as he felt a creeping migraine. "I met the woman when she was stalked by a fan, a construction worker who was put under a restraining order. I might've also been one of the last people to see her on the day she disappeared."

"How does that make you responsible?" Chris asked. "She was bitchy. I met her, too, remember?"

With some exasperation, Ray said, "Chief Gerard held a press conference in the afternoon and insisted that I attend. McCall asked very pointed questions the chief tried to sidestep. She cornered me as I tried to leave through the back door. I'm afraid I was very rude to her. She returned to the station and prepared her story for the five o'clock news. She was last seen after the broadcast."

"Yes," Larkin interrupted the argument. "I usually listen to my TV rather than actually watch, except for *Lost*. I watch that religiously, but I remember your comment. You said that instead of accusing the local police of not doing their job, maybe she should look into why the feds had only seen fit to send one agent."

"That's exactly what I said, and threatening to go to the press finally got three more agents. I should've pushed it then, but I didn't," Ray said. "And she was killed June 21st and had a sun with a face painted on her. McCall lived alone with her Rottweiler."

"That's because only a dog could love her," Chris grunted.

The two law officials exchanged stabbing glares.

"Ray," Larkin interrupted again, "McCall's death was *not* your fault."

He cocked his head to the side. "I didn't say it was."

"No, but you think you should've been able to do more. You've done your job well. Don't blame yourself for this psychopath's work."

Ray nodded. "Until now, I *have* felt useless and frustrated. But now, I have something to go on." Annoyance tinged his voice.

"I hope I can give you more. You mentioned knowing about the solstices and equinoxes. The sun's face represents the summer solstice. I have another question. Your notes say you think Molly Jensen's employer was in love with her, but he wasn't a suspect. Why?"

"He was so torn up over the girl's death I'm certain he was in love with her even though he was twenty years older and recently divorced."

"Was there any evidence they were sleeping together?"

"No. From what I could gather, his divorce was ugly, and his ex-wife was looking for something to drag him back to court."

"Okay," Larkin said under her breath and read on. "Here." She pointed. "You note you think Rochelle Waters was lesbian. What evidence do you have?"

"She lived with a roommate who may or may not have been her girlfriend. The evidence supports that she was probably lesbian. The girl relocated here with Rochelle and worked as a telemarketer."

Chris interjected from her place on the floor, "According to Rochelle's coworkers, they were affectionate during the company picnic on the last day Rochelle was seen."

"Explain affectionate. I hug my female friends often," said Larkin. "That doesn't make me gay, just affectionate."

Chris said, "More intimately affectionate than hugs. They kissed in public. Then, I asked. The girlfriend confirmed."

Ray looked shocked. "You asked?"

"How else do you get the truth?" Chris rolled her eyes.

Larkin looked back and forth between the two officers. "Okay," she said. "My intuition grows stronger. And all these women were found in the same place?"

"Yes," said Ray. "We've been staking out the cemetery since the third victim and haven't seen a thing. Of course, it's a big place with several entrances, and I only have four officers to help me.

"Finally, the FBI has sent someone besides Chris, though she's awesome." He nodded toward her. "The FBI profiler says the killer has probably had some kind of medical or scientific training, is very religious, probably raised Catholic, and patriotic, perhaps even former military. Journey, the profiler, also believes it could be a woman who needs an accomplice and then gets rid of the man. Assuming Latrice is the woman, and Baker's victims were her accomplices, the men have been someone who could be easily manipulated as you've already pointed out. Sorry, Raif, but even you were manipulated when you were confused."

"That's the past." Raif nodded. "But no more."

"No, no more," assured Ray. "Well, Larkin, you know everything I know. What do you think?"

"One question." She held a finger aloft. "Had any of the women ever been married?"

"No, why?"

"The seven deadly virtues," she replied softly.

"Excuse me," said Ray. "I've heard of the seven deadly sins, but not the seven deadly virtues."

"I have," Chris said. "In the musical, *Camelot*, Mordred sings about them."

"Yes!" said Larkin excitedly. "The seven deadly virtues: courage, purity, humility, honesty, diligence, charity, and fidelity. I think my theory is right. We're looking at the deadly virtue of purity." She shifted to sit on her knees.

125

"Ray, you said that none of the women were sexually assaulted. They were sacrifices. They had to be pure. They were wearing wedding dresses. Were they all virgins?"

"What?"

Slowly and with precise articulation, Larkin repeated, "Were...they...all...virgins, Ray?"

Before he could respond, Chris was already on her cell phone. "Dantzler, look through the M.E. reports quickly. Were all the victims virgins?" She stood and paced.

Everyone waited in silence. "Thanks," Chris said after several minutes. She disconnected and looked at those with her. "Ten reports of 'intact hymen.'"

"Which two weren't?" asked the detective.

"Waters and Winters." Chris shrugged. "Broken hymen doesn't mean they weren't virgins. Winters was an equestrian. Horseback riding is notorious for breaking the hymen, even in small children. Waters?"

"She was gay," said Ray.

"And?" argued Chris. "She might not have ever been with a man. This loon might equate virginity with heterosexual sex only."

Ray turned to Larkin. "How did you think of that? Are you?" He shook his head and hand at the same time. "That's none of my business."

Larkin laughed. "Why is that so hard to believe, Ray? Because I'm twenty-seven? I must not be normal. Maybe not in our society, but it's my *choice* to wait until marriage."

Ray's mouth gaped. Larkin laughed again, even harder than the first time, but she could feel a burn in her cheeks. "You should see your face. All of you should see your faces."

"*That's* why Latrice asked if I'd touched you," Raif commented.

"I'm sorry," mumbled Ray, "but how did that fact escape me?"

"You didn't expect it. Just like you *assumed* I was sexually active."

"I'm sorry," Ray said, feeling his own flushed face. "I wasn't being judgmental. I find it admirable, but, forgive me, you're very pretty. How can you not have ever had a lover?"

She rolled her eyes and turned half her mouth down. "Trust me, I've had opportunities. It's my choice." She put her hair behind her ear. "I've also scared a few men away with that choice." She shrugged. "So be it. The man who loves me will accept me."

Chris muttered, "Yeah. We met Brad. He's a prick."

"You did?" Larkin asked.

The FBI agent nodded. "We questioned him briefly after Dr. Fairchild reported you missing."

Larkin beamed. "I *knew* she'd be looking for me." *She'll make sure Cyclops is okay too. Thank you, God.*

"Again," said Ray, "admirable, but back to business. How did you figure that out about the others?"

"This is how I drew my conclusion." Talking as much with her hands as her voice, she explained. "I know I'm a virgin." She touched her chest. "Raif said several times Latrice wanted me to be pure and unblemished. Obviously, from the things in your notes unblemished couldn't mean without scars or markings. Even *I* have piercings and a tattoo."

"You have a tattoo?" asked Ray.

"Yes," she replied.

"What is it?" he asked, his stomach suddenly doing loops.

"A Celtic guardian."

His mind wandered for a moment. "Where?" he asked as the other three looked at him.

"My left shoulder blade. Why?"

"I just didn't expect you to have a tattoo." *Especially not the same one I have.* He subconsciously touched his own left shoulder blade where a Celtic guardian dragon tattoo was located. His thoughts fell to the day he got it.

Mardi Gras with several fraternity brothers during my senior year in college. My roommate and I were lit. We stopped at a tattoo parlor on a side street off Bourbon Street. Half a dozen other brothers wandered on. Rob chose a bizarre two-headed serpent. He unconsciously shivered. *I felt a connection to the Celtic guardian, thought it might actually offer protection. It must have because when the brothers rejoined us, they bragged about beating up some guy that looked like me. Said the guy locked his girlfriend in the car when they went for her. I thought it just a drunken tall tale, but still felt I might've been spared something by my Celtic guardian.* He glanced toward his twin. *Now, I've met my twin who was mugged in New Orleans during the same Mardi Gras. Why would Larkin have the same tattoo? Does she feel the need to protect herself? Will it actually protect her? Oh, I hope so.*

"Hello, Ray," Larkin said. "Are you listening?"

The detective shook himself. "I'm sorry. Please, enlighten me."

"As I was saying, it couldn't be without physical blemish. It had to be something else—moral purity, at least sexual purity." She counted off each victim with her fingers as she spoke. "LaQuesha's car accident might've kept her pure. Her scars from all the repair work might've kept men away. Sister Mary Michael was a nun, the Virgin Mary, the Christmas or Yule sacrifice. Betty Kim came from a fairly traditional Chinese family. If they're old school, they'd expect her to remain a virgin until marriage. Chinese culture places a high value on female virginity. Lucia Torres's limited English was a barrier to her dating. I know how much she struggled with English because she served me several times at the Mexican Cantina, and she seemed very shy. Mira Samir was a devout Muslim. She *definitely* would've been a virgin. Isabeau's fiancé is in Iraq according to your notes. I guessed on her. Molly Jensen's

128

diabetes most likely made her very cautious even if she was in love with Dr. Epps. She might've been extra afraid of getting pregnant. Diabetics often have serious complications. You note how conservative the Winters girl was, and she was away at an all-girls' boarding school. She didn't sound like the type to sneak out and disappoint her father. Your reporter was too much of a 'B' word to be involved with anyone but herself from what I've read in your notes. The Waters girl was lesbian, but that was still an assumption on my part. The Native American"—She shrugged—"I know the reservation she lived on in Mississippi offers free abstinence courses. Maybe she was waiting; again, a guess. Bianca was a baby who was *planning* to have sex from what you wrote down, which means she had *not* had sex. The wedding dresses, the sacrificial element." She struck a pose as if to say, *Ta-da!* "Voila! Virgins."

Ray nodded thoughtfully. "All right. I see your logic, but how would the killer have known all these women were virgins?"

19
Investigation

The four people in the old wine cellar of the deserted monastery exchanged glances. After a short time, Chris offered a conjecture. "Their gynecologist."

Ray countered, "I don't think Bianca had a gynecologist."

"No, but she went to the health department where I met Latrice. Latrice might've started working there before Bianca's visit," Raif offered.

"Good thinking," concurred Ray. "All we have right this minute though is theory and the fact that this woman manipulated my brother in his weakened state into snatching Larkin. We need a lot more in order to bring her down."

He addressed Larkin. "First, we need to get you somewhere safe."

"This is the safest place I can be right now," argued Larkin.

"*Fooyay!*" Ray snapped and jumped to his feet. "Don't you wanna get out of here?"

"Of course I do, but Latrice expects Raif to keep me here. If we give her no reason to suspect complications to her plot, both Raif and I will be safe. In addition, it'll give you time to build your case. I just have one request. Make sure my cat is okay."

"Already taken care of," Chris said with a grin.

Ray rubbed his temples. *Not now. No headache allowed.* "I've got reservations, serious reservations, but I'm gonna pull the stakeout on the cemetery and put a watch on this place."

"All right," agreed Larkin and Raif in unison.

Ray whipped out his cell phone and made the call before he addressed his brother again.

"Raif, what do you know about the rest of this place?" The detective looked around the cellar. "This room is obviously not where the murders took place, but I smell decay."

"I have no idea. Latrice forbad me to go anywhere but here. I don't know what's above us other than what you'd expect a church to have."

Ray turned to Chris, "Go get everybody else to work on finding out about these women's doctors, and I'll get us a search warrant for this place. I want every jot and tittle in place so this maniac doesn't get off on a technicality."

"We could just bring her in for questioning," Chris suggested.

"Yeah, but that would alert her that something is going on, and without some more concrete evidence, we couldn't hold her for more than seventy-two hours. If she's the one we want, she could do something once she's released and hurt somebody or disappear." Ray shook his head. "I hate to agree with the notion of letting y'all stay, but you could be on to something. We'll be back as soon as possible."

"We'll be fine," assured Raif and Larkin together.

"And, I'm sending somebody here to baby sit the two of you. Chris, which little stooge would be best?"

"Patrick," she answered." He wouldn't stand out in a crowd."

"I agree. Arrange it with him." Reluctantly, Ray and Chris left, after speaking with the reassigned patrolmen. He instructed them to look for Agent Swift soon.

As he drove back to the stationhouse, Ray phoned Judge LaVigne at home and was assured his search warrant as soon as the judge had enough information in his hands to issue one.

Back at the station, Ray sent Baker to the Hall of Records to find out who owned the old monastery. "I hope you get the sweet little college co-ed who works part time. The clerk is a bitch." Ray shrugged at Baker's scowl.

Chris immediately began investigating who the victims used as gynecologists and sent Swift to the monastery. The agent entered with a sleeping bag and burgers for the evening meal. His two charges found him down-to-earth and delightful company.

Disgruntled officials who had already gone home grudgingly returned to their offices for Baker to look through records. The same woman who had given Ray and Chris grief about the birth records let Brian Baker in. She grumbled, "Couldn't this have waited until tomorrow?"

"No, ma'am," said Brian, remembering Ray's warning. "If we wait, another woman might die. Do you want that on your conscience?"

"Humph!" grunted the woman. "Will it go faster if I help you look, Detective Baker?"

"Yes, ma'am," he said with an uneasy feeling. *She rubs me the wrong way.* "That would be quite helpful, but I think I need to do this more discreetly. Thanks for the offer."

He gave her a disarming smile, causing her to shrug and open a novel from beneath the counter. She read while Baker searched.

His hunt complete, Baker called Ray in transit. "Investigation turned up the owner of the monastery to be Restoration and Revival, Inc."

"Who owns the company?" He held his breath.

"None other than Latrice Descartes." Baker chuckled. "Get this, pal. It's the 'Mark of the Beast.' The woman's address is 666 Causeway Annex, Eau Bouease, Louisiana. You got everything you need to obtain a valid search warrant. I'll be there in twenty minutes."

"Who came to let you in?"

"Your friend. I ignored her. I didn't even tell her exactly which property I was looking for."

"Good call."

Chris's inquiries by phone to the victims' relatives found that three of the women had used Dr. Bill Sullivan, just as Larkin had. Two of them had used Dr. Sessums, and six, Dr. Jimenez. Bianca had gone to the health department. Knowing there would be great resistance to personnel records being handed over, Dantzler pulled some strings and got court orders for personnel files at each of the doctors' offices.

As soon as physicians' offices opened the next morning, Dantzler, Chris, and Ray each went to a different office. Dantzler visited Dr. Sessums and Chris took the doctor's office with the most victims.

Unable to explain his need to interview the man personally, Ray felt compelled to see Larkin's doctor, almost as if a voice guided him. He shivered at the thought. He did not approach the personnel office. Rather, he went directly to Dr. Sullivan, an amiable giant at six-six and a good two hundred fifty pounds.

Ray broke the ice by saying, "You should be on the football field."

"Was," he clipped. "Played five years as a defensive lineman for the Chargers. After three concussions, I came to my senses before I lost my senses. I changed direction in life. Delivering babies brings me joy. What can I do for you, Detective? You do *not* appear to be pregnant." The doctor gave his unusual patient an impish, but good-natured grin.

"I'm not," laughed Ray. "I need to ask you about a possible employee, Latrice Descartes."

"Oh, yes. Latrice. She was a trip." He opened a candy dish and popped a lemon drop into his mouth, offering Ray one. The detective declined with a hand wave. Dr. Sullivan characterized Latrice around his lemon drop. "I often wondered if she should be named Larry. Latrice was former military, a Marine. She was most unladylike. More like a lumbering bull. I had a hard time believing she wanted to be an obstetrics nurse, but she was highly qualified.

133

However, the only position I had at the time was in billing. She worked several months part time here and at the health department. She left us to go full time at the health department. She was a good employee. Is she in trouble?"

"She might be of real help in an investigation. I need her file."

"Do you have the proper documents compelling me to give it to you?"

"Of course I do." Ray handed the court order to Dr. Sullivan.

The doctor gave the paperwork a quick read and nodded. "Come with me, Detective Reynolds." As the two men walked down the hall, the doctor asked, "Detective, does this have anything to do with Larkin Sloan?"

"Perhaps. Why do you ask?"

"Intuition." The doctor shrugged. "*She's* a trip, too. You'll fall in love with her when you meet her."

"Are you in love with her?"

Dr. Sullivan laughed. "I'm married, Detective, but if I weren't, Miss Sloan would be my kind of gal. I don't remember all my patients so vividly. She's unusual. Of course, I'm also nearly twenty years her senior. If Latrice has had anything to do with Larkin's disappearance, find both of them, whatever it takes."

He pulled a file and handed it to Ray. "Good luck, Detective. If I can be of any further service, let me know."

All three investigators obtained information showing that Latrice Descartes had worked for each doctor at the time the various victims had been kidnapped and killed. She had indeed had access to all their records for medical billing purposes. She had only worked part time at the health department until a month before Larkin disappeared.

Dantzler frowned looking at Ray and Chris. "You two don't look as if you had any trouble getting information."

"I didn't," Chris said. "Why do you think I took the office with the most victims?"

"Beats me."

Chris chortled. "Really, Lawrence. I'm a woman. Sometimes it does have its advantages. I talked openly and showed the proper documentation. The human resource coordinator gave me just what I needed."

Dantzler looked at Ray. "How'd you fare?"

"I made a new friend, one that really likes Larkin Sloan. You?"

"I met with serious opposition—patient confidentiality. I had to prove I didn't want patient information, just employment confirmation. I got what I needed even if the HR person in that office probably will never speak to me again. And she was hot and not wearing a wedding band."

Chris rolled her eyes. Ray caught the look and raised an eyebrow in question. She just shook her head.

Ray and Chris returned to the wine cellar two days later to find Raif, Larkin, and Patrick having a relaxed late breakfast. "Perhaps, you should've waited to eat," suggested Ray. He held up the search warrant. "Do you wanna see what's upstairs?"

All agreed they did, and Ray cautioned the civilians not to touch anything. However, he gave them rubber gloves just in case.

The unusual assortment of sleuths made their way up the creaking stairs to a locked door on which Ray deftly picked the lock, thankful he had trained with a locksmith. They entered a corridor lined with cells where monks had once slept. The cubicles appeared to have been undisturbed for eons. A thick layer of dust covered everything, and cobwebs invaded the corners and spaces. The small narrow rectangular windows covered in decades of grime allowed very little light to filter in. Feeling certain it would be a mistake to use the electric lights installed around 1900, Ray distributed flashlights. The beams sent rats and roaches scurrying. Sandwiched between Ray and Raif, Larkin shivered at the scratchy noises. Ray touched her hand. Raif caressed her shoulder.

Further snooping found a kitchen and dining hall in the same condition as the small bed chambers the monks and acolytes had used. Out the other side of the kitchen rose another set of stairs with a locked door at the top. Once again, Ray picked the old lock.

The group entered the side door of the sanctuary, and the pungent odor of decay sent them back into the stairwell. Ray reached into his back pocket and pulled out a packet of scented wipes. He gave one to each person and asked, "Shall we try again?"

Inside with the wipe against their noses, the group could not believe what they beheld. The stained glass windows, which should have drawn breaths of awe for their craft and beauty, instead cast eerie dancing shadows and a deathly pall over the room. The dark pine pews remained undisturbed, but the marble altar and communion utensils stood defiled and cursed, caked with dried blood.

Ray, Chris, and Patrick snapped pictures from every angle of the room and scraped numerous samples of the dried blood into evidence vials. "Do you think she drinks the blood?" asked Larkin in innocent disgust.

"How repulsive!" Chris gagged.

The group made their way back to the relative safety of the wine cellar. With a severe scowl on his face Ray said, "We have a lot of circumstantial evidence. Unless our victims' DNA turns up in these blood samples, all we can get her for right now is conspiracy to kidnap, and *that* on the word of a man a good lawyer could make seem completely unreliable. I'm sorry, Raif, but you know it's true."

Raif nodded.

His brother continued, "She could say all the grossness upstairs was there long before she bought the place, and we would be hard pressed to prove otherwise. Right now, we can't say for certain it's human blood. Santeria practitioners kill chickens. Some Voodoo rituals might use animal blood. We need more than this if we want to nail her. What we need is to catch her in the act." He handed Patrick all the evidence vials and envelopes. "Get this stuff to the lab ASAP. I want to get these two housed somewhere safe."

Larkin opened her mouth to protest, but Ray put his index finger against his lips in sharp command. Her eyes widened at his audacity to order her to do anything. The detective told Patrick, "We'll be close on your heels. Take care of this."

The FBI agent left with the evidence. Once the door closed, Ray looked around at the others. "I have a plan, but it involves a great deal of deception and could prove to be very dangerous."

20
Laying a Trap

"What do you have in mind, Ray? Are you considering using me as bait?" Larkin asked, planting herself in her usual spot near the headboard of the old bed.

"Well, sort of," he admitted.

"Should I be prepared to be led away like a lamb to the slaughter?" A hint of fear and annoyance tinged her voice.

"You won't be alone. I'll be with you." The detective looked toward his twin. "My plan really has more to do with my brother and me trading places."

"What?" gasped Raif, his already fair face blanching. His sapphire blue eyes exuded both anger and apprehension.

"I told you my plan involved deception." Sitting patiently at the foot of the bed and looking at the cheap blanket, he smoothed a wrinkle. "How good a liar are you, Raif?" The detective made eye contact with his brother.

Wrapping his arms tightly about himself, Raif answered, "Well, I really don't know. I've never made a habit of lying."

"I'll have to do more lying than you. You'll simply need to follow Chris's lead."

"Oh, my God!" Chris hollered. "Are you serious, Ray?"

"Do I look as if I'm joking?" the detective responded, lines etching his brow.

Chris paced in agitation waving her index finger in a tick-tock motion. "Let me get this straight." She paused. "You want *Raif*"—she pointed at the cop's twin—"to pretend to be *you*"—the point turned to her partner—"while you stay here and pretend to be *him*." A perfectly French manicured index finger jabbed into Ray's chest. "So *you* can be here when this Latrice person finally comes onto the property?"

"You know it." He looked at the fingernail poking into his chest. "Do you mind?"

"You've lost it." The FBI agent snapped her hands to her hips, arms akimbo, muscles taut.

"I want to catch the nutcase in the act."

"We have enough to bring her in for questioning now!" Chris shrieked.

Ray sighed. "But not enough to nail her. And I'm sure she'd try to pin it all on Raif."

Ray turned to Larkin. "I swear I won't let her hurt you, but if you don't agree to this charade, I can't pull it off."

"I know you won't let anything happen to me, Ray." Larkin looked at the other twin. "I worry more about your being able to fool Latrice. I'll go along with your plan *if* you can fool me into believing you're Raif."

"You're on!" he chuckled. "This should be interesting. Raif, let's get started."

With arms crossed, Raif said, "Well, the first thing we need to do is to get you very scruffy looking." He held up an index finger and waved it back and forth. "No shaving. As a matter of fact, before you meet Latrice, you might get a makeup artist to make you even rattier. I think for all our sakes we'll let you walk through a stink bomb rather than not bathe. Of course, she did tell me to take a bath, but I'm nuts. Remember, Latrice thinks I'm off my meds and gone completely off the deep end." He flipped his hands into the air and grinned. "I'll have to get you to hear voices."

"I'm sure I'll be hearing yours. As a matter of fact, I'll need to meet this woman before Halloween. I'll probably wear a hidden ear piece so I can hear your instructions."

"This is crazy, Ray." Chris voiced her objections again. "It's too dangerous. The boys upstairs will never agree."

Ray mumbled, "They don't have to know."

"Not just crazy—*stupid*!" The FBI agent paced back and forth across the room, stopping in front of Raif. She glared at Ray's mirror image. "I thought *you* might be more sensible."

Raif smiled. "I'm not worried about Ray's being able to fool Latrice. I'm concerned about being him."

"That's easy. Act like a stubborn jackass." She glowered at her partner. "What's the Cajun word you use—*fooyay*? This is foolish!" she finished with a crescendo.

Raif sighed. "I tried so hard to lose the Cajun accent. Now I have to get it back."

"I don't sound Cajun," the detective argued.

Everyone else in the room laughed as he took umbrage.

"*Fooyay!*" joked Raif.

"Yes, foolish action," agreed Ray's temporary partner. "I'll say it again—foolish, foolish, foolish."

Larkin nodded. "Yes, you *do* sound a little Cajun. In a charming way."

The FBI agent put both hands to her head. "It's not funny." The woman continued to argue. "Ray, this creature is capable of killing you. I mean, she's physically capable of overpowering a man your size. She's done it to several victims. What did you learn about her? She's a former Marine. She's trained to kill. If she suspects anything, this could blow up in your face. Not to mention get you fired."

"Not if you have my back. Chris, trust me. This is our best chance to put the nail in her coffin."

Larkin shivered at the use of that particular idiom.

"You okay?" Chris asked.

"Yeah. Just use a different phrase. There's been enough death."

"Sorry," Ray mumbled before presenting more arguments for his case. "We've run her fingerprints. She's smart. The only place we've found her prints is on the outside doorknob. She owns the place, so we would expect that. We have to wait on the DNA from the blood samples. By the time the results get back, it could be too late. She has coerced and manipulated men in a weakened state to help her and then killed them, just like a black widow."

140

Raif grunted under his breath, "I thought black widows killed the male after mating. Latrice might be a virgin herself. I can't imagine a normal man being attracted to her."

Everybody looked astonished at Raif's comment.

"What?" Raif asked, standing up straight and spreading his arms out wide, palms facing his brother. "You haven't seen her. She's five-ten, a hundred sixty pounds, hair shorter than yours, very masculine features, and very muscular. This woman has biceps almost as big as mine. She's scary, Ray. I'm saying this to you while I'm totally in control of my faculties."

Ray nodded. "I believe you. That's why you're going home with me for a couple of days. Chris will stay with Larkin. She'll shoot first and ask questions later if anything unusual happens."

Chris looked around at the other three. "You're all nuts." The agent stomped to the small refrigerator, grabbed a bottle of water, and chugged half of it. "Damn you! Count me in."

Pleased with himself, Ray grinned with smugness. "When you and I return, brother, and I pass Miss Sloan's test, we'll set the snare, lay the trap, and catch this poisonous snake."

The two Raifords left Chris and Larkin well supplied for a couple of days. Baker and the FBI agents were left with the impression that Ray and Chris were hiding Raif and Larkin in a secure location. Ray felt it would be prudent for the fewest people possible to know about the change of identities until the last minute.

However, Ray made one phone call to his boss. "Chief, I need a little trust for the next several days," he said.

"What the hell are you up to?"

"I don't want to tell you so that you can claim complete ignorance if it fails."

"Are you going to get both of us fired?"

"I don't think so. Just back me up when the time comes."

"Ray, I swear." Chief Gerard took a deep breath. "Does this have anything to do with the man that came in who looks like you?"

"You heard about that, huh?"

"Yeah. Baker mentioned it to me."

"Yeah. It has *everything* to do with him and the missing woman. Please have some faith in me."

"Okay. I don't feel easy with whatever secrecy you're planning, but I'll trust you—for now. But I swear if anyone else dies, I'll fry your ass."

"As you should."

21
Getting to Know You

As Chris and Larkin waited for the twins to make their transformation, they became well acquainted. Chris put herself in charge of their physical needs. Larkin took control of their social interaction. After two days, they felt a sisterly connection. Chris got out Styrofoam cups and plugged in the coffee pot the second morning. She asked, "Larkin, are you sure you wanna go through with Ray's lame-brained plan?"

"Want to? No. But I think it might be the only way to pin down Latrice. And Ray will be wired and there'll be agents, including you, stationed strategically to be in the door within seconds on Ray's code word."

"I'm worried about Raif, too," Chris confessed. "He's really a good guy. I don't want him to get hurt anymore."

"Chris, what's going on?"

"Nothing. I just have a soft spot for him. Working with Ray and getting to know both of them makes me want to know what happened to my daughter after she was adopted. She'll be turning sixteen next month."

"So, track her down. Abuse your authority a little."

"That's what Ray would say. Finding out he has a twin has made him more thoughtful. Don't misunderstand." She held her hands in the air in a stop motion. "My partner's great! That's just it—he's my partner. He's as hardheaded and headstrong as I am. We would kill each other. Raif seems sweeter and needier."

Larkin interrupted, "And a part of you wants to take care of him. I understand. I've seen how vulnerable Raif can be. I just think you've missed that part of Ray. He tries so hard to hide his insecurity. I sense he needs somebody to look after him, too. The difference is he won't admit it.

Well, *maybe* when he finds the right woman, he'll admit he needs her."

"Ray's very proud, or at least self-reliant. He's afraid of failure. He's the type that says, 'If you want it done right, do it yourself.'" Chris mimicked Ray.

Larkin laughed. "Yeah, I get that impression, but he sure seems to rely on you."

"That amazes me, but we've truly become partners. I'll find it hard to leave when this is over."

"Don't go."

"What reason would I have to stay? This is my job."

"If God wants you to stay here, He'll find a way."

"Larkin, you astound me." Chris poured two cups of coffee and handed one to her new friend. "Considering everything you've been through, how do you remain so strong and positive?"

For a moment Larkin looked at the cross at the top of the wall as if seeking inspiration. "I have a true abiding faith," she responded.

"I wish I could feel that way."

"You can. You must simply trust in God."

"I believe, but I was brought up in the Eastern Orthodox Church. It's very works-oriented. Strict obedience is the key." Old hurts resonated in her voice. "I'm sure after my rather immoral past, I'm bound for Hell."

"Works come as a result of faith, Chris. Faith first; works come later. And you can never be perfect, but you can be forgiven."

"I've done some pretty…um…shall I say *loose* things?" She stirred sugar into her coffee and took a sip. "I haven't been celibate like you by any means."

"Have you ever asked God to forgive you?" The early morning sun flickered through the cross in the window and made a reflection on Larkin's hair like a halo.

"Yes, and I've reformed over the last few years. I've become much more selective. I keep hoping for someone to

144

actually love me." The agent sighed. "I wish it *was* that simple."

"It is," Larkin said with conviction. "And with the love of the Heavenly Father, other kinds of love seem to come easier." She paused with a slightly dubious look on her face, dipped brows and a half frown. "Well, I think romantic love might come easier. I'd like someone to love me, too."

Chris laughed a little. "Like Brad? I didn't like that jerk."

Larkin shrugged. "He didn't like the fact that I wanted to wait for marriage to have sex."

"I'm really glad I met you. 'The love of the Heavenly Father,'" Chris repeated what Larkin had said. "Nobody has ever made this much sense to me."

"Raif said the same thing. Like I told him: I'm just the messenger. Listen to the message."

"Ray needs to hear the message."

Larkin giggled and put her coffee cup down. She made the sign of the cross and looked heavenward. "If he pulls off his little switch-a-roo, he will. Be assured, my friend."

Chris sat on the bed beside Larkin. "Mind if I ask you something else?"

"Of course not."

"Do you believe in the supernatural?"

Larkin thought before she spoke. "Yes. Why?"

Chris heaved a sigh. "I dreamed Raif asked me to help him find his heart before I ever met him."

The two women locked eyes without speaking as Larkin considered all the dreams she'd had, especially since being abducted. She clutched Chris's hand. "Let me tell you about the dreams I've been having…"

Meanwhile, both Ray and Raif were becoming rather scruffy as each tried to master the other's mannerisms and speech patterns. They found they did many things the same way. They liked many of the same foods. They chose the same cologne. However, there were differences. Raif tended to be more easygoing but more formal in his speech and interpersonal interactions. He liked his life orderly, with little complication, but he was flexible and adapted. Ray had a quicker temper and was impatient. Ray was also brutally candid. He had been known to hurt feelings. Both were analytical as their choices of professions showed.

Their lives had been similar, yet different. Both had been adopted by families who loved them dearly. Both had affectionately called their sisters "Ronnie." And both had had their hearts broken by a woman who could not handle a difficult situation, but when that topic came up, both balked and shared very little.

Ray said, "I don't like to talk about Mia."

Raif nodded. "I understand. Talking about Abbey hurts too much. We'll get there one day."

"Yeah, just not now," Ray agreed. "Hey, did you know you're older by thirteen minutes. You were adopted a few days before me. I was still in incubation."

"Good to know I'm the big brother." He grinned. "I was brought up on a farm. My family often struggled financially, yet their love never faltered." Raif told his brother, "Because of a severe case of mumps, Louis Gautier was sterile. When I was six, the Gautiers adopted a little girl that they named Rhonda. My dad, sister, and pet dog died tragically seven years later in a car accident. Mom worked hard to get me through high school, and I won a scholarship to Tulane University to continue my education and became an architect as Dad had encouraged."

Ray asked, "Did the two of you actually frame a house when you were about ten?"

Raif laughed, eyes crinkling at the corners. "Yeah. I designed it with a ruler and a protractor. It was a simple ranch style. That's when Dad told me to be an architect. How'd you know?"

146

"I dreamed about it."

"I dreamed about you my whole life."

"I know. I did, too."

Ray already knew all that had transpired with Abigail Bertram even if Raif didn't talk much about it and how Raif had come to live in Eau Bouease. Raif spoke fondly of his childhood. Though not wealthy, he had been happy, and his short time with Louis Gautier had been a firm foundation of unconditional love. Maria, his mother, only strengthened that love as the years went by. Ray was satisfied his brother had been as well loved as he had.

While Raif's family struggled with some financial hardship, Ray's was well-to-do. Ray's parents had had a daughter they named Veronica. Ray explained how he was adopted. "Due to complications during childbirth, my mom couldn't have any more children. When Veronica was four, the Reynoldses adopted *moi*." He grinned and placed a hand on his chest. "I grew up a bit spoiled. Life was pleasant until Veronica disappeared and was murdered when I was thirteen. That incident made me determined to become a detective to protect others from my sister's fate."

Ray sighed. "I've done a miserable job so far, haven't I?"

"No," argued Raif. "You've done all that you knew to do. Now, God, at His appointed time, has sent you the means to stop this evil."

"Is part of your illness to sound like a religious fanatic?" He arched an eyebrow.

"No!" Raif laughed. "But I *have* discovered real faith. Larkin explains it so simply. After you spend a few days with her, you'll be a changed man, too."

A burn filled Ray's face. "I already feel changed because of her. I think she's an angel."

"She definitely has heavenly guidance, brother. Be careful, or she'll totally bewitch you."

"Has she beguiled you, Raif?"

"Yes, indeed, but I'm not attracted to her in a physical sense. She reminds me too much of a little redheaded girl that was my sister. Now, Chris!" He stretched his eyes wide. "That's a woman!"

"Oh, ho!" cheered Ray with a clap of his hands.

"Don't you think Chris is beautiful, Ray?"

"Yes, Chris is very attractive, but I could never think of her like *that*. She's my partner."

"Only temporarily."

"Then, she'll be over a thousand miles away." The detective shook his head. "No, Chris and I would never work."

"Good."

"Raif, she'll be leaving when this case is over."

"Who says I have to stay here?"

"I...I thought...You're my brother, my family. My mom wants you to be part of *our* family. What about Walter Bertram? I thought...Oh, never mind." Ray waved his hand as if trying to erase something. "Let's get down to business. We both need a little more facial hair if we're to fool first the angelic being and then Satan's spawn." He touched his right cheek. "I have this little scar to cover up. After we convince Larkin, you can go clean cut while I continue to look like a reject from the sixties."

"Ray?"

"It's fine, Raif. I've always been self-sufficient. I've never admitted this to anyone else, and I probably never will again, but I need you in my life. Losing you now would devastate me."

"I'm not leaving. Even if I did, I'd only be a phone call away. You're a part of me, a part that has been missing for a long time. Now that I've found you, I'd hate to leave you. But you're right; we have something more important than our feelings to deal with right now. We have a killer to catch and God's messenger to save."

The two brothers embraced and Ray said huskily, "Where's that makeup artist?"

148

Well," quipped Chris as they heard footsteps. "Let the games begin."

Forty-eight hours after Ray and Raif left Larkin and Chris, the two men returned. When they entered the wine cellar, identical twins in every detail stood before a pair of astonished women.

"Larkin, who's who?" Chris asked.

"At a cursory glance, I can't tell. Let me pose a few questions Raif would know from having been with me for more than two weeks. What's my favorite breakfast food?"

The men answered simultaneously. "Rice Krispies with fresh fruit."

"What's my favorite fruit?"

Again the answer came in unison. "Blueberries."

"Oh, this will never work. Chris, ask something that only Ray would know."

"You know, Larkin, they've discussed possible scenarios. I'll try this one though." She took a deep breath. "What's my biggest regret?"

Larkin gasped. She hurt for her friend and her heart sent up a prayer. *How will Chris handle this? It's so personal.*

Ray looked sidelong at his brother as he felt a pang of betrayal, but for a higher cause.

Raif made eye contact with Chris and gave her a look of sympathy as he replied, "That you gave your daughter up for adoption."

Chris looked at Larkin and shrugged. "Either that's Ray, or Ray divulged my deepest, darkest secret to a stranger in order to stop a killer. Either could be true. If he didn't tell Raif, well, everybody knows now. But Ray would do whatever it takes to stop this maniac. So, my assessment as a trained FBI agent is that *Raif* just answered my question."

Both men said, "Chris."

She shook her head. "Sympathy from either of you is *not* required. I did the right thing then although it hurt like hell; just as Audrey did the right thing thirty years ago. Now, it's time for us to do the right thing. Let's lay an inescapable trap."

"Agreed," Larkin said.

Revealing the truth, Ray said, "Really?"

"Yes. I'll be in very good hands."

Raif and Chris left Ray with Larkin. The time would soon come when Ray would need to deceive a very cunning and perceptive jackal, not an innocent, trusting angel or a dear friend.

In Ray's car, Raif, at the wheel, simply asked, "Where to?"

"Ray's place. I have to keep you safe while we wait for Halloween."

"Will we be going into the police station?"

"I hate to send you in there alone, but all the guys know Ray would never leave you and Larkin unguarded. We'll have to put in an appearance now and then. I'll go most often, but you'll have to show up two or three times. Keep your conversations short. Be grouchy." She nodded with high-arched eyebrows. "They'll buy that. I'll lay out the plans for Halloween night."

Raif released a long puffy sigh. "What about all the other time? I don't mind telling you this whole act worries me."

"I'll stay with you, Raif. Heck, Ray's sleeper sofa is as comfortable as the hotel bed."

"Thank you," he said with deep humility.

"For what? Doing my job?"

"This is above and beyond the call of duty."

"Now, I don't think you're as big a challenge as you do."

"You're not afraid of the psycho?"

"You are *not* a psycho." She gave him an affectionate punch in the arm. "As a matter of fact, I think you need to see a neurologist. After what you went through in New Orleans, your problem could be physical, not psychological."

"You really think so?"

"Yep."

Raif glanced at Chris and could tell she was serious from the firm set of her jaw and her narrowed eyes. "All right. When this is over, I'll go if you'll hold my hand."

Chris winked. "I'd love to." She reached out her hand. "I'll start right now."

He squeezed her offered hand. "I think this could be the start of something very nice."

As they pulled into Ray's parking place, she affirmed, "I agree, but first let's get you looking presentable."

"Yes, ma'am." He scratched his chin. "This mess itches. I can't wait to get it off. I feel for Ray. He has to keep it for *Latrice*." He said the name with derision.

Upon entering Ray's apartment, they were greeted by enthusiastic ankle rubbing. Raif picked up Cyclops and rubbed his head soothingly. "Larkin is just fine. She'll be home soon." He turned to Chris. "I was surprised to see Larkin's cat here."

Chris waved her hand. "Ray's a softie. He won't admit it, but he's very sensitive."

"I'm glad I've met my brother, but I do wish it were under better circumstances."

"Me too."

The FBI agent made her way through the small, functional apartment. The living area consisted of one large open room with the living room and dining room running continuous and separated from the kitchen by a bar, which had cabinet space accessibility from both sides beneath it. The color scheme ran the gamut of the beige spectrum: wheat colored walls, ecru trim, grayish-tan Berber carpet, and tan linoleum with white octagons in both the kitchen and the bathroom. All countertops were off-white, tan-flecked Formica, and every appliance and every piece of plumbing was basic white.

Raif's eyes crinkled as he chuckled. "You can tell I didn't design this complex. It's satisfactory, but sort of cheap."

Chris laughed. Rummaging in the refrigerator, Chris said, "Yes! Go clean up, and I'll make us something to eat."

When Raif returned from the shower, he felt and looked like a new man. He found popcorn shrimp, tater tots, and coleslaw waiting.

"This looks great." He took one of the four non-descript light brown chairs around the matching circular table.

Placing the food on the table and sitting beside her charge, Chris observed, "So do you. A definite improvement."

Deep dimples showed as he smiled. "I'm glad you noticed."

Over the next week, Chris and Raif talked and bantered. Raif pulled off several visits to the police station, to his relief. The morning after the switch, he even facilitated the press conference in which Steve Journey delivered the killer's profile to the public.

Taking the podium, he kept his statement short. "Let me introduce Special Agent Steve Journey, a profiler with the FBI. He has put together a psychological description of the person we think is responsible for twelve brutal slayings. He will answer any questions you might have." He indicated the microphone with his hand as he stepped back. Journey delivered the news, leaving out the actual suspect and the fact that they knew the killer to be female. Behind his colleague, Patrick Swift whispered something to the detective, who lifted an eyebrow. On *Ray's* other side, Baker whispered something. To the press it appeared to be an exchange of information, but Raif's heart raced. He left as soon as he could without drawing more attention to himself. Walking off the platform, Chief Gerard placed a hand on his shoulder and whispered. Raif's whole body stiffened. He hurried away.

Raif entered the apartment, which Chris had domesticated, with a sigh.

"What's up?" she asked.

"Patrick and Baker know."

"Know what?"

"That I'm not Ray. And Chief Gerard suspects."

She gave him a questioning look. He shrugged. "They won't say anything. Patrick thinks it's funny, but he says I'm not as arrogant as my twin. Baker noticed I don't have a scar on my lower right cheek. At least Ray has a beard right now so Latrice won't notice his scar."

"It'll be fine," Chris assured. "I think they should *all* know before the actual day."

"You're probably right, but I still have to keep fooling the other two agents until then."

After another visit to the station, Raif returned with a deep scowl, which made him look even more like Ray.

Anxious at his expression, Chris asked, "What happened now?"

"I'm not sure."

"You look upset."

"Well…" He hesitated. "May I ask you something?"

"Of course."

Raif sat on the tan leather sofa, hugged an earth-tone paisley throw pillow to his chest, and stared at the floor. Chris recognized the barrier. She fretted. *Will we have to start over? I thought we'd broken down several walls.* "Have I done something wrong?" she asked.

"What's your relationship with Lawrence Dantzler?" he asked, looking up with his captivating eyes without raising his head.

"Excuse me?" Chris shook her head as if she didn't understand. "What relationship?"

153

"You don't have one?"

"No!" she barked.

"He...intimated otherwise."

"Jackass! I'll put him in his place." She sat beside Raif but hesitated to touch him because of the barrier he still held against his chest. "Lawrence Dantzler is a player. Likeable, but he strings women along."

"You know this how?" He cocked his head to the side, but made eye contact with Chris.

"We dated about five years ago. The big problem was he had three or four other women he dated at the same time."

"So, there's nothing *now*?"

"No. Why?"

"It's just...I wouldn't want to step on his toes. He's Herculean."

Chris laughed. *I hope I'm interpreting Raif's dialogue correctly.*

He said, "After Halloween, I think, I'd like to ask you to dinner since you're not with Dantzler."

"I am *not*," she assured him. "And I'll go."

He put the pillow against the back of the sofa.

Through their time, Raif's admiration and respect for Chris deepened. He wanted to open up fully to her, but he kept up his guard. Old wounds ran deep.

She tried everything she could, including talking about her dark childhood after her mother's death when she'd had to shoulder the responsibility of helping parent six younger siblings. She shared about becoming involved with a boy no older than she was and how his parents had forbidden him to have anything else to do with her when she got pregnant. She related how her father had forced her to give the baby up for adoption. She talked about her own child she'd never held and wondered about every day. Her words were factual, but anguish and heartache showed on her face. Although a friendship blossomed, Chris was quite aware there was a shield, harder than the throw pillow Raif

154

had held in front of him, over his heart. Only a miracle would make him lower it. Chris was angry with Lawrence Dantzler for replacing the mortar she had managed to chisel loose.

Even as Raif and Chris bonded, Larkin and Ray grew close despite Ray's resolve not to become involved any further on a personal level.

The ice broke the first day as they sat down to eat on the bed. Sitting cross-legged, Larkin joked, "All right! So, you deserve an Oscar. However, you can leave the playacting for Latrice. I would really like to get to know Raiford Reynolds."

"What would you like to know?" the detective asked.

"Everything. I want to know about your childhood. I want to know your likes and dislikes. Then, you can choose an adjective that begins with each letter of your name that describes your personality."

Shocked by her reply, Ray asked, "Yes, Teacher. Ray or Raiford?"

She grinned. "Raiford. Ray is too short, and Y is hard anyway."

"I will if you will," he challenged.

"Bring it on!" she teased.

Ray set about giving Larkin a synopsis of his childhood and family, including the death of his sister and the impact it had on his life. He became quiet and thoughtful for he wanted to be honest without being offensive. Then, he seriously said, "Now, for your adjectives."

"Not mine—yours," countered Larkin.

"You know what I meant," argued Ray, "but I just might do some for you and tell you what I think of you." His cheeks dimpled teasingly.

"Go for it, if I get the same privilege." Her eyes danced with mischief.

155

Ray laughed. "Oh, this I have to hear. Here I go: First of all, Y wouldn't've been that hard. I would've chosen yare. I think yare describes me. I'm just like a Boy Scout; I was a Boy Scout, an Eagle Scout. I'm always prepared."

Both of them laughed before he began in earnest. "Rakish or Roguish—I couldn't decide, but I confess I have a wild side, so either will work."

She snickered. *I have a hard time seeing you, so bent on justice, being a rake, although you are pushing the boundaries of the rule book with this double identity farce.*

Face blank, he deadpanned, "I like beer and tequila, and I can tie one on."

"Okay." *Trying to get my goat, huh?* "Please, don't let me stop you. I want to hear what you think of yourself."

He nodded and kept on. "Alert—I pay close attention to details. Independent—I'm used to depending on myself and I find it difficult to let other people make decisions for me or about me. Fallible—I make mistakes. Opinionated—And I will argue my point to the bitter end. Reliable—you can depend on me. Determined—I don't give up easily. How did I do, Miss Sloan? Do I get an A?"

"Well, all the words were adjectives, and you explained yourself quite well. I guess I'll pass you." The teacher pretended to write in a grade book and took a deep breath. All the while Ray had talked, she had weighed her options to describe a man that took her breath away. "But you might consider these: Restive—you're quite impatient. Affable—you're very kind and friendly, but. Irascible— you have a quick temper. Familial—your family and those you care about are important to you. Objective—although you're opinionated, you must keep an open mind and weigh all the evidence. Rational—you have a great ability to reason. Daedal—you are very intricate and complicated. You're not so hard to read, Raiford Reynolds, and you're not as awful as you pretend to be. On the contrary, you're one of the genuinely good guys."

156

"Thank you, ma'am," Ray said deferentially. *Interesting. Damn, and I thought of those too.* "Now it's your turn."

"As you wish," Larkin conceded. "Loquacious—I love to talk."

"I can tell," he said in a smart-aleck tone.

Larkin rolled her eyes, but did not let him deter her. "Ardent—I'm full of emotion in all that I do. Reserved—I keep a lot of my thoughts to myself, especially negative ones, which has caused my colleagues to think I don't struggle as much as they do when I do. Keen—I'm sharp as a tack. Individualistic—I don't conform simply to conform. I am myself. Take me or leave me. Novel—I'm far from ordinary."

"Um," mused Ray. *I want to say just the right words.* "You're Likeable—I like you."

"I like you, too."

"Let me finish, Miss Loquacious."

Larkin giggled.

He went on. "You're Angelic—there's an ethereal aura about you. You're Refined—you've been purified by fire and emerged clear and delicate and cultured. Dr. Fairchild would agree. She told us about all you've endured. You're Kind—a simple word, but as uncomplicated as you are. You're Indulgent—ready to forgive and forget, most of the time. I see how you've already forgiven Raif." He paused, not certain he should say exactly what was on his mind, but he couldn't help himself. "I'm waiting to hear what you have to say about Dupree Parks."

She started to speak, but he wagged his head and shook his finger at the same time. "I'm not finished. I still have your N." He stared at her a moment. His voice took on dreaminess. "Last, you are Narcotic—spending time with you could become very addictive."

"Take me off that pedestal right now, Ray," she asserted. "I'm merely a sinner saved by grace. Anything good does not come from me, but from Above."

"Like I said, angelic. How could you want to spend time with a rogue and rake like me?"

"Rogue! Rake! Right! When was the last time you were a rogue or a rake?"

"Do you really want an answer to that?"

"Yes."

"I've never told anybody but my priest this. Why am I telling you?" He rubbed his head as if one of his migraines might be coming on. "I have no idea," he answered himself. "But it was the night I hired a call girl after my fiancée decided she couldn't handle being a cop's wife."

"Why did she decide that?"

He sat back with a curious look on his face, mouth slightly ajar. "Aren't you appalled I hired a hooker? I'm a cop. I broke the law."

"No." She shook her head. "It's understandable. Like you said, you're fallible. You made a mistake. Now, why did your fiancée leave you?"

"I got shot on a domestic disturbance response before I became a detective."

"Ah. I've heard that's one of the most dangerous calls a policeman can respond to."

"Yep. You never know just how volatile the situation might be."

"She really hurt you, didn't she?"

"If she had just decided she couldn't marry me, I could've dealt with that, but she went straight to the arms of the man I thought was my best friend. He was a lawyer—much safer and more money." He rubbed his stubble. "When his philandering broke her heart, she wanted to come back. Sorry, babe. No can do. I realized then I'll probably grow old alone. It'd take a very strong, special woman to be my wife, a cop's wife. It's who I am."

"And after all this time, you're still angry. You need to let it go."

158

Ray looked at Larkin in disbelief. *How can this woman see through me like that?* "I suppose you think I should go to confession."

"Would it help?"

"No. I actually went after the night with the prostitute." He displayed the defiant look of a naughty little boy who should feel sorry for something he had done, but didn't. "I was told to say ten 'Hail Mary's' and ten 'Our Father's.' They were empty words. I haven't been back. That was four years ago. My mom worries I'll go to Hell."

"Perhaps if you confessed your feelings and sin to the Real Father, it would help."

"The Real Father? Directly to God?" He sighed impatiently. "Just tell God how I feel? Sin? Ask him to forgive me?"

"Yes, face to face before the Throne."

Words coated with bitterness, he said, "Are you preaching to me now?"

"Not my intent." She sat back with her hands raised in surrender.

"Honestly, I'm not sure there's anyone listening." Ray looked contemplative. *Is this what Raif meant? Will this woman's words change my life?* "I'll have to think about that. Right now, I need to talk to Chris for a minute. Excuse me."

Ray stepped out the door and called Chris. They talked several minutes, not about the case, but about what Larkin had said.

"Trust what she says, Ray," assured Chris. "Try it. I did, and I'm changed from the inside."

She got to both of them? "That's what Raif said."

"My dad always said that confirmation comes in threes. So, try it."

"I don't guess a prayer can hurt. 'Bye."

Before he returned to Larkin, Ray paused at the door. "Okay, God. I've had my doubts about you even being up there. I've been very angry and bitter for a long time. I've

159

tried to make it go away by myself. I'm sorry. Forgive me. Please, help me to let it go. Help me to find a better way. Whew! Amen."

When Ray came back in, Larkin had washed the dishes they used. She asked candidly, "Just how close are you and Chris?"

The detective chortled. "Are you asking if I'm in love with Chris? The answer is no. She's probably the best friend I've ever had. I love her to death, but I am *not* in love with her. We're too much alike. One of us, or maybe both, would end up dead."

"That's what *she* said. I just wanted to make sure you weren't setting yourself up to get hurt again."

"I can take care of myself, Larkin, but thank you." His tone abruptly ended the conversation.

"If you insist." Larkin let the matter drop. *The time hasn't yet come,* she told herself.

After three days of chess, gin rummy, and *Scrabble* with Larkin, and losing every time, Ray announced, "I have to go to the health department to make contact with Latrice. I need to see her at least once before Halloween. A tail was placed on her, and I've kept in touch with Chris."

Larkin looked terrified, her eyes wide and misty.

"I promise I can pull this off. Raif and Chris will be around the corner and will be listening and giving me advice," he said confidently. "I do need your help though." He opened a small case, which contained the tiniest microphone and recorder Larkin had ever seen. He produced a roll of medical tape and took off his shirt.

Her eyes were drawn to his finely chiseled and defined physique, innocence momentarily overwhelmed by the involuntary reaction of her own body. Face flushed, heart racing, she was sure she betrayed herself when she spoke.

"What do you need me to do?"

He handed her the tape as he connected the microphone cord to the recorder. Placing the recorder in the small of his back just inside the waist band of the grungy jeans Raif had worn at the last visit to Latrice, the detective said, "Tape the recorder to my back."

Larkin's eyes widened when she observed Ray's tattoo. *A Celtic guardian, in the same place as mine. A sign?* That fact alone made her hands shake as she taped the recorder down securely. "How's that?" she asked, unsure of what was racing through her mind. *For the first time in my life I've found a man to whom I could give myself and possibly break a vow I made with you, Lord.* The fleeting thoughts scared her. *But here is all I've dreamed about—the dark hair and the blue eyes have a face and a name and a matching tattoo. Is this what God's planned all along?*

He felt the recorder. "Nice work." Ray ran the cord along his rib cage. With his thumb, indicating where, he said, "Put a piece here."

She taped the cord, and he positioned the microphone between his pectoral muscles against his breastbone, being careful to place it just to the side of the small patch of ebony hair on his chest.

"And here," the detective instructed.

Before she taped the microphone, Larkin gently touched a scar in Ray's left shoulder.

"That's where I got shot," he explained without her ever asking. "It wasn't life threatening, but it hurt."

She taped the microphone as asked, terrified this man would be able to read her thoughts, lustful thoughts as never experienced before. Ray said, "Thanks." He then put on the same filthy hoodie Raif had worn. "How do I look?"

Her nose crinkled. "As revolting as you smell." Impure thoughts vanished.

"Thank you again. I'll be back very soon." Ray reached into his bag again and handed Larkin a gun. "This is my backup .38. If anyone besides Chris, Raif or me comes

161

through that door, shoot 'em. All you have to do is point and pull the trigger."

A new worry struck. *Might I have to kill someone?* Her face drained of blood.

"Don't worry. It's just a precaution. We're watching Latrice. Let's hope you don't have to pull the trigger." He smiled. "But be sure you *don't* when I come back in."

Larkin tremulously asked, "Ray, have you ever had to kill someone?"

He became pensive for a moment before he answered. "Yes, and it haunted me for a long time. I hope I never have to do it again, but I know I can if it comes to protecting an innocent victim or myself. Let's hope you won't have to pull that trigger." He kissed her on the forehead and left.

Larkin prayed.

Latrice came out of the health department right at five. She saw Ray in the gathering dusk. "What do you want?" she snarled through clenched teeth.

Raif's voice buzzed in his ear. "Act confused and a little incoherent."

"Lar...Larkin needs food," Ray stammered. "The three hundred dollars is gone." He remembered the story his brother had told him about giving the money to a homeless man.

"Lord! How I look forward to Halloween!" Latrice muttered.

"Talk about the voices," Raif instructed.

"Me too," Ray whispered. "The voices will stop on Halloween, right?"

"Trust me, Ray. After Halloween, you will never hear voices again, just like all the other useless pieces of societal refuse." She slapped a hundred dollars into his hand. "I'll be there at ten. Have her washed and ready to get dressed.

And do *not* come here again. You have been a thorn in my flesh just as I was warned from day one. Momma could be right about you, but I don't have time to change plans now. I swear if this can't hold you two days, I'll take over and finish without you. I cannot wait to be rid of you." She stalked off.

What a piece of work, Ray thought. It took every ounce of control not to strangle Latrice on the spot. *But I have some very incriminating words on tape.* He stopped by the car where Raif and Chris were and handed the money to his partner. "I'm tempted to tell you to give this to the nearest homeless shelter, but bag and tag, partner."

Chris opened an evidence bag and Ray slipped in the money.

Ray returned to the wine cellar with a smug expression on his face. "Listen while I bathe," Ray said as he gently squeezed the frightened woman's hand and exchanged the recorder for the gun. She had held it ready from the moment he had left.

A curtain had been rigged around the tub. Ray came out wearing fresh clothes, clean jeans and a snug-fitting Kelly green pullover sweater, which showed every ripple in his chest and abdomen; but he would not shave until the ordeal was over. As Ray held the repulsive clothes away from him, Larkin's eyes became like saucers, and her heart skipped a beat. Ray grimaced and said, "We're gonna start a bonfire with these in a week."

Larkin smiled and held up the recorder. "Nice work, Detective Reynolds. Raif said the same thing about those clothes."

Ray laughed and bowed flamboyantly. "You may begin my official fan club."

♣♣♣

Ray made arrangements with Chris about how to set up in the sanctuary. He knew the FBI agent would attend to the details.

The day before the appointed date arrived. Ray and Larkin made a pilgrimage to the sanctuary where they met Raif, Chris, Patrick Swift, and Baker.

Ray pointed at the other FBI agent and his former partner with raised eyebrows in question. "They know the whole story," Chris said. "Patrick figured it out at the press conference, and Brian noticed Raif didn't have a scar on his cheek. The man has known you a long time. I'll tell everyone else tonight anyway."

Raif added, "And Chief Gerard suspects.

Ray groaned. "Of course he does."

Chris showed them the hidden voice activated surveillance equipment and the places where the other officers would be hiding. "These little dark cubbies are nifty," stated Patrick.

Ray was pleased with the setup, and all parties returned to their places to wait.

For the first time, Larkin showed she was not a pillar of stone. As bedtime approached Ray noticed she was crying. *This is my angel. How could I have put her in this much danger?*

"Hey, what's this?" he asked as he took her by the shoulders. "You know I'm gonna protect you."

"I know, but I'm still scared. So much could go wrong."

"Where's that faith of yours?"

"Oh, Ray." She put both her hands on top of his. "God doesn't always keep bad things from happening. Sometimes it's His test for us."

"Not this time." He pulled her into his arms. "We've already been through the test. Now, it's time for justice."

She looked up at him. Before he realized what he was doing, Ray whispered, "My angel," and kissed Larkin deeply and passionately. She responded without hesitation, her hands moving up his back.

Coming to himself, he gently pushed back from her and said, "*Mo chagren.* I shouldn't've done that. It was totally inappropriate."

"I disagree," she countered. "It was totally perfect. Do it again."

Ray kissed Larkin again, and held her in his arms all night.

22
Samhain

Morning arrived all too soon. Ray made breakfast, but neither he nor Larkin had much appetite. They set about making the place as desolate as it had been when Larkin had arrived. With the small amenities Raif had added gone, the room was barren. In the light from the three lit candles, the slate-colored baked dirt walls glistened with moisture from both the humidity and being below sea level. Cobwebs draped the rough wooden beams above them. The ceiling hung low; Ray could touch it with his fingertips if he stood on his toes. The original blankets on the bed were devoid of color and threadbare. Their feet left prints in the hard dirt floor. Ray shuffled around to hide the fact there had been more than two sets of prints and got Larkin to walk back and forth to the restroom.

Ray looked around and in disgust blurted, "God! How desperate Raif must've been to think bringing you here could be anything but utter evil!"

"Don't blame him." Larkin defended the man who had become her friend.

"Oh, I don't," he assured her. "Raif's my brother. He has a problem and was manipulated in a weakened state." His jaw clenched. She could almost hear the grinding of his teeth. "That psychotic wench is gonna pay for Raif, for you, and for twenty-four dead people."

"Ray, channel the anger."

"This isn't anger, Angel. This is righteous indignation."

"So? Now you get to dispense the wrath of God?"

"Absolutely," he responded with a laugh. "Seriously, I'm ready for this day to be over. I'm ready for Latrice to be behind bars. I wanna take a sixty-minute shower, get a haircut, shave, and sleep in my own bed."

"You'll be all alone."

Ray grinned mischievously. "I have Cyclops. I'll hold him for ransom so that you have to come and get him."

"You have my cat? You didn't tell me that before." Larkin remembered her dream of Cyclops with the blue eyes. *Here, again, is a sign Ray is the man in my dreams— the man of my dreams.* "Chris just said he was being cared for. I guess I assumed Dr. Fairchild took him."

"He put a paw down and wouldn't take no for an answer. He even insisted on riding along to lockup while I questioned Dupree."

She laughed at the thought, then said, "About Dupree."

"Just what I've been waiting for. Don't tell me. Let me guess." He raised his index finger. "Here goes your indulgence. You wanna give him another chance."

"Yes, I do."

"We'll talk about that when all this is over."

"Ray, I'm very stubborn. It would be the perfect word for the S in Sloan." Her voice firm and even, she shook her auburn head for emphasis. "Don't *even* try to tell me what I should or should *not* do."

"Whoa! Trick or treat. Snap on me." Thumb and middle finger added sound effects.

The fiery redhead couldn't help but laugh. "Well, I really do want to return to my students. I think Dupree was as duped as Raif."

"All right. I see your point." He nodded his head reluctantly. "Maybe the kid deserves a break." He held his hand up in a blocking motion. "But"—the word was edged with objection— "He also needs major counseling."

"I won't disagree with that."

"Whew!" Ray wiped his brow. "Middle ground. But now, I want to check out 'hallowed ground' again." He used his fingers to make quote marks around hallowed ground. "Let's get this over with."

He held Larkin's hand as they navigated the dark stairwells. Just outside the sanctuary, Ray put his finger to his lips as they heard humming within the auditorium. Inch by inch he cracked the door, hoping it would not squeak. His blood froze when he saw Latrice arranging candles, a chalice, and a wicked, curved dagger on the altar. With great caution, he closed the door and motioned Larkin down the stairs. Back in the uncertain safety of the wine cellar, Ray said with a heavy sigh, "That's not a trick I expected. She said ten."

"It's lunch time. Maybe she came over on her lunch break," Larkin rationalized.

"Maybe," he agreed in an attempt to comfort her. "Come here."

Frightened, Larkin slid into his embrace. He kissed the top of her head and said, "We have to prepare just in case."

Ray retrieved handcuffs from a gray backpack. Nodding understanding, she sat on the bed. He cuffed her wrist to the long chain attached to the headboard, hastily changed into the grimy clothes from before, and stuffed his under the bed. He strapped his gun to his back beneath the baggy sweat shirt and his spare to his ankle, finally calling Chris to get over there.

"Don't fret." He took Larkin's free hand. "Maybe you're right. And if she comes down here, I'll play dumb and say I thought she meant ten at night. I'm sure she meant night. I can't imagine she would attempt anything so heinous and gruesome in broad daylight." He kissed her fingertips. "Or, Angel, we can call this off right now. I'll wait alone here for her to come."

"No. We have to do this." She smiled. "God told me I'd be the one to stop this. I'm not schizophrenic," she added to his questioning look.

"Okay. We stick to the plan."

Ray's phone vibrated. "Yeah?" he answered.

It was Chris. "I'm outside. Everybody else is on their way. I had to bring Raif. He's as stubborn as you." She cut Ray's twin a look. He stared back and bared his teeth in a mock snarl. "But I guess for those still in the dark, he had to pretend to be you a little longer. You're a bad influence rubbing off on him."

"It'll be fine," assured Ray. "Stay alert. If I call you before nightfall, don't even answer. Just get in here."

"Gotcha!"

For what seemed an eternity, Ray paced until Larkin said, "You've made a believer out of me."

"Huh?"

"Well, you do appear a little insane right now. What time is it?"

Ray looked at his phone because he had stashed his watch in the pocket of his jeans. "Half past three."

"You've been pacing without a word for almost three hours. I don't think she's coming down here right now." She jerked her head upward. "Go check."

"How could Chris *and* the stakeout *and* the tail by the FBI have missed her?"

"I don't know. Maybe there's a secret passage. It would explain how she could get to the cemetery undetected."

"Now that's scary," Ray said, arching his brow. "Shit. You think?"

Larkin pointed. "Check."

Ray sneaked back to the sanctuary. He eased the door open. No one was there.

At seven, Ray's phone vibrated. "We're setting up," Chris said.

"Thanks," he replied and closed his phone.

169

He turned to Larkin. "Come on, Angel. Let's get as ready as we can."

Larkin bathed and allowed herself to be re-shackled. They settled in to wait. She talked for a while about her annual haunted house. "How disappointed the kids will be."

Ray's dimples etched his face. "You like Halloween?"

"It's my favorite holiday. It fuels the imagination. I hope the substitute Dr. Fairchild secured for my classes followed my lesson plans. Yesterday and today the students should be reading their original horror stories and sharing treats." She sighed. "I would be doing a haunted house tonight. I usually have at least fifty kids show up." She asked, "Ray, do you know why we have the Halloween traditions we have?"

"No, why?" *If teaching me keeps her calm, I'd lie even if I knew every detail—which I don't. This could be interesting.* "Tell me," he encouraged.

"Well, it's called Samhain."

"Saw what?"

She laughed lightly. "Saw-wen. I promise it looks nothing like it sounds."

"Okay. Go on."

"It's the celebration of the Celtic New Year. Long ago before Christianity came to Ireland and Scotland, the Druids were the religious leaders—they understood the balance of Nature and conducted religious rites. They were healers, judges, teachers." She grinned. "Like me."

"So, it's a religious holiday of sorts?"

"Yes. The Celts believed this is the day when the barrier between the spirit world and Earth is at its thinnest."

"Yeah, Journey mentioned that for Wiccan beliefs."

Larkin nodded. "The people believed that on Samhain the spirits of those that had died the year before came back to look for a new body to inhabit. So, in an attempt to scare away the spirits, they would disguise themselves and carve gourds with faces with a candle inside, and bonfires were built. That's why we wear costumes and have jack-olanterns today." She smiled. "I have many happy memories of Halloween.

"Many Christians deplore the holiday and consider it satanic," she went on. "Ironically, October 31st, is the day the Protestant Reformation began. On that day in 1517, Martin Luther nailed his ninety-five theses on the church door in Wittenberg, Germany. Many Reformed denominations celebrate Reformation Day in place of Halloween."

She tilted her head to the side. "For Catholics isn't 'All Hallows' Eve' the day before All Saints' Day?" she asked.

"Yeah, it is, but I'm not a very good Catholic these days. How do you know all this stuff?"

"I *read*, Ray," she said with a little exasperation in her voice.

He sat beside her and put his arm around her. "It's fascinating. Tell me more."

Before they could continue their conversation, the chamber door rattled. The detective jumped to his feet and checked his phone for the time before stashing it in the pocket of the grungy old clothes. He nodded toward Larkin and mouthed, "On the dot."

Promptly at ten o'clock, Latrice, wearing a long, black, hooded robe, entered the dungeon. Larkin *did* know the woman, and her insides quivered. "You!" Larkin said with a start. "I know you! You worked in Dr. Sullivan's office."

God, I told her things about myself. I thought she was a nurse.

171

23
Looking Death in the Eye

Wearing a long inky robe, the figure that stood before Ray and Larkin looked like a ghost from the Spanish Inquisition. The very comparison terrified Larkin. She shuddered, her face blanched, her eyes stretched wide.

Latrice, in a smooth, even voice, said, "What's wrong, my little lamb? Are you afraid? I promise tonight you'll help bring the world to where it should be. You *must* feel honored to have been chosen."

"Chosen for what?" squeaked Larkin.

"Ah, relax, my dear. I have something for you that'll relieve all your concerns. Now, you must get dressed."

From a hanging travel bag, Latrice removed a medieval patterned wedding dress. Brocade flowers outlined the rounded neckline and the deep V waist. Long flowing tippets draped delicately over tight-fitting sleeves beneath.

"I'm not getting married," said Larkin defiantly.

Latrice scowled. "No, no, you're not, dear," she agreed. "Just put it on. Unlock her wrist, Ray. If you choose to be uncooperative, I can have Ray dress you. Would you like him to see you naked, dear?" Latrice said condescendingly.

Ray unlocked the cuff and gently, discreetly rubbed Larkin's wrist in assurance. *If you only knew what I would like from Ray*, she thought. Her jaw clenched.

Larkin slipped behind the curtain and put on the dress. It was an exquisite article of clothing, made of the finest linen and silk. If she were donning it for another reason, she would have been ecstatic. The dress would have been exactly what she would have chosen for her wedding.

Larkin stepped out, Ray drew a sharp breath, and Latrice cooed, "Oh, my! You are perfect. Come now." She

172

motioned with her fingers. "I have something for you." She thumped a syringe.

Larkin backed away. "I think not!"

"Come now. Everything's fine. This is just a little artificial relaxation."

"You are *not* sticking me with that needle. I have been locked up and chained up, but I refuse to be doped up."

Latrice's demeanor changed abruptly as she commanded, "Ray, hold her."

"No. I won't hurt her."

"Hold her. Now!" Latrice snapped. Ray stood still.

Latrice grabbed Larkin's wrist, but Larkin squirmed away. It took several minutes for the former Marine to subdue the smaller woman. During the struggle, Larkin saw Ray's hand at his back, but she managed to shake her head.

Shit! Shit! Shit! raced through Ray's mind. *God, I'm really praying. Please don't let that kill Larkin. This is my fault. I'm an idiot. Please help me keep her safe.*

With a sharp movement, Latrice twisted Larkin's arm, pinning her against her body, forcing the other arm straight. With her free hand, the nurse injected something directly into Larkin's median cubital vein located in the crook of her elbow on the straightened arm. It took over a minute to inject the liquid. The solution was not enough to render her unconsciousness; but becoming like a rag doll, Larkin slumped onto the bed.

That done, Latrice glared at Ray. "You useless, crazy bastard! Bring her with us and don't argue."

He lifted Larkin gently in his arms. "Be brave," he whispered. "I'll take care of you."

"I know, but be careful," Larkin whimpered, her words slurring. "She'sh shtark raving mad." Unable to fight for herself, her head drooped onto Ray's shoulder.

Well, that explains why the victims didn't struggle, he thought. *It has to be some form of tranquilizer. With all the blood drained, a tox screen was near impossible on the victims.*

173

The sight that met Ray's eyes as the odd trio entered the sanctuary was bizarre beyond anything he could have imagined. A panel slid open behind the platform where the priest would have conducted mass—*a secret passage as Larkin thought.* Lighted black candles formed a pentagram around the altar. An ebony chalice and an onyx-handled dagger with a sharp curved blade adorned the holy water basin. A baphomet was suspended over the altar. But the most appalling addition to the scene was twelve more robed women waiting with anticipation.

Larkin's heart sank. *They're waiting for me.* A small sob caught in her throat.

Ray was so shocked by the sight he could hardly have a coherent thought and could not find a way to comfort Larkin except to pull her closer to his heart. Scanning the robed women, he muttered, "Fuck. I know one of them."

"Place her on the altar, Ray, with her head toward the door," Latrice commanded. "Then, you wait downstairs until I call for you."

"I'll stay," Ray said. "You promised to make the voices stop. I have to stay." He kept his face averted from the women as best he could.

Latrice shot him a peeved look. Somehow, she realized an argument would be futile. *What kind of voice is this fool hearing?* Her mother's warning not to use him came back to her, but it was too late. "Very well, stand toward the back. Don't say a word."

He gingerly laid Larkin on the icy marble slab, keeping his head down, and shuffled toward the back. Ray was sure he heard a slight gasp from one of the women. His insides felt tied in knots. He stole a glance toward where Chris was supposed to be. *There you are, so well hidden I almost didn't see you.* A glimpse of his partner calmed his nerves.

174

Lying like a sacrificial lamb upon the altar, Larkin tried to lift her arms, but they felt like lead. A glance up toward the suspended goat's head, made her stomach churn. She rolled her head to see Ray. He stood with a hand behind his back. Knowing that hand was on his gun, flooded her with relief.

As midnight approached, the women made a semi-circle on one side of the altar while Latrice stood with her back to Ray. The ceremony began with Latrice sipping something from the ebony goblet and passing it to the left. Each woman drank until the cup got back to Latrice. The women began a low, rhythmic chant, "Adveho, meus dominus, adveho." ("Come, my lord, come.") From the folds of her robe, Latrice retrieved a handful of dried flower petals and sprinkled them over Larkin's torso at the same time saying something Ray recognized as Latin.

Once Latrice began to speak, the temperature plummeted. Ray saw his breath. He cut his eyes toward Chris and saw she had pulled her black spandex sweater over her mouth and nose. *She feels the chill too.*

A rumble beneath his feet brought Ray's eyes to the floor and back up toward the ritual being performed. The air around the women visibly moved. Ray jerked his head upward at a flapping sound, as of large wings thumping.

Larkin's eyes darted about as she heard the same sounds and felt the vibrations through the stone. Even though she was helpless, she understood much of what Latrice said as she recalled her high school Latin. *Expio quod restituo ordo, vitualamen para virgo. Cruor of tredecim mos pario Gremory protelo quod debello chaos.* ("To purify and restore order, the sacrifice of a virgin. The blood of the thirteenth will bring forth Gremory to lead and vanquish chaos.")

175

Larkin's mind raced. *Gremory? Is that an actual demon? Lucifer can't be the only fallen angel with a name. Angels have names. Do these nuts think sacrificing a virgin will summon a demon? They're calling for one to come. I feel spirits here, moving.*

The women's chant reached a crescendo. Latrice raised the dagger above her head as she spoke, louder and louder, repeating the phrase six times. At that moment, Ray heard only one word, Larkin's almost inaudible, "Ray?"

Ray pulled his nine millimeter. "Drop the dagger and turn around, you psychotic bitch," he demanded. Silence fell. The temperature returned to normal.

"You idiot!" Latrice snarled through gritted teeth. "You interrupted the ritual! He was almost here!"

The other women began to murmur and move a bit. One whimpered, "Latrice, what's happening?"

Another voiced concern. "You said this was legal."

A young girl began to cry. "I'm scared."

The woman Ray recognized mumbled, "Damn it! Reynolds!"

Ray repeated, "Drop the dagger and turn around. The rest of you don't move a muscle. Mikayla, shut the fuck up. Latrice, I said, 'Drop it!' *Or,* I can shoot you where you stand."

Latrice slowly lowered the dagger. She turned around. Ray had advanced to just out of her reach. "Who are you?" she said in utter bewilderment. "You're not Ray."

"That's not quite true," said another voice as Raif stepped from the shadows along with Chris, Baker, and the three FBI agents, all with their weapons drawn.

"What the?" was all Latrice managed.

"Feel a little confused?" asked Raif sarcastically. "So did I, until a Providential God used you of all people to

176

bring Larkin into my life. Let me introduce myself. Raiford Gautier, architect, and a man with a condition which requires medication that you, a health professional, deliberately kept from me in an attempt to control me. You failed. The voices of reason and righteousness are much stronger than your insane wickedness." He looked around him. "I have no clue what I just witnessed, but it was pure evil."

Latrice looked from one twin to the other.

"Who's the ragamuffin?" Raif jerked his head toward his brother. "Another blessing that came out of this. I really think you should officially meet him though you've already dealt with him. No, that was not I at *our* last meeting. This, Latrice, is my twin brother, *Raiford*—yes—*Raiford*—*Raiford* Reynolds—Detective *Raiford* Reynolds." His voice increased in intensity with each repetition of their name, but he never shouted. Contrarily, the intensity was accentuated by a lowering of volume.

"And now, I think you're under arrest." Raif looked her squarely in the eye. "I'm sure you'll be charged with twenty-four counts of murder, thirteen counts of kidnapping, thirteen counts of conspiracy to kidnap, and what? One count of reckless endangerment? God only knows what else. Now, Ray, may I, *please*, say it?"

"You know it, Raif."

"Cuff all the..." He paused to find the right word. "*Ladies*," he finished with reluctance and disdain. "And be sure to read them their rights. We don't want them to slip by on a technicality. Oh, Latrice, it *is* Halloween, but your costume is lacking. You have the black robe and a miniature sickle, but where's the skeleton mask?"

She stared daggers at Raif as Lawrence Dantzler roughly placed handcuffs on her wrists.

"Yes, Latrice, look at me." Raif took a step closer to the woman who would have killed him. "Look me in the eye so I can proudly say, 'I looked death in the eye. And *I* won.'"

24
Homecoming

While Latrice was unceremoniously shoved into the back of a squad car and the other twelve women were herded into two police vans, Ray helped Larkin stand and held onto her protectively. "Can you stand? Do I need to carry you? An ambulance is on the way to take you to the hospital.'

"I don't want to go to the hoshpital," she argued in a weak voice. "I jusht want to go home."

"And home you'll go as soon as a doctor pronounces you fit."

"I'm fine. You and Raif have taken very good care of me. I've probably gained ten poundsh from all the food and no exerchishe. Pleashe, take me home."

"Larkin, that nut job injected you with something. Listen to yourself. You're slurring your words. Let's get you checked out. Then, I will personally take you home. Humor me. After all, I'm the reason you let yourself get put in this situation."

Brian Baker jerked Mikayla Pickett past his former partner to get her into the police van. The woman balked beside the twins. "Two of you?" She laughed. "Latrice thought not to use Geminis, but you're actual twins. Who knew?"

Ray glared at the woman who worked for the mayor. "Baker, get her out of my sight."

"Gladly."

Ray signaled to Patrick Swift to check out the open panel. The FBI agent took the two patrolmen who had been watching the monastery with him through the opening.

Ray turned to Chris, "Will you take care of Raif? Get him home, and I'll be by later."

"Not a problem."

Ray looked at his brother. "*Fooyay!* What were you thinking? You put yourself in a dangerous position. It's bad enough you were even here. Don't ever do something like that again."

"Sorry, bro, but I had to unload on that crazy bat, or I would've exploded."

"Well, I hope it was cathartic. I have to say it felt good hearing you put her in her place. Now, go home." He jerked his head toward the exit. "I'll come by later."

"By the time you get there, it'll be time for breakfast," Raif joked. "Bring something delectable."

"You know it."

With a gentle push on his shoulder and a stern look, Chris prodded Raif out the door to her waiting car, and Ray insisted Larkin go to the hospital.

Raif unlocked the door to his townhouse about one thirty in the morning. He stopped in the middle of the living room and breathed deeply. "God! It feels good to be home."

Chris said nothing for a moment. She just looked around. "It's very...um...manly. Neat, but manly," she said.

"Are you saying it needs a woman's touch?"

"It's just so plain, so sparse."

"Leave it to a woman to want to clutter up with little doodads." He laughed.

"Knickknacks make it homier."

"I suppose my space is rather functional," he admitted. "And needs a good cleaning. I barely had time to wash the dishes when I came by. This dust has to go."

"You apparently got rid of the rotted meat in the fridge."

"You went in my refrigerator?"

She nodded.

He walked around his home as Chris followed. "Where's my computer?" he asked.

"We took it. I'll get it back to you tomorrow. I promise."

"Please do. I'll function better with all my tools."

She inclined her head toward the drafting table. "I saw some of your work. Who are you designing that fabulous house for?"

"The love of my life," Raif replied.

"And who is that?"

"I don't know, but that house will be my wedding gift to my wife. I have forty acres to build on about twenty miles out into the boonies toward the old train trestle."

"Wow! That'll be one lucky lady. She'll get the house *and* you."

With a slight frown he said, "That last part might make the house just a drawing."

"Na. You still have to see a neurologist. Remember?"

Raif nodded. "You promised to hold my hand."

"Indeed, I did."

He yawned behind his hand. "Well, Chris, would it be possible to consider all this after a good night's sleep in my *own* bed?"

"Yes, of course. I'll leave you for my wonderful hotel."

"You can stay."

"Excuse me?"

Unaffected, Raif explained, "I have a lot of things in common with my brother. The sofa is a sleeper. Stay and eat breakfast with Ray and me. I've kind of gotten used to having you around. Don't cut the apron strings just yet."

"All right," agreed Chris. "Let's get some rest. Maybe we'll actually sleep tonight."

As Raif and Chris made up the sleeper, he thought, *I'd rather have you beside me, but I'm scared of offending you. You think I have walls? You are a goddess if only you'd lower yours. No—you remain the consummate professional, even in your attire.* He sighed, but said not a word. Raif slept alone and dreamed about Chris beside him.

Meanwhile in the emergency room at the hospital, the attending physician drew Larkin's blood and checked her from head to foot while Ray waited patiently. Finally, she was pronounced quite fit despite a massive, unwanted dose of valium. The doctor scowled though. "You say she pushed this directly into your vein?"

Larkin nodded.

"You're one lucky lady. If she had gone too fast, your heart would have stopped. The best thing you can do is go home and sleep it off."

She looked at Ray with an impish, sideways grin. "May I *pleashe* go home now?"

"After a quick stop at my place."

She rolled her eyes. "There's something there I think you might want," he said

"Shyclopsh!" She brightened as she remembered Ray had her cat.

"I'm gonna miss him," admitted Ray. "But now he has become attached to my brother. That poor little guy won't know what to do."

"He'sh a trooper," she bragged. "He'll know eshxactly what to do. He'll come to hish momma. Uncle Ray can vishit."

They had very little conversation in the car. Larkin leaned her head against the window and dozed. Once they got to Ray's apartment, the two were greeted with enthusiastic meowing, and just as Larkin had predicted, Cyclops leapt straight into her arms.

"Let's go home," she said rubbing her cheek against his head. "I want to sleep in my own bed." She yawned drowsily and held Cyclops closer.

181

"Hey, I understood what you said there." Ray grabbed the cat's food, and the trip continued to Larkin's house.

Larkin stood on her porch a minute in the pre-dawn. She took a deep breath of the crisp autumn air and listened to the tinkling of her wind chimes as the gentle fall breeze blew them. "That helps clear my head," she said. She inhaled the fragrance of the fall flowers. "Oh, it smells so clean and fresh. I thought I might never smell fresh air again."

Ray touched her shoulder after he unlocked her door. She stepped through. Inside her home, Larkin was suddenly overcome with tears as the tension of the last several weeks found release. Ray steered her to the sofa, put an arm around her, and offered comfort, letting her cry. "Now, now. It's over. You're home safe and sound."

Cyclops bumped his nose into Larkin's cheek. She wiped her eyes as she sniffled. "I feel so silly."

"Nonsense," snorted Ray. "You needed to let it all out. But now you're safe in this wonderful old house." He looked around. "You know, Raif could probably help with your restoration."

"That's a good idea." She nodded. "It's on the historical register, so I'm limited in what I can change. I want to stay as original as possible though. The place housed captured Union spies before they were hanged. One was extremely interesting. His name was Baxter Pryor. After two failed attempts to hang him, the people around here thought he had some kind of magical powers, and he was kept prisoner here until the war was over."

"Fascinating. Did he have magical powers?"

She shrugged. "After what we witnessed tonight, I don't know."

"Do you tell your students these things?"

"Sometimes. I'm sure they'll have a thousand questions on Monday."

"You're going back so soon?"

"Absolutely." Her voice was soft but determined. "I'm sure you'll be at your desk tomorrow."

"Yes, but I have loads of paper work to do to make sure that lunatic doesn't get off on some technicality. I really should get going. I need some sleep, too."

Her mouth dry, her throat tight, Larkin hesitantly asked, "Ray...do you think you could stay here tonight?"

"I think it would be better if I called Chris to come and stay with you."

"Why?" she said, suddenly affronted.

"It's just not ethical for me to be this close to you."

"Ethical?" Larkin said shrilly. "Is this because you *kissed* me?"

"I shouldn't have let that happen."

She pushed herself from Ray and glowered at him. "Do you regret it?"

"Larkin, please." He patted her arm. "You have to understand my position."

"Oh, I *do*!" She stood, walked to the door, and opened it. "You hide behind that stone wall of ethical conduct." Her legs wobbly, she grasped the doorknob to steady herself. "Out! Go home! See how much comfort and love your ethics can give you. Maybe you should hire a *hooker*."

"Larkin!" Ray said as he stopped in the doorway.

She shoved him out the door, slammed the heavy wood in his face, and turned the deadbolt hard enough to wrench her wrist. A loud, "Meow!" that sounded like scolding brought her attention to her feet.

She picked up Cyclops and cradled him in her arms. "Come on, buddy. I know I can count on you."

Larkin headed to her bed but sank onto the stairs, head spinning. Staring at the door, she chastised herself for ever being tempted by Ray's presence. She buried her face in Cyclops's fur and wept, emotions in complete disarray. In addition to captivity and valium, it was time for her cycle, and the added stress just made her feel worse. "What should I do?" she sobbed.

On the other side of the door, Ray's fingertips touched the wood lightly before he sighed, got in his car, and drove away.

25
The Accused

After only a couple hours sleep, Ray was awakened by his phone ringing. "Reynolds," he answered sluggishly.

"My office, thirty minutes." The mayor's voice made the detective bolt from his bed.

"Oh, on my way, sir." *Oh, shit. There goes my job.*

Ray walked into the mayor's office to find Chief Gerard waiting also. His stomach was in knots.

"Sit," said the mayor sternly.

Ray sat in the chair beside the chief of police and began, "Let me explain."

"Explain what, *Detective?*" the mayor demanded. "That you had my full knowledge and approval for an unorthodox undercover operation?" An age-spotted hand slid a folder across his desk. "Open it and sign, but if anyone ever finds out you did this bullshit without proper authorization, I'll bury you."

Ray read over the documents quickly. He looked from the chief to the mayor. The chief looked away and grunted, "I can't believe you didn't trust me enough to give me details. Why didn't you tell me? I would've objected, but you would've convinced me." The chief's eye twitched as he looked at his detective.

The head official, furrowed bushy gray eyebrows and turned his lips down beneath a neatly trimmed mustache. Ray signed without comment. The mayor reiterated, "That crazy bitch best go away forever, not to mention my assistant. Damn it, Ray! I'm covering *all* our asses and hoping for under-the-table justice. Now get out of here."

Mid-morning found Ray, clean-shaven and with a haircut, ringing his brother's doorbell. When he entered, he dropped a box of assorted Krispy Kreme doughnuts on the dining table and plopped himself into one of the chairs.

Raif cackled. "Leave it to the cop to think a box of doughnuts would make a scrumptious breakfast."

"Oh, shut up!" snapped Ray.

Raif and Chris looked at each other warily before Chris prodded, "Sounds like somebody woke up on the wrong side of Larkin's bed this morning."

Ray snarled in reply, "I'll have you know I didn't wake up on either side of Larkin's bed."

"Oh, for God's sake!" hissed Chris. "What did you do to offend her?"

"Nothing. I was a perfect gentleman," sulked the younger twin.

"Let me guess," continued Chris. "Honor and ethics. You idiot! You colossal fool!"

"Never mind!" griped Ray. He stood. "We have a lot of paperwork ahead of us to ensure Latrice goes away for a long time—and her coven." With a head shake and a snort he went on, "Who'd've thought there were practicing witches—not some Voodoo practitioners, not true Wiccans, but witches—in Eau Bouease trying to summon a demon no less. Let's go."

The agent sighed. "Ray, *witches* have nothing to do with demons or Satan. That's TV and movie hocus-pocus." Chris patted Raif's shoulder. "Enjoy the doughnuts while I go deal with Attila the Hun."

Raif sniggered and squeezed Chris's hand as they all walked toward the door. "Thanks for last night."

"Anytime. You have my number."

Opening the door to leave the townhouse, they were greeted by a shrill squeal. "Mr. Ray! Momma, there are two of them."

Raif chuckled and held out his arms. "Come give me a hug."

Sheena Johnson hugged Raif. Picking up the little girl, he felt her face. He asked, "Are you sick, honey? You're very hot."

Carol Johnson unlocked their door as she answered, "She has strep. We just came from the doctor."

"Well, I have some doughnuts in my house to share with you and I'll get you some ice cream later." Raif furrowed his brow. "What flavor do you want?"

"Double Dutch chocolate," the child answered. "Did you forget? Are you the right Ray?" She pointed at Ray. "His name is Ray, too."

"Yes." Raif hesitated. "Little Miss Sheena, this is my twin brother, and his name is *Ray*. I have decided to call myself *Raif*. Can you remember that?"

"You know I can." Her voice had a foot-stomp sound to it.

"Yes, I do." Raif let the child down. "You're just too smart."

Carol Johnson smiled. "It's good to have you home. It appears all the trouble is over." She looked toward Ray who nodded. "Terry is gonna like you. He'll be home from Iraq before Christmas, maybe by Thanksgiving. Thank you again for last Christmas."

"It was my pleasure. Maybe one day soon, I can do that for my own."

"You'll make a great father," affirmed Carol Johnson. "Well, let me get this little bit in bed. It was good to see you again, detectives."

Ray and Chris exchanged pleasantries. They headed for the police station after Ray told his brother he would call later and that he would have his car and computer delivered after midday. On the way to the cars, Ray's frown looked like a grimace. He asked, "What happened last night?"

"Get your mind out of the gutter. I merely stayed the night like you should've done." Chris gave him a crooked grin. "Not that I would have said, 'No.'" She slid behind the steering wheel. "Ray, Larkin didn't want you to sleep

187

with her last night. She just wanted you there. You should've stayed."

"Chris, I wasn't thinking about what she wanted. I was thinking about myself. That woman is more tempting than the fruit Eve gave to Adam, and she doesn't even mean to be. She just is. Besides, this case is open. It isn't ethical. I've already bent so many rules and been reprimanded before I could wake up this morning. I have to have *some* principles." He snorted. "I'll tell you all about it sometime."

"Even if those principles mean losing something you so desperately desire? Honestly, I wish Raif had asked. Damn ethics!" She drove off before Ray could speak.

Ray and Chris spent the next several hours completing paperwork. He leaned over her shoulder close to her ear, whispering. "Listen up. The mayor called me in early this morning. He had bogus documents saying our undercover operation was approved. Thought you should know."

"Told you that you might get fired."

"Yeah, well, I still have a job—though I probably shouldn't. I should've pulled Latrice in long before."

"Yeah, but then we wouldn't have the other twelve. Stop sweating it. You're secret's safe with me."

"Speaking of the devils…"

Then they began interviewing the women from the night before.

Although it was the weekend, Judge LeVigne slipped into his robe, determined to see an end to the horror that had been taking place. By three in the afternoon, the thirteen women had been arraigned and denied bail. The interrogations began in earnest. Over several days, the detectives and the FBI agents gathered information and questioned the women.

The twelve coven members ranged in age from fifteen to forty and came from many walks of life and backgrounds. Some were professionals while others were unemployed. All seemed to think their practices were protected by their Constitutional freedom of religion. The most disturbing information to the interrogators was these women did not see the deaths of twelve women as murder.

"Gotta be the strangest damned thing I've ever heard," Chris said, rubbing her head as if she had one of Ray's headaches. "For them, the deaths were sacrifices—their way of consecrating their temple and purifying America. That's a new one. It's not as if they were chopping off chicken heads."

All twelve confessed complete ignorance in the deaths of any men.

At the end of a long week, psychologists who evaluated the accused determined the women were experiencing the same thought patterns as many cult members. They handed their assessments to the taskforce.

The taskforce made up of Ray, Brian Baker, and the same FBI agents reviewed the files and discussed their findings. Chris plopped down the first file as she came in last to sit around a conference table. "Maureen Pope, forty, is a certified public accountant who's frustrated with the nation's economy. She felt pulled to Latrice to set the country on the right course. Do you believe this crock of crap, Ray? She's an accountant, for God's sake! Did she seriously believe pennies would fall from Heaven?"

"Or spring from Hell?" muttered Dantzler. "Maybe that's what the rumbling was."

Baker barely whispered, "That had to have been a train that forgot to blow its whistle."

Patrick asked, "How does that explain the drop in temp?"

"Why didn't it get hotter if something was coming from Hell?" argued Baker.

Journey interrupted, "I won't pretend to understand the weirdness, but all kinds can be lured into a cult. A lot has to do with their emotional well being, not IQ or social status. Latrice found a need or a fear and preyed upon it."

"For both the men and the women she recruited." Ray opened another file. "It seems Lilah Steen was in an abusive relationship and thought Latrice offered her an escape. She filed more than one report with the force, but she always dropped the charges." Ray rubbed his head.

Journey commented again, "Normal behavior for an abused person. So often, they die before anything is actually done."

"Listen to this." Dantzler read a summary. "Michelle Knowles is a burnt-out stripper looking for something other than a life in the gutter. She seems to think Latrice could provide security for her future. She said Latrice took care of all her bills. What is this witch—a sugar momma?" He opened another file. "Sydney LeRoc has been unemployed for over a year. Latrice promised her financial stability. She paid for an apartment for the woman. Where'd she get all this money?"

"Good question. It could not be from military retirement." Baker read a file. "Mikayla Pickett works for the city in the mayor's office. Latrice promised her advancement and success."

"Jeez Louise!" Ray exclaimed. "Thank God she didn't know about the investigation into Latrice's holdings. If she'd found out, this whole scheme would've backfired. When I saw her at the monastery, my heart almost stopped."

"Yeah, mine, too," agreed Baker. "She commented during her interrogation that she didn't think the youngest coven member would stay and she had been trying to recruit a friend who worked in the Hall of Records." He lifted an eyebrow toward Ray.

Raising a cup of coffee to his lips, Ray almost choked as he surmised which employee it had to have been. His palms began to sweat and his stomach churned as he realized how close his plan had come to disaster. "That crazy woman that Chris hates?"

"That's who my money would be on," affirmed Baker.

"Thank God you didn't let her research with you." Ray flipped open another file. "Sabrina Hatch is an educator at a local community college. She's teaching our kids, folks. She reports being intrigued by Latrice's approach to religion. I think the woman a cretin to be duped by Latrice. She has never been diagnosed with a mental condition. She obviously doesn't have the intellectual capacity of Larkin Sloan."

Dantzler winked at Chris; she rolled her eyes at him and mumbled, "Yeah, Raif has a problem the bitch exploited. But she got Larkin to talk to her in the doctor's office. She has some form of charisma."

Journey nodded and reiterated, "I've already said a person's mental capacity has no bearing on their need for safety or the need to feel loved. Hatch must've needed some sort of affirmation. She has admitted letting Latrice borrow her SUV and reporting it stolen as Latrice requested." He read from the interrogation he had conducted. "Valerie DuBose worked as an entertainer at a gentleman's club. Her sexual preference drew her to Latrice. They apparently had a little tryst going on. She even said Hatch participated with them. Love is a powerful motivator."

"Ah," Ray gloated. "Dr. Sullivan said he thought Latrice might have been gay."

Journey shrugged. "People will grasp at straws to feel safe and loved. It's in Maslow's hierarchy of needs. Cults in general prey on people's fear and need to be accepted."

Patrick Swift, said, "Raif's a nice man. He's intelligent, but he had a need that Latrice exploited. Once he got control of himself, he certainly fooled all of us." He sniggered. "Especially Lawrence. When he told *Ray* all about the time he dated Chris, I saw steam coming from

Raif's ears. Lawrence thought he was laying the bullshit on thick for *Ray*."

"Oh, shut up!" snapped Dantzler. "Raif was convincing. He fooled the press, too."

Patrick nodded. "That's the day I realized who he really was. He's nicer."

Chris laughed at the scowl on Ray's face. Patrick quickly got back to the discussion of importance. "Latrice manipulated all these people. Kelly Delacroix, a hostess at a local upscale restaurant was hoping for a better life. Here again, is the promise of stability, wealth, safety. Aisha Forbes worked with Kelly who apparently lured her into the fold. She figured her friend was just trying to help her."

Ray asked, "What about that passage? Anything useful there?"

Patrick replied, "It's like catacombs under there. We did find where steps led to a secluded parking area and all their cars, which have been impounded. One tunnel led to the cemetery, and one to the hearse bay in the mortuary."

"That explains a lot," said Ray. "Like why the stakeout missed Latrice placing bodies and going and coming."

Chris rustled through the pages of another interrogation. "Catina Dukes is a homeless recovering addict. Latrice made her believe she was an easy way off the streets. I can see how some of these women needed what Latrice offered. I have to wonder if the woman kept any of her promises."

"She actually did," said Journey. "At least some of the financial stuff, a safe place to live, those things. If she hadn't, some of them would've broken ranks. I found a house she rented where several of these women were living together. In some way, I think she was trying to create a family of a sort, maybe to meet her own need."

"Francesca Melton was a student in Sabrina Hatch's class," observed Baker. "Her professor enticed her. It makes me concerned for my children's minds. College is a time of searching for answers. This girl found the wrong answers."

Journey nodded. "Her mind was fertile for brainwashing."

Ray read the last file. "Alicia Steen, fifteen, is Lilah's daughter and came to the group via her mother. She's a child who is really messed up. I'm surprised and appalled at the same time that she wasn't one of Latrice's victims. Obviously, the little girl is *not* a virgin." Ray scowled. "I want her father investigated. She has two younger sisters. If he *is* the abusive son-of-a-bitch the mother claims, he might be hurting those children."

"I'm on it, Ray, right now." Baker, the only father among them, left the group.

Journey tapped the child's folder. "She's the only rational one in the group."

"Why do you say that?" asked Ray.

"When I talked to her, she said her mother made her go, and that Latrice gave them all some *potion* to drink."

"Potion?" asked Chris. "What the hell was in that goblet?"

Journey nodded. "I ordered a tox screen on all of them and an analysis of the concoction." He looked toward the door Baker had just used. "I'm glad you're checking out the father. The kid mentioned Latrice promised *to take care of* her father."

Most of the women seemed to be under an unbreakable spell cast by the wicked witch of the South—Latrice Descartes. They were completely loyal to Latrice and would go to jail or die before they betrayed her.

On the other hand, Ray was convinced Latrice was totally bonkers. Looking at the file in front of him, he read, "Latrice Descartes, forty-three, born in Germany. Her father was an army officer and was transferred a dozen times before Latrice left home and joined the military herself. She's one of a few highly trained female Marines in covert operations. She was involved in a number of them, of which even now, the government won't reveal details."

He looked up. Dantzler shrugged. "I called the Pentagon. Can't get 'em to budge, but I'd bet she's still an operative, and that's where her money comes from."

"Doubt it," argued Patrick Swift. "CIA, maybe, but I checked for a money trail and found none."

Ray dipped his head to the side. "She's a registered nurse, and tests show her IQ to be in the genius level, well over one-fifty. She was brought up in a very strict Catholic home with a father who appears tyrannical from documented reports. Got a number here. Let's see what Daddy has to say. Chris, try to find Mom again."

Ray contacted Latrice's father in Guam, working as a contractor on the Navy facility. He gave the detective some background information. "Her mother was a Baltic gypsy who secretly practiced black magic and introduced Latrice to her dark religion behind my back. All I know is that bitch cost me my security clearance years ago."

"At what age did Latrice get involved in the stuff?"

"Teens, and she became a hellion. I divorced Edyta. Last I heard she was in Germany. Latrice joined the military as soon as she turned eighteen. I hoped it would straighten her out."

"Reports say you were abusive, sir."

"Define abuse. Did I whoop her? You *bet*. Lesbian, bisexual—Hell bound." The man laughed and said, "She's getting her just desserts and I want nothing else to do with her." He hung up the phone without further ado.

Ray muttered, "Asshole."

Chris glanced up from her phone conversation trying to find Latrice's mother. "Edyta Descartes was deported not long after Latrice came to Louisiana and the State Department has no idea where she is now." She closed her phone. "But, I do have a theory—if Edyta was of the Roma—you know, Gypsies—finding that woman will be a waste of time."

Journey gave the detective a questioning look.

194

"Latrice's dad is an asshole," said Ray. "No wonder she turned out like she did; couple him with a woman who was into the occult. She didn't stand a chance."

Comparing notes, the taskforce members realized that no matter who questioned her, Latrice was belligerent and believed herself an emissary of God who had been ordained to purify America. Each officer, local and federal, tried to break her. They shared their findings.

Latrice had served in the first Gulf War, and prior to that, had a spotty service record that said virtually nothing.

"But she's dead certain the attacks of 9/11 were God's warning that America had to be purified through blood sacrifice," Journey said. "Covert operations," he mumbled. "Something smells about that. Mostly it's the timing."

"Explain, Steve," Ray said. "Timing?"

"Well, if she was involved in covert operations—let's assume it was the CIA pulling her strings—or was at least exploiting her madness. Anyway, the only time she would have been effective was 1984 to 1989, that is, before the fall of the Soviet Union." Journey nodded. "Plus, the only places she could have moved through without being obvious would be Europe, both East and West, the Soviet Union or the U.S. I see no indication of language skills. Not that they don't exist, but...probably that's part of the blacked-out sections of her service record." He sighed. "Anyway, for Latrice, dealing out death is natural, and of course, there's no remorse, not then or now. She felt *called* to find the appropriate sacrifices. Called by what deity we'll never know. But, because of her absolute conviction she's doing something holy and righteous, she will *always* refuse to admit that she had ever *murdered* anyone. In her mind, the deaths of both the women and men were a part of the cleansing process. Latrice mumbled on several occasions, 'Momma told me number thirteen was wrong. "Don't use a twin," Momma said. I thought she meant a damned Gemini.'"

Delving into her background showed she had been ritualistically sexually abused in her mother's coven and warped religious beliefs abounded in her past. She related many stories to Steve Journey. He said in their meeting, "The woman is a raving lunatic. First of all, she doesn't believe the things that happened to her were abuse. She relates them as worship rituals."

The state's psychiatrist, the defense's psychiatrist, and an independent, non-partisan psychiatrist concurred with all law enforcement officials: Latrice Descartes should be ruled insane and a serious danger to society. Nonetheless, the state needed more proof than the fact the woman was delusional to commit her to a facility for the criminally insane rather than take her to trial and seek the death penalty.

26
Proof

"Hey, Parks, Agent Milovich is back and your teacher came to see you with the FBI," grunted the guard outside Dupree's cell Monday afternoon after Halloween.

Dupree sprang from his bunk with great excitement. "You mean Miss Sloan is here? Is that who you mean?"

"I guess it's Miss Sloan. It's a little redheaded white lady."

She's safe! Dupree reached under his bunk and pulled out a folded piece of paper. "I'm ready. Take me to her."

The guard escorted Dupree to the same interrogation room where Ray and Chris had questioned him. As the door creaked open, Larkin Sloan looked up to see the boy who had put her in a struggle with life and death. This time she noted no belligerence in the young man's face, but a certain fear that anyone could read. Dupree walked in and gushed, "Miss Sloan, I'm sorry. I'm real sorry. I had no idea you was in such danger." He handed the folded, crumpled paper to Larkin. "I wrote what you asked for. I hope it's good enough."

Larkin unfolded the paper and read silently:

Miss Sloan wanted me to write about what I'm afraid of. I told her I wasn't afraid of nothing. That was a lie because I'm just plain scared all the time. I'm scared of being on the streets. I'm scared of ending up here in jail. I'm scared of dying before I turn twenty-five. I'm scared to see the tears in my momma's eyes. I'm scared of being nobody. I'm scared of never having my dreams come true. I'm scared of having my dreams dry up like a raisin in the sun.

197

But I don't want to be scared all the time. I want to be like Walter Lee and rise above my circumstances. I want to be somebody, not a thug. I want to make my momma proud. I want Miss Sloan to be found so I can tell her I'm real sorry. I want to tell her that I really am afraid, but I just can't put my finger on just what. I think I'm just plain scared. That's all. I'm just plain scared of being scared.

Larkin looked toward Chris who stood near the window then back at Dupree who had sat down across from her. "Dupree, do you mean what you said in this piece?"

"Yes, ma'am. And I'm real sorry. I didn't know that man was gonna hurt you."

"That man *didn't* hurt me. Someone was using him and hurting him. Detective Reynolds and Agent Milovich arrested the woman who was behind all of this. Dupree, what do you know about *A Raisin in the Sun?*"

"It's a real good story. Walter Lee, I guess he's my hero. He was at a real bad place, but he became a man, a real man."

Shaking her head with her mouth agape and her eyebrows knitted together, she extended her hand in a pleading gesture. "Why do you pretend to be stupid and bad when I can tell from this one piece of writing that you have great potential?"

"Miss Sloan, people like me either die or get a miracle. Mostly, they die."

With a catch in her voice, she said, "I have a proposition for you, young man. It can be your miracle if you'll agree."

"Whatcha want me to do?"

"I won't press charges on you *if* you'll come back to school, behave, and do *whatever* any of your teachers ask. I'll tutor you and help you find your dream if you'll cooperate. Well, Dupree?"

"Yes, ma'am," he answered excitedly. "I'll do whatever you want me to do. And, Miss Sloan, I won't let nobody ever hurt you neither."

She stood and held out her hand to seal the bargain with a handshake. To Dupree, she knew his word was his honor. Not only did he grasp Larkin's hand, he reached across the table and engulfed her in a bear hug.

Once all the coven members had been questioned, the authorities turned to witnesses. Both Raif and Larkin were scheduled to make official depositions the first Friday in November.

Robert LaFontaine, the handsome assistant prosecutor, was heading the state's case. His eagerness to prosecute this case gleamed in his pale blue eyes. He knew this one would catapult his career in politics. Sitting in his office on the fourth floor of the Plaquemines Parish Court House, LaFontaine ran baby-smooth, well-kept hands through thin blond haired as he looked over files. He stood to his full seventy-one inches and stretched his firm hundred seventy pounds when he heard the outer office door open. Knowing the importance of the case for him, he personally planned to take Larkin's and Raif's statements.

Chris accompanied Raif to the prosecutor's office for his appointment. The agent knocked on the prosecutor's door. "Come," LaFontaine called.

Raif and Chris entered a rather ostentatious office furnished completely in dark mahogany and bright brass. "My God!" the prosecutor verbalized at his first encounter with Ray Reynolds's twin. He offered a handshake to both parties.

"You knew Ray discovered he had a twin, right?" asked the FBI agent.

"Yes, but seeing it…Well…Please sit, Mr. Gautier."

Raif sat in the chair in front of LaFontaine's desk and looked around the room. "Do you have another chair?"

"Excuse me?"

"I want Agent Milovich to stay."

"No problem." LaFontaine got a bright brass folding chair from a closet and opened it. "Here you go, Agent Milovich.

Raif stifled a snigger. *About as pretentious as I've ever seen. What lawyer doesn't have at least two chairs for clients or other visitors?*

Chris narrowed her eyes at him, halting the laugh. "Thanks." She sat.

Retaking his seat LaFontaine pulled a recorder from his drawer. "I need to record your statement."

"Of course."

"So, talk to me." LaFontaine listened with minimal interruption.

Chris listened intently while Raif explained. "During the time I was off my medication, Latrice convinced me she could help me if I would bring Larkin to her. I paid one of Larkin's students to be my accomplice, but Larkin was able to communicate with me and got me back on my medication."

"Why didn't you take her with you when you went to the police?" asked the prosecutor.

"Once I was in control of my faculties again, I became aware of the real danger. As long as Latrice thought she was getting what she wanted, Larkin was safe. I worked with my brother to gather evidence against Latrice."

"You know, I could arrest you," commented LaFontaine.

"Whoa," interjected Chris. "Does Mr. Gautier need a lawyer here?"

The prosecutor waved off her comment and gave a slight headshake. He stopped the recorder. "Reynolds really should've held you, Mr. Gautier. And he should have brought in Latrice the second he had a suspect. He let his personal relationship get in his way."

"Yes," Raif said, "you could arrest me, but what would it accomplish? Do you really think the public would support your punishing one of this woman's intended victims? Besides, Larkin would have to testify against me, and she won't do it."

"Don't be smug, Mr. Gautier," LaFontaine warned with a stern look.

"That's not smugness," Raif argued. "That's confidence in friendship."

LaFontaine frowned. "You're sure of that, aren't you?"

"Absolutely. You haven't met Larkin yet, have you, Mr. LaFontaine?"

"No," the lawyer answered. "She's coming in after school."

"Just wait. You'll see," he said confidently and grinned. "She's stubborn and would probably go to jail herself for contempt before she'd compromise her values."

Chris slapped her hand on the prosecutor's desk. "Mr. LaFontaine, I think you'll find signed documents by both Chief Gerard and the mayor of Eau Bouease authorizing Detective Reynolds's undercover operation, no matter if it was a bit unusual. Don't try to intimidate Mr. Gautier. He cooperated fully with law enforcement." She stood. "And he's said all he's going to without representation. We're out of here. I can't wait for Larkin Sloan to put you in your place."

"Agent Milovich, I'm fully aware of Mr. Gautier's immunity and a farce of undercover work that I pray holds up. I meant no insult." He extended his hand. "Mr. Gautier." Raif shook the man's hand.

Chris crinkled her nose as if smelling a foul odor and walked out. *Social-climbing slime ball. He's worse than Brad Tisdale.*

As Raif was leaving LaFontaine's office, Larkin came in. She greeted Raif with an affectionate embrace, as she

201

did Chris. LaFontaine saw Raif was, without a doubt, correct in his assessment of his relationship with this woman.

On the elevator ride down, Chris said to Raif. "I listened to you. You have total recall of everything that happened while you were off your meds. Most schizophrenics don't. It's all the proof I need. I'm convinced you need to see a neurologist. The drugs could be masking your real problem and preventing you from getting the treatment you need."

"I'll make that appointment." He smiled. "Are you still going to hold my hand?"

She nodded and discreetly slipped her hand into his.

LaFontaine sensed immediately the specialness of Larkin Sloan.

She came confidently and alone to give her statement. LaFontaine observed her self-confidence and found her attractive. He began sympathetically. "Miss Sloan, don't you want a friend here with you?"

Larkin smiled. "I can do this alone, Mr. LaFontaine. I'm a big girl, and I learned to stand on my own two feet a long time ago."

He nodded. "Very well, then. Let's make it a little easier. Call me Robert."

"Row-Bear? Are you really French?"

"Oui, Mademoiselle. Mon grand-père marié ma grand-mère pendant la Seconde Guerre Mondiale à Marseille. Il a fait partie de la résistance Française et elle a été une infirmière marine. Il a choisi de venir en Amérique avec elle quand la guerre était terminée." ("Yes, Miss. My grandfather married my grandmother during World War II in Marseilles. He was a part of the French resistance and she was a Navy nurse. He opted to come to America with her when the war was over.") He nodded again. "I speak fluent French, and not the Cajun variety."

"Très bien, Robert. Et vous devez m'appeler Larkin." ("Very well, Robert. And you must call me Larkin.") She flashed a smile, but had a pang of uneasiness. Her flirtation did not seem natural to her.

"Okay, Larkin. Tell me your story, and, *please*, tell me why you aren't pressing charges on Dupree Parks and why you would hesitate to testify against Raiford Gautier. Parks hurt you and Gautier paid him to do so and then abducted you and held you for weeks."

"I know it might seem odd." She smiled. "So, I'll answer the last part first. They were victims, too. Since Dupree has been back in my class these past four days, he has been a model student. He's a lot brighter than anyone has ever given him credit for, and he has a talent for music."

She sighed, full of emotion. "Raif? He's a sweetheart. I truly like Raif. He would never have hurt me in any way if he hadn't been manipulated. He'll never let himself get to that point again."

"All right, Mother Theresa!" Robert laughed, his hands raised in mock surrender. "Now, tell me what happened after you answer one more question. Will you have dinner with me tonight?"

"Isn't there some *rule* against having dinner with me while this case is open?" Her right eye twitched.

Reading a bit of anger in her face, Robert shrugged. "Rules are made to be broken. You're fascinating, and I'd like to get to know you."

"In that case, yes."

"Great! Now, tell me what happened." He pointed to his recorder and received a nod from the redhead.

Larkin told her story from her really bad day that got worse after Dupree hit her with a book to Latrice's being cuffed and included how she knew Latrice. She finished, "I don't think I left anything out."

"One thing." He turned off the recorder.

"What's that?"

"Do you have feelings for Reynolds?"

She thought a moment before she replied huffily, "It wouldn't be ethical." She clamped her jaw tight.

Robert was a little confused by the remark, but he let it go, thinking he had grabbed a tiger by the tail. As she left the prosecutor's office, Raiford Reynolds came in with a folder.

"Hello, Larkin," Ray said awkwardly.

"Ray. How have you been?" she replied.

"Well, and you?"

"Great. I'm back at work where I belong."

Even-toned, Ray asked, "Dupree is behaving?"

"Perfectly." Larkin nodded. "He might even get the male lead in the spring musical review."

"Well, if anybody can bring out the good in him, it's you."

"I'll take that as a compliment."

"It is."

Ooh! Take this! She turned back to the prosecutor and asked in a sugary voice, "Robert, did we decide seven?" Her eyes cut to Ray.

Robert gave a crooked smirk. "I'll see you then."

Ray flinched.

"I'm looking forward to it." She walked away, head held high.

There was a pregnant, uncomfortable pause in the room for several seconds after Larkin left. Ray shook it off.

"LaFontaine, I think we have all the proof we need." He held up the folder triumphantly.

The prosecution had already established the fact that Latrice had access to all the female victims' medical files while working for their doctors. Latrice's credit card purchases included thirteen wedding dresses. The ceremonial dagger matched as the murder weapon in all the female slayings. Twelve coven members could attest to the "necessary sacrifices." In addition, they had the botched ritual on tape, along with the tape of Ray's meeting with Latrice, as well as Raif's and Larkin's testimony. Now, Ray proudly pulled out the forensic and DNA reports.

LaFontaine read, and a smile spread across his face. "Good stuff."

The blood scrapings contained DNA from every female victim on the altar of the old monastery, which Latrice owned. The altar had an etched groove where the women's necks had lain and the blood drained to collect in a reservoir around the base of the slab. That accounted for the lack of blood on the garments. Coven members admitted to drinking a swallow of blood for empowerment.

Hair fibers found on the wedding dresses belonged to Latrice. Blood specks on the robe Latrice had worn matched every victim. A garrote and a hand gun discovered in Latrice's home were linked to two of the male slayings, and Latrice had frequently volunteered at the local missions and homeless shelters. The black SUV used in the hit-and-run belonged to Sabrina Hatch, one of the coven members. She had confirmed Latrice asked to borrow her car but told her to report it stolen.

"Reynolds, I think you're a prick, but you really did your homework this time. Good job."

"The feelings's mutual, but let's put that aside and lock this whacko away."

"Agreed."

Robert walked the detective to the elevator. Ray turned. "Larkin's special," he said quietly. "She's innocent and sweet. She's angelic. Don't pull your philandering on her."

"Reynolds, I don't know what you did, or maybe it was what you *didn't* do, to her, but thank you."

A feeling of triumph coursing through his veins, Robert LaFontaine returned haughtily to his office, and Raiford Reynolds angrily kicked over the standing ashtray outside the building.

27
Criminally Insane

The state's psychiatrist, the defense's psychiatrist, and an independent psychiatrist interviewed Latrice Descartes, as well as the twelve coven members over a period of weeks before they released final reports. The general consensus regarding the women who had followed Latrice was that they were suffering the same kind of brainwashing that members of other cults, such as Jim Jones's or Charles Manson's followers, experienced. Additionally, the blood work came back to indicate a strong hallucinogenic combined with the hypnotic sedative Methaqualone in each one's system. The only one who seemed to be letting go of her infatuation with Latrice and feeling remorse was Alicia Steen.

Judge LeVigne ruled, "Gullibility does not negate responsibility in the deaths of twelve women. Nobody forced you women to drink a concoction that affected your minds. You are hereby bound over for separate trials within six months. You will be notified of your court date. I want Alicia Steen evaluated further. Miss Steen, I'll see you in the morning at nine sharp." He banged his gavel and dismissed.

Ray whispered to Chris who sat beside him in the courtroom. "Damn it. LeVigne means well, but those comments were stupid. Notice that the defense didn't object, but those words could be construed as bias upon appeal. My improvisation will be moot."

"Shh. We can hope and pray."

The same afternoon, a juvenile advocate met with Alicia Steen and asked for an immediate bench trial, not a simple hearing. The judge listened intently to arguments from both sides the next morning. He watched the child closely throughout the proceedings to get an accurate reaction from her about her involvement. During her trial, she broke down and told the court about her sexual abuse and desperation to feel safe, which is what Latrice offered her and her mother. "She said she'd make him stop forever," the child sobbed. Turning her tear-stained face toward the judge, she said, "I think she planned to kill him. I can't say I'm sorry for that." Her next words came in gasps. "He...hurt...me...so...much."

Judge LeVigne read the reports and reviewed the child's background. He sent Alicia to a juvenile facility to be treated for mental illness until she turned eighteen, at which time the case would be reviewed to determine what, if any, further action was warranted. His suspicions confirmed from the scant information Baker had obtained, Ray stayed long enough to hear her verdict before he filed the paperwork to arrest Alicia's father and have her two siblings taken into protective custody.

On the other hand, the mind of Latrice Descartes was complicated and convoluted. There was no disagreement among the psychiatrists that Latrice was guilty of multiple counts of murder, but there was a great deal of disagreement about the degree of mental illness the woman suffered and how her case should be adjudicated.

Attorneys for both the prosecution and the defense sat down with all three psychiatrists. After reviewing the physical evidence and hearing the psychiatrists' reports, Latrice's public defender convinced his client to plead guilty and seek the judge's mercy in sentencing in a bench trial. He told her a jury would be much harsher than Judge LeVigne. Mr. VanDevere, the defender, was surprised at the ease of his persuasion. He had to wonder what this ingenious, but insane, woman was up to. He honestly wanted her locked away because he was afraid of her. After only three weeks of testing and interviewing, Latrice Descartes waived her right to a trial by jury and appeared before Judge LeVigne in a bench trial. She pled guilty and begged for mercy.

The state's psychiatrist believed Latrice to be a sociopath with no conscience and a menace to society. LeVigne read the file presented by the state. His scratchy voice grunted, "Criminally insane—a mental defect or disease that makes it impossible for a person to understand the wrongfulness of his acts or, even if he understands them, to distinguish right from wrong. Defendants who are criminally insane cannot be convicted of a crime, since criminal conduct involves the conscious intent to do wrong—a choice that the criminally insane cannot meaningfully make." He motioned Dr. Culpepper to the witness stand. "You are under oath," he reminded the man. "Talk to me. This psycho-babble means little to me. Say it in English. Is this woman mentally competent to stand trial?"

"It's arguable."

"Don't jerk me around. Tell me your diagnosis."

"Very well. I have determined that Latrice's upbringing with a very strict military father did influence her need to control and dominate as she was dominated. However, her mother's secret involvement with a satanic cult to which she exposed her daughter and the decadent sexual practices of the group jaded and corrupted Latrice's idea of perfection. Her overexposure to so many cultures helped to confuse her understanding of religion because she didn't have guidance or formal religious foundation in the standard realm of religion although her father required her to attend mass every Sunday." He looked at the judge to see if he was being clear. LeVigne waved both hands in a forward sweeping motion for the doctor to continue.

"In her distortion, Latrice created her own religion in which she is the supreme authority. Her misinterpretation for the need for cleansing through blood sacrifice prompted her foray into black magic and ritual sacrifice. She feels no remorse for her actions. Indeed, she voiced her intent to continue purification of America and will have to start over because the process is 'cyclic and must be done in stages at the given times.' Those are her direct words. In addition, she repeatedly mentioned her mother's warning not to use a twin. Mother seems to have vanished back to Transylvania."

"Please," grunted the defender. "Objection. For the record Mrs. Descartes was deported before anyone was killed. Her visa expired sometime ago."

LeVigne nodded. "Miss Descartes's mother is not on trial. Sustained. Tell me about the defendant." The judge held up a finger and spoke to the bailiff. "It's freezing in here. Check the thermostat. Now, Doctor, go on."

Dr. Culpepper nodded. "The only emotion she seems capable of is rage. She is obsessed with finishing what she started. I recommend that Latrice Descartes be declared criminally insane and be confined to an institution for the rest of her life. I would recommend capital punishment for her crimes if the *U.S. Constitution* allowed the execution of the insane. The State of Louisiana would certainly desire the ultimate sentence."

"So," the judge asked, "you think she's insane?"

"Yes."

"Is she capable of standing trial?"

"Not at this time."

"Step down. Rousseau, your turn. Don't forget you're under oath as well."

Dr. Rousseau, the psychiatrist for the defense agreed that Latrice was criminally insane, but she sought leniency for the person she perceived as a victim of her upbringing and harsh war-mongering influence. The vapors of her breath hanging in the air, Rousseau said, "She herself has been brainwashed into thinking that only blood would cleanse America. I ask that Latrice be committed until such time that she be diagnosed sane."

Listening to the procedures, Ray muttered to Chris, "Which would be never." He shivered. "Damn, it's as cold in here as at the monastery."

The FBI agent whispered, "Spirit world?"

"Shit." Ray's stomach roiled.

The judge glared toward law enforcement, prompting silence. LeVigne asked, "So, am I to understand, you think Miss Descartes is not competent to stand trial?"

"No, she's not Your Honor."

"You would declare her insane?"

"Yes."

"Step down. Petra."

Dr. Petra, an independent psychiatrist appointed by Judge LeVigne, diagnosed Latrice as a sociopath. He took the stand when the judge called him forward. LeVigne asked, "Well, do you concur with the other two? What do you mean when you say she's not a psychopath?" He tapped the file in front of him.

He nodded. "Yes, Your Honor, I agree that her harsh, unstable childhood might have warped her perception of reality, but she poses a terrible danger to society. She is not psychopathic. A psychopath often feels guilt and shame. She has no conscience, which played perfectly into her military duties. Uncle Sam won't tell us what she did, but I'd put money on her being an assassin. The government cannot acknowledge sanctioned murder. They used her mental illness for their own purposes and then turned her loose on society. I tried to read her psychological history from the Marine Corps. Half of it is blacked out." The psychiatrist shrugged. "She transferred often and was assigned to 'other agencies'. That could explain a lot."

The psychiatrist took a deep breath after his diatribe and went on after noting the defense attorney whispering to his client. "She is a consummate sociopath with the ability to see what a person needs and to become that thing, which is how she manipulated thirteen men into doing her bidding and convinced twelve women she could save them from their circumstances. She is obsessed with completing her task, and she will kill again. I recommend her incarceration in a maximum security facility for the criminally insane for life. Dr. Rousseau is overly optimistic to think Miss Descartes will ever be declared sane."

"Is she competent to stand trial?"

The doctor shook his head. "She has no concept that what she did is wrong."

"Yes or no?"

"No."

"Insane?"

"Absolutely."

Judge LeVigne reviewed all the evidence. He listened to every word and dismissed the group until three in the afternoon.

As they waited Ray asked the defense attorney, "What did she say to you while Petra was testifying?"

"You know I can't tell you that. I'll say this, if her mother comes back to the States, the U.S. government could be looking at a lawsuit."

Steve Journey, standing with Ray, said, "If it could be proven the military capitalized on her illness and made her worse, they could be held liable."

"You think?" Chris asked.

Journey shrugged. "Possible, but a long shot." He fidgeted. "Honestly, I think she's been hired as a mercenary, maybe by someone with underworld ties, since she got out. A paid assassin can make a *killing*." He chuckled softly.

"Bad pun." Ray grunted, "Real *underworld* ties."

"That too," agreed the agent.

When court reconvened, Judge LeVigne requested that Latrice stand with her lawyer. He shivered. "Why is it so damned cold in here?" He addressed the defendant with a measure of respect for her past service to her country. "Master Sergeant Descartes, do you have anything you'd like to add before I make my ruling?"

"No, Your Honor," she replied, her voice low and gravelly, her breath visible like ice crystals on the air.

"All right, then. I pronounce retired Master Sergeant Latrice Descartes criminally insane. You are hereby sentenced to incarceration conditionally for the rest of your natural life in a maximum security facility for the criminally insane. However, I will see you one year from today to be re-evaluated since *The Constitution* requires you to be given the chance to be cured. If, and I emphasize *if,* you are declared sane and competent to stand trial, there will be a trial. Bailiff, take her into custody to await transport." He noted in his calendar. "Schedule transport for the Monday before Thanksgiving, November 24th, seven P.M. Court adjourned. I need a hot toddy."

The moment Latrice left the courtroom, the temperature leveled.

Detective Raiford Reynolds, Agent Christine Milovich, Prosecutor Robert LaFontaine, Raiford Gautier, and Larkin Sloan left the courthouse feeling both relieved and victorious. Two of the other FBI agents and Brian Baker gloated with them. Journey's brow creased. "It was too easy."

28
Things that Go Bump in the Dark

Upon leaving the courthouse, the unlikely quintet comprised of Detective Raiford Reynolds, Agent Christine Milovich, Prosecutor Robert LaFontaine, Raiford Gautier, and Larkin Sloan went to dinner to celebrate the resolution to a very trying time. The other agents and Brian Baker, along with Olivia, his wife, joined them for a short time before the agents prepared to head back to FBI headquarters. Chris had made arrangements to stay longer to ensure Latrice was properly incarcerated.

Dinner consisted of never-ending pasta at the nearest Olive Garden, along with numerous glasses of champagne, prompting Raif to declare, "I guess we all know why we brought my car. I'm the DD."

Nobody differed with Raif's statement. The agents ate, toasted victory, and left. Baker and his wife left shortly afterward. However, after a couple of hours, Ray finally snarled at LaFontaine, "For God's sake! Get your hands off the woman!" when Robert took Larkin's hand in his.

"Ray! Mind your own business," Larkin hissed.

"I am," Ray argued.

"No, you're not. You're minding *mine*. I think we've celebrated long enough." She calmly placed her napkin on the table.

With the check paid, the group left the restaurant. Raif whispered to Chris, "Sit in the back with Robert and Larkin *please*. I'd like to avoid bloodshed in my car."

Chris nodded and whispered, "Just don't put me between Ray and Robert."

Raif delivered everyone safely home beginning with Larkin. He dropped Robert at his apartment and Chris at

214

her hotel. He scowled at Ray, whom he intended to take home with him. He passed Ray's turnoff.

"What are you doing?" Ray groused.

"Being your big brother. What the hell is wrong with you? If you want Larkin, go for her, but stop making a fool of yourself."

"Hasn't she made it clear that she doesn't want me?"

"No, but she has made it quite plain she doesn't want to be with a jerk."

"Ha!" Ray laughed sardonically. "Then why is she letting LaFontaine fondle her?"

"Jeez! Ray, what is it with you and Robert?"

"Nothing. I don't like him." He grunted. "That's all."

"No, it's not." Twin intuition kicked in. "It's Mia, isn't it? Your former fiancée went to Robert when you and she broke up. He's *Rob*, that so-called best friend you mentioned." He glanced at his brother. "Am I right?"

"Yeah! You're right!" shouted Ray. "Then he went to a hundred more women, and Mia was too self-absorbed to realize she threw away someone who loved her. Larkin is doing the same thing, and he'll break her heart."

Raif pulled onto the shoulder of the road and stopped the car. "Talk to me, Ray. What really happened? You know everything about me. You know all about Abigail. Why can't you share this with me?"

Ray laughed bitterly. "Raif, you don't even know all about you and your ex, and I don't want to lose my brother now that I've found him."

"What are you babbling about?" Passing headlights illuminated Raif's confused frown.

"What happened to you in New Orleans is at least partly my fault."

"How do you figure that? What the hell are you talking about?" Irritation began to edge the brother's tone though his volume remained low.

"Robert...Your mugging...If I hadn't stayed with him to get a tattoo, I could've stopped it. I know who did it. I

215

was there at Mardi Gras. They were my fraternity brothers. Maybe being associated with me is the problem. Maybe I'm the monster that goes bump in the dark."

"*Fooyay! Fooyay! Fooyay!* You are so full of bullshit." Raif hit the steering wheel in frustration. "Or maybe it's just booze tonight. Are you trying to drive me away? Is that what you want so you can wallow in self-pity? Ray, absolutely nothing that has happened to me is your fault. *Nothing*, Ray. Absolutely nothing that happened to Larkin before you met her is your fault. What happens to her from here on out might be your fault if you don't get over what happened with Mia and Robert. One of the best things you can do is talk about it. Stop keeping everything bottled up inside."

Ray drew back his fist all the way to his shoulder for maximum force and started to punch the windshield.

"Whoa!" Raif barked. "If you break my windshield, you *will* pay for it, brother or not. Now, stop acting like such a damned idiot and talk to me."

Ray grunted, slouched back into the seat, and folded his arms over his chest, looking like a petulant child.

Raif unsnapped his seatbelt and pivoted in the driver's seat to look squarely at his brother. "We are not budging from this spot until you talk to me."

Ray released a deep, heavy, almost tearful sigh. "Four years ago, I was still a patrolman. It wasn't long before I became a detective. Brian Baker was my partner. We responded to a domestic disturbance call. The woman's drugged-out husband was holding a gun to the head of her child, a boy about thirteen or fourteen. The man had his arm around the boy's throat, dragging him backwards. Boy and Mom were screaming. The guy turned his gun on us." Ray dropped his arms and stiffened his back.

"Then what?" Raif prompted.

"The kid was gutsy. He jostled the jerk's arm, and we were able to disarm the low-life." He paused.

Raif encouraged, "Go on."

216

"Yeah, yeah. But not before the gun discharged and struck me in the shoulder. It's ironic," Ray continued. "The kid was Dupree Parks. I recognized him in lockup, but he didn't recognize me out of uniform. He came between his mother and her slug of a husband and almost got killed for it. Dwight Funchess, that was the slug's name. He had used her for a punching bag for a long time. The poor woman was covered in scars. Her eye was almost swollen shut and her lip was encrusted with blood." Ray clenched and unclenched his fists. "I got shot, not life threatening, but Mia completely freaked out." Recounting the event had taken him back to the place and time. He hit his shoulder where his scar was located.

"Freaked out how?"

"We had only been engaged a month. I wasn't even out of the hospital when she walked into my room and announced she couldn't handle being a cop's wife." Ray snorted. "She handed me her engagement ring right in front of a damned nurse. When I was discharged, I went to talk to her." He held up two fingers. "Two days. That's all it took. Robert was there, shirt unbuttoned, hair tousled; and she was wearing lingerie. I'm not a fool. I put two and two together. It was going on before I got shot." Ray ran his fingers through his hair.

Raif listened with little interruption. With a low whistle, he said, "Finish, Ray."

After a great sigh, Ray continued. "Two months later, Mia caught Robert cheating on her. She wanted to get back together. All I could do was to ask her how it felt. I just couldn't do it. Not only had she betrayed me, but with my best friend. Robert and I were fraternity brothers and roommates at LSU. We had been friends since we were six. I think his actions hurt more than hers. I'm sorry, Raif, I just can't get past it.

"And, now, he's after Larkin." Ray shook his head as if trying to shake the thought from his mind. "Raif, she's a virgin. He'll hurt her in more ways than one. God! When I think about him and her, I get nauseous. I could kill him."

"Ray, Larkin is not a fool," Raif consoled. "She will *not* sleep with him. Give her some credit."

"He's as charismatic and persuasive as Latrice." Ray continued to sulk. "That's why he's such a damned good lawyer. I'll give him his credit where it's due."

Raif stared at his mirror image. "Tell the woman you love her for Pete's sake."

"You're a fine one to talk! Now, take me home. I wanna wake up with a hangover in my own toilet. And don't you say a damned thing to Larkin."

Raif didn't argue but drove his brother home. Back at his place, he called Chris. "I just wanted to tell you good night," he said when she answered.

"Is everything all right?"

"It is now."

"Well, good night then," Chris said, confusion weighting her words.

"Good night."

"Sweet dreams."

"Yeah, finally."

After retrieving his car the next day, Ray dragged into his office. Chris was already there packing her things.

"What's going on?" Ray snarled after popping some more aspirin.

"I'll be leaving as soon as Latrice is transported to the state mental institution."

"That's not until Monday."

"Yeah, I'm just getting prepared." She paused as she held a snow globe of Santa using alligators rather than reindeer, a gift from some of the officers. She shook it and watched purple, green, and gold snowflakes fall before packing it in a box. "Dantzler, Swift, and Journey have already gone back. They'll be back to testify. Steve's analyses of the defendants are crucial. Did you notice that Patrick and Raif have become friends?"

"Yeah. So what?"

"You're in a horrible mood. I knew you drank too much last night."

"I needed more to watch LaFontaine paw Larkin."

"Jealous?"

"Forget me. Let's talk about you and my brother."

"There's nothing to discuss. After all, he took you home last night." Chris winked and went to get coffee, leaving Ray to stew.

To make Ray feel even worse, his mother paid him a surprise visit. She met Chris with warm affection and demanded to meet the man who should have been her other son and the girl who had captured Ray's heart.

Ray said, "You already met Chris."

Dorothy Reynolds furrowed her brow and scowled at her son. "Don't play games with me, Raiford Michael Reynolds. I want to meet *Larkin*."

"I don't know if she's even speaking to me."

"What did you do?"

He moaned, not wanting to answer. Mrs. Reynolds glanced at Chris with hands outspread.

"He acted like a jealous fool last night at dinner," offered Chris.

"Did he?" said Mrs. Reynolds. "Well, suck it up and call. I want to meet her."

Ray obediently called since it was ten in the morning and he knew from Dr. Fairchild that Larkin would not be in a class and could answer her cell phone. "First," he said, "I apologize for being rude last night. Second, my mother is in town and wants to meet."

"I'll make dinner. I'd like to meet your mother. Bring Raif and Chris as well."

"That sounds good," said Ray. "Larkin, are you inviting LaFontaine?"

"It's better if you two aren't together. I'll cook for him another time."

Ray sighed deeply. "I wish you wouldn't."

"Why? What reason do I have for not seeing Robert socially?" *All I want to hear is that you want to see me socially.*

"Never mind. I won't bad mouth the man. It would only blow up in my face. What time do you want us?"

"Eight works for me. It'll give me time to cook. Bring some white wine."

"Yes, ma'am. Larkin I…"

"Yes, Ray?" she responded hopefully.

"I'll see you tonight."

Ray took his mother to Bertram and Associates and introduced Raif. Dorothy took him by the shoulders. "It might be a little late, but I have every intention of spoiling you as much as I did Ray. Call me 'Momma Reynolds.'"

"Yes, ma'am."

She pulled him into a warm embrace. Raif could only return the affection. *It feels natural*, ran through his mind.

Ray interrupted, "Raif, Larkin is making dinner tonight. She wants you to come." He grinned. "Chris will be there."

"I'd love to. What time?"

"Eight."

Dorothy patted both men's arms. "Well, until then, I'm going to Ray's place. My boys. Yes, indeed."

Raif covered his mouth to hide an amused grin as Ray shrugged and followed his mother out the door.

By the time dinner with Larkin arrived, a storm raged in full force. Larkin's company practically floated into her house. Dorothy Reynolds met Larkin with the same affection she had shown Raif and Chris. The two felt they had known each other forever.

Ray watched every move Larkin made. She wore a fitted burgundy sweater dress that bared her left shoulder, revealing her matching tattoo. She pulled her hair back in burgundy and flowered cloisonné combs with matching earrings dangling gracefully as she moved. The darker shade of lipstick she wore accentuated her perfect smile. And she smelled like a rose garden. He would have given anything to bury his face in that scent and those copper ringlets, but he sat across the table from her. Ray could hardly taste the rotisserie chicken, wild rice, and broccoli with cheese sauce for the memory of the sweetness of Larkin's lips.

Halfway through dinner, glaring lightning flashed. Resounding thunder shook the walls. The party was thrown into total darkness. The gloom was instantly followed by a crash and a yowl. Cyclops bounded over Mrs. Reynolds to get to Larkin.

Mrs. Reynolds gasped as Larkin passed the cat to Ray and retrieved candles and a lighter from the buffet drawers. Dorothy Reynolds asked, "Larkin, honey, aren't you scared to live way out here by yourself?"

"No, I like the peace and solitude, especially when I write." She laughed as she lit several candles.

"So, you're an author as well as a teacher?"

"I hope so. I've been compiling an anthology of poetry. I'm ready to look for a publisher."

"That's very commendable, but I'm afraid I'd jump at every little sound in the night if I were out here alone."

"I'm not afraid of things that go bump in the dark, Mrs. Reynolds. I've survived a true monster, and Psalm 56:3 is my motto: 'What time I am afraid, I will trust in Thee.'"

Just as she spoke, the wind howled fiercely and someone pounded on the front door. Mrs. Reynolds started in fright. "Mercy!"

"Who could that be?" mused Larkin as she headed for the door, taking a candle from the table.

"I bet I know," muttered Ray. "I thought you weren't inviting him."

"Robert?" Larkin shook her head. "I didn't, but his cell has been off all day."

Sure enough, Robert LaFontaine stood on the porch. "I didn't think I'd make it out here tonight," he said. "I had to run to Baton Rouge and got caught in the deluge." He entered the foyer and although Larkin was not alone, he did not seem to think anything of barging in. Rather, he asked pointedly, "Why wasn't I invited to the party?"

"Because you and Ray don't get along," answered Larkin frankly. "You should've *called* before you came, and I left you three voice messages if you'd bothered to check."

"The storm completely knocked out my cell phone reception. I didn't realize I'd be unwelcome."

"Don't sound so wounded," Larkin chided. "I do have friends besides you."

"Friends? Raiford Reynolds?" Robert hooked his thumb over his shoulder. "That *is* his car out there."

"In person," Ray said sulkily from the doorway to the living room. He stood in the shadows with his arms folded across his chest.

"Hello, Reynolds."

"Dispense with the pleasantries. The lady said you should *not* have come." Ray jerked his head toward the door. "Get back in that nice Mercedes and leave."

Larkin held up her hand. "Ray."

"What's the matter, Reynolds? Afraid of the competition?" Robert gloated.

"You are not *competition.* You're a forked-tongued, venomous snake. I will *not* allow you to sink your fangs into Larkin."

"Whoa!" she commanded. "This stops now! I'm not some golden statue to be won by the best jouster."

By this time, Mrs. Reynolds, Chris, and Raif had arrived in the foyer.

"No, you're not," Robert agreed. "You're an invaluable prize that someone as vulgar as Reynolds doesn't deserve."

"You philandering, back-stabbing, loathsome, two-faced..." Ray advanced toward LaFontaine.

"Stop it!" said Larkin shrilly as she verged on angry tears. "Raif?"

"I'm right here." Raif placed a restraining hand on his twin's shoulder.

Ray became rigid and clenched his fists. He looked at his brother and mother. "I'm getting out of here before I kill the son-of-a-bitch." He turned to Larkin. "I'm sorry, but I cannot and *will not* go through this again." He walked into the rain, oblivious to its icy chill.

"Again?" Larkin asked in confusion.

"I'll tell you later," said Raif as he went after his brother. Mrs. Reynolds and Chris reluctantly followed.

The weekend found Chris continuing to pack her belongings in the police station. Ray really did hate to see her leave, and he encouraged her to stay.

Chris grinned and tried to placate her temporary partner. "I'll visit at Christmas," she teased. She didn't want to be serious about departing because she did not want to leave. "Don't worry, Ray. I'll be here with you while the state police transport Latrice Monday evening. I promised to stay until she was locked securely away. Actually, I won't be leaving until Wednesday. I also promised to hold Raif's hand when he visited a neurologist. His appointment is Tuesday morning. I have to go. I have all kinds of reports to write."

"Well, you can at least stay until *next* Monday. Mom wants you to come for Thanksgiving."

"I could do that." She became thoughtful. "I'll have to put in for leave. I have enough days to get me through the holiday." She nodded. "I'd like a family Thanksgiving.

Yeah. Okay." Her excitement rose with each determination. "I'll do that."

Monday evening, Chris walked into Ray's office with a Bumper's Biggie Bag and a deck of cards. "Gin rummy while we wait?" she asked as she set the bag on Ray's desk.

"Sure." Ray nodded. "And food, too. I see you have all the answers."

"No, just something to keep you busy until the asylum calls to let you know our little loon is locked up tight."

"Thanks. I won't sleep until she's gone away."

"I know. Me either. Have you talked to Larkin?"

"No."

"Chicken."

"Don't start. I know she's having dinner with Robert at this very moment."

"And why not you?"

"I could ask *you* why you aren't with my brother."

"I was. Then, I came to babysit you because you're too chicken to go after Larkin." She spread the food on the detective's desk. "Take off the gloves, man. LaFontaine has nothing better to offer her than you do."

"Chris, I've lost a woman to him before. Honestly, it hurts too much."

"You lost a woman, not a *Larkin*. Isn't she worth the fight, Ray?"

He finished his fries without answering. Finally he mumbled, "Deal the cards, Chris. They're on their way. In two hours, I'll be free to fight."

Larkin toyed with her meal although Robert had ordered her favorite enchiladas. She drank her margarita and asked for another.

Robert ordered another margarita and took her hand. "What's wrong?"

"I just can't relax until Ray calls to tell me Latrice has been locked away."

"I hoped dinner with me would take your mind off Ray's calling you for anything."

"I'm sorry. It's not you." She withdrew her hand. "I'm truly frightened of that woman. She's living proof monsters are real."

Larkin finished her second margarita and managed to eat one enchilada before she asked, "Robert, will you, please, take me home? I want to take a hot bath, snuggle up with Cyclops, and watch a movie with a happy ending."

"I'd *love* to snuggle up with you and Cyclops." He smiled winsomely.

"Robert, please? Cyclops hates you. I don't know why, but he does. Besides, I've told you I'm not ready for that kind of relationship with you."

"But you are with Reynolds?" he snapped.

Get a grip. I am not your property. "That's not it. I can't force feelings." She firmly placed her napkin on the table.

"I apologize. I'll admit I'm jealous of the bond you have with Raiford Reynolds."

Larkin sighed. She and Ray had been through a lot. She had begun to doubt there had ever been a bond, just lust, a purely physical attraction.

Robert huffed. "Of course I'll take you home. Do you want a doggie bag so you can eat later?"

"That works for me. I don't have much appetite right now."

The drive to Larkin's home was silent. Robert left Larkin at her front door with an aloof kiss and the promise to call her the next day. He drove off into a quickly gathering freezing fog.

Larkin ran a steamy bath filled with bubbles and slipped in up to her neck as Cyclops sat on the side of the tub. She put her headphones on and turned Debussy's "Claire de Lune" up. She gave way to complete relaxation.

"Ray!" Chris grumbled after winning yet another hand of gin. "You are no competition tonight. Concentrate, for Pete's sake."

"I can't!" He banged his fist onto his desk.

The phone rang, startling both of them. He snatched the receiver. "Reynolds."

After a short interval, Ray sprang to his feet and bellowed, "Are you fucking serious? Goddamn it!" He slammed the receiver down.

Ray grabbed his jacket. "She's escaped, Chris. The two troopers escorting her are dead, and she has the cruiser and their guns."

Chris's stomach clenched. "Oh, my God!" The FBI agent threw on her coat. "You go to Larkin's. I'll go to Raif's."

"I can't believe I'm glad she's having dinner with LaFontaine," said Ray as he sprinted to his car.

Raiford Gautier hunched over his drawing table reviewing his latest blueprint. He rubbed his arms with his hands to warm them as the room had become cold. Pounding on his door brought a scowl to his brow. "Stop banging! I'm coming!" he said as he bounced down the stairs and headed for the door. "That had better be Chris coming to babysit me early."

Raif jerked the door open and tried to slam it closed just as fast as he stared at the muzzle of a hand gun in the grasp of Latrice Descartes. Before he could shut the door, the barrel exploded in his face. The bullet caught the edge of the door and then the right side of Raif's head. He fell backward with a thud.

A faint scream came from the townhouse next door. "What was that?" Carol Johnson asked her husband as they lay in bed.

Lieutenant Terry Johnson jumped up. "A gunshot. Get Sheena and stay in the bathroom." He reached atop the highboy, snagged a black case and spun a combination, grabbed his nine millimeter, and popped in the clip. He raced to his front door.

"Terry, be careful!" Carol cried.

"Dial 9-1-1."

Latrice stood over Raif and gloated, "I'm finally rid of you. Now, I can finish what I started." As she started to fire another bullet, this one into Raif's chest, the Johnsons' door flew open and Terry trained a gun at the escaped prisoner.

Latrice shouted, "What the fuck? Who the hell are you?" She whirled and fired at the soldier freshly home from Iraq. Terry Johnson ducked behind the door jamb as the bullet splintered wood. Latrice snatched Raif's keys from the hook by the door, dashed down the walkway, and sped away in Raif's Nissan.

Chris passed the Nissan driving at a high rate of speed. She recognized both car and driver. Her heart skipped a beat in her anxiety. She whipped out her phone. Seconds after another emergency call, Christine Milovich summoned an ambulance. She dreaded what she might find. She shivered in the sudden chill of her rented vehicle.

Please, God? Don't let him be dead. The FBI agent sprang from her car without cutting the engine. She rushed inside the townhouse, dropped to her knees, and hovered over Raif. "Don't you die on me," she commanded. Cradling Raif's head in her lap, she called Ray.

His throat constricted, Ray answered. Before he could speak, Chris shouted, "She's got Raif's car. She shot him. The ambulance is here. We're going to the hospital."

"I called the restaurant. LaFontaine already took Larkin home," Ray informed Chris in a thin, tight voice. "She's not answering her phone. I'll call you. Take care of my brother." *Please, God? Don't take him from me. Protect Larkin.*

"Be careful," Chris said. "I don't need both of you hurt. The fog is thick."

"Thanks." He clicked his phone shut.

Ray gunned the Mustang down the long dark road that led to Larkin Sloan's house. The fog was so dense he could hardly see the road in front of him, and small ice crystals dotted the windshield. He let the GT out as far as he could and turned the wipers on high.

Larkin fluffed her wet hair with a towel and shuddered in the cold air. She heard a racket at the front door. Cyclops arched his back, his hair standing on end. Warily she dropped the towel and listened. Hearing nothing else, she descended the stairs cautiously. She pulled her robe more tightly about her when she saw her front door wide open, the lock shattered. She looked beyond the door to see Raif's car pulled onto the lawn, leaving deep ruts in the pristine landscaping.

Larkin called, "Raif?" as she reached the door. Her breath hung in the frosty air.

"You wish," answered a menacing voice behind her.

Larkin started to run for the yard, but Latrice grabbed her hair and yanked her backward. Latrice pinned the much smaller woman to the floor and brandished Larkin's own butcher knife. "You don't get to die as fast as that weasel of a traitor, Gautier," Latrice hissed. "No. You're the final offering. I suppose your white terrycloth robe will have to do as a sacrificial gown."

Larkin struggled fiercely beneath Latrice's weight. A piercing yowl stabbed the air as a large one-eyed black ball of fur landed on Latrice's face. The woman flung Cyclops from her, but his attack gave Larkin enough leverage to get free.

She stumbled to the fireplace and grabbed the fire poker. Latrice, blood streaming from her face, advanced on Larkin. Larkin swung the poker with all her might. She caught Latrice across the left arm, but the former Marine wrenched the poker from Larkin's grasp.

As Latrice hurled the fire tool across the room into a lamp, Ray's Mustang screeched to a halt beside Raif's Nissan. Larkin screamed. Latrice punched her in the face. Larkin fell to the floor, stunned and dazed.

Latrice sprinted to hide behind the open kitchen door as Ray entered, weapon drawn. Larkin watched the scene in a blur.

Seeing Larkin on the floor, Ray momentarily let down his guard, starting toward her. Latrice sprang from behind the door. She plunged the butcher knife into Ray's side and abdomen again and again.

Larkin roused and screamed. Ray toppled to the floor. His gun slid across the wood. Latrice bragged, "And I got the twin, too, Momma. Now, the sacrifice."

Like a slow-motion movie sequence, Latrice started toward Larkin again. As if by reflex, Larkin inched to Ray's fallen weapon, clutching it in desperation. She pointed the gun at Latrice who cackled like a classic cinematic witch.

You are the one who will end this echoed in the frigid air, along with the sound of large fluttering wings.

Larkin closed her eyes. She pulled the trigger until the gun made no more sound.

All was silence; the air, comfortable. When she opened her eyes, Latrice Descartes lay dead only inches from her.

Larkin dropped the gun and crawled to where Ray lay still as death. She gathered the man into her arms and sobbed, "Ray, don't leave me. Please, don't leave me."

Larkin did not hear the sirens or see the police or rescue personnel burst into her house.

All went black.

29
Healing Balm—Festering Sore

Larkin smelled antiseptic and heard muffled voices; one was a familiar, comforting female voice. She bolted upright and uttered one word—"Ray!"

"Larkin, honey, you're all right." Chris took her hand. "You're in the emergency room. The doctors say you're fine. You were in shock and lost consciousness. You'll have a nice shiner, but there's no lasting damage."

Larkin focused on Chris's face. "Where's Ray?" she demanded.

"He's in surgery. He's in pretty bad shape."

"What about Latrice? And Raif?" Larkin became agitated and tried to get out of bed. Chris gently restrained her. "Where's Raif? She had his car."

"Relax, honey," Chris soothed. "Latrice is dead. She can't hurt anyone anymore. Raif's in surgery, too. He's in much better shape than Ray. Latrice tried to kill him, but luckily the bullet grazed the door before it hit him in the face." She patted Larkin's shoulder reassuringly. "The doctors are doing some reconstruction on his cheek. And something good came out of it. They discovered an aneurysm when they did the CT scan to check for bullet fragments since it was a hollow point. Dr. LaSalle, the neurosurgeon in partnership with the neurologist Raif was supposed to see tomorrow, is repairing it. I told him he wasn't schizophrenic." Chris smiled triumphantly. "I knew there was a medical reason for his behavior."

"I remember." Larkin breathed shakily. "I killed her."

"Yes, honey, you did the only thing you could've done."

"Ah-hem, I'm Dr. Stephenson." A young intern cleared his throat in the doorway. "I see Miss Sloan's awake. I've brought you some scrubs to change into. You can wash up across the hall." He handed them a couple of towels. "Then, you can join the waiting committee in the family room. You might want to trash those clothes unless Agent Milovich needs them. In that case, there's a bag in the bathroom."

Larkin realized she was covered in blood. *Ray's blood.* Unwanted tears escaped scrunched eyelids.

Chris squeezed her hand. "Come on. Let's get you cleaned up."

Larkin allowed Chris to lead her across the hall and washed off in the lavatory. A short time later, bathed and in clean scrubs, she joined the FBI agent and they found Mr. and Mrs. Reynolds and Walter Bertram in the family waiting room.

Dorothy Reynolds stood. "We just flew in by helicopter from Biloxi."

Walter Bertram took Chris by the elbow. "Thanks for calling me."

"Of course. You're Raif's family."

Mrs. Reynolds had just introduced her husband when Dr. LaSalle, the surgeon who had been operating on Raif, entered. He asked, "Where is Mr. Gautier's family?"

"Here," asserted Mrs. Reynolds.

Dr. LaSalle knitted his eyebrows together. "I thought you were Detective Reynolds's parents.

"Didn't you notice they're twins?" Mrs. Reynolds asked.

"No. I haven't seen Detective Reynolds."

"Well, they are. Those are my boys, and these are my two future daughters-in-law."

With surprised expressions on both their faces, Larkin and Chris stared at Mrs. Reynolds.

"You'll see," she said to the women. "Now, Doctor, how is Raif?"

"He'll be fine. This attempted murder has proven to be his salvation. We were able to repair the aneurysm. He

232

should only hear the voices of people who actually talk to him from now on and without medication. He'll need one more cosmetic procedure in a few weeks, but there should be no extensive scarring. The door saved his life from what I've heard. He's in recovery if you'd like to see him."

"You go, honey." Mrs. Reynolds patted Chris's arm. "You're the one he'll want to see. We need to wait to find out about Ray, but we'll be in soon."

Chris sat by Raif's bed. She held his hand and stroked his brow along the edge of the bandage. His head was completely bandaged, along with the right side of his face. "Hmm. I'm trying to picture you without that lush charcoal hair. Bald, you won't look like Ray for a while."

Raif groaned, and his eyes flickered open. "Chrish?" he said groggily.

"Hi," she whispered. "It's nice to see those baby blues again."

"What happened?"

"Latrice managed to escape during transport. She killed her escorts, but you don't have to worry. She's dead."

"Ray shent her to the pit of Hell, huh?" he slurred.

"Not exactly."

"Huh?"

"Larkin killed her."

"Larkin?" Several seconds elapsed before he finished his thought. "Ish she all right?"

"She's fine, but…"

"But what?"

Chris stood and heaved a sigh.

"What aren't you telling me?" His body stiffened. "Ray! Where's Ray? I don't feel him." More coherently, he demanded, "Chris, answer me." When she didn't reply, he tried to get up.

233

"Lie down," she commanded as she pushed on Raif's shoulders.

He argued, "Tell me, or I'll find someone who will." He lay back, his body rigid. "Ooh. There he is. I feel him again, but he's weak. He needs me."

Chris stared at him a minute. *You really are as stubborn as Ray.* She said, "Ray's in surgery. I want to say this so you'll understand." Battling her own feelings, she caressed Raif's arm. "When Ray raced to Larkin's, Latrice ambushed him. She did a great deal of damage to his intestinal tract and right kidney with Larkin's butcher knife. Larkin emptied Ray's nine millimeter into her." Her voice trembled. "He's in bad shape. There's no doubt he'll lose his kidney." She watched him closely to be sure he was handling the news all right before she continued. "He's in really bad shape. They're reconstructing his large intestine, and maybe some of his small."

Raif relaxed a bit. "How can I help?"

"You can't. Get well yourself. If you think Ray needs you, be strong for him."

"Okay." He drifted off again for a brief time. "I'm glad Latrice is dead," he said as if he had never stopped talking. "Is that wrong?"

"No. She can't hurt anyone anymore. But I guess you could say she kept her word to you."

"How's that?"

"You won't be hearing voices anymore. When they ran a CT scan of your head, they found an aneurysm. They used this technique called coiling to repair it, but you still might have a little short term memory loss for a few days. They shaved your head just to get a few pieces of the bullet that, thank God, did not pierce your skull. Do you remember what we've been talking about?"

Raif nodded. "Yeah. Ray's in surgery because Latrice almost killed him."

"Good. Now, why are you here?"

"She tried to kill me too. But apparently I'm not schizo. I have an aneurysm."

"Had. That's why you were in surgery for several hours. They called Dr. LaSalle. He came and repaired it. He says you won't need medication, and you won't hear voices. He's pretty certain there was some heightened sensitivity caused by it, but even if you sense some kind of emotion, no more voices."

"That *is* good news." Raif smiled weakly. "I'd rather hear your voice."

"There might come a time when you'll tell me to shut up."

"Never." He held out his hand to her. "Stay with me after you find out what's happening with my brother."

At that moment, Dr. LaSalle pulled back the curtain. "Well, you're wide awake."

"Mostly. I don't think I'm having much memory loss. Chris told me everything. What's happening with my brother?"

"Brother? Oh, yes—Detective Reynolds. All I know is he's still in surgery. It's been touch and go. If I hear anything, I'll let you know. Now, you're going to a room."

"I'll go see what I can find out." Chris squeezed Raif's hand. "I'll be back. What's the room number, doctor?"

"Three-thirteen, unless you're superstitious."

"No, three-thirteen is good." Raif laughed. "I am one lucky thirteen. Thirteen anything is good."

Raiford Reynolds looked down upon the surgical suite. He felt himself being pulled toward a light, and he wanted to walk into its warmth. A voice in the light told him, "Not yet, Ray. Why are you so stubborn? You give new meaning to the term free will. I sent you an earthly angel. Go back and accept the gift I sent to you."

Ray heard many voices. "Clear!" He felt electricity pulsing through his body.

The light beckoned again. He heard the heavy flutter of large wings. The gentle voice said a second time, "Go back. The next time we meet, I will not be so lenient. I will not send you back a third time."

The six-hour wait while Ray was in surgery seemed interminable. Finally, as the new day dawned, Dr. Shue, Ray's surgeon, stepped into the waiting room. He looked exhausted while everyone turned toward him in dread. "Well, he's alive," the man practically whispered. "We had to remove his spleen, right kidney and several sections of his intestines and reconnect them to undamaged areas. We lost him twice, but he's a real fighter. Somebody's prayers kept calling him back. He's in ICU. Y'all may visit him one at a time for five minutes each hour. I know that seems like a very short time, but Ray doesn't need any excitement right now. So, who goes first?"

It was agreed that Ray's mother should see him first, and the vigil for Ray to wake up began.

After two days, Raif was released from the hospital. However, he refused to leave the premises until Ray woke up. He joined the family vigil. Day and night he sat in the waiting room with only brief periods of sleep until Momma Reynolds forced him to go home for real rest and a shower.

Twelve days after surgery, Ray remained in a coma. Every hour for five minutes one of the people who loved Ray sat by his bed. Nerves frayed and fatigue set in.

At midnight on the beginning of the thirteenth day, Larkin took her turn in the rotation. As she bent over to kiss Ray on the forehead, his eyes popped open. He seemed to look directly at her and said, "What the fuck are you doing here? Get the hell away!"

As quickly as Ray's eyes opened, they closed. Larkin grabbed her purse and fled the hospital.

Raif took his turn by his brother's bed the next morning. Resting his chin on his fist as his elbow rested on the bed, Raif was startled when a voice said, "You look like The Mummy, big brother."

Raif clasped Ray's hand. "Welcome back. You tried to scare us all to death."

"Oops. Sorry, but I took on the psycho bitch from Hell up close and very personal. Where is she anyway?"

"With Gremory where she ought to be—Hell. Larkin sent her there with every bullet in your gun."

"Good for her. Where is she?"

"I guess she went home for a little while. That's what we've been doing—going home to rest a little in between our turn to sit with you. Momma and Daddy Reynolds have been sleeping at your place. You might have lost your car. Daddy Reynolds loves driving it."

Ray tried to laugh. "Oh, don't make me laugh. It hurts."

The nurse stuck her head in. "Mr. Gautier, time's up."

"He's awake," Raif informed her.

"It's about time." Relief spread across her face. "I'll get Dr. Shue here immediately."

Raif added, "And I'll get everybody else. I'm glad to have you back, Ray." He paused at the curtain as he said emotionally, "Ray, I love you."

"Me too, bro, me too," Ray whispered.

Raif spread the exciting news. When he called Larkin, her response shocked him. "I won't be coming back to the hospital."

"For heaven's sake, why?" he asked.

"Ray doesn't want me there."

237

"Yes, he does."

"Then why when he opened his eyes last night, did he tell me to get out? I'm honoring his wishes."

"Something strange is going on here."

"I am *not* coming. That's final."

Several days passed before Dr. Shue released Ray, just in time for Raif's next reconstructive procedure, which only required an overnight stay. Raif went to his brother's place as soon as he was released.

Ray pretended to be content with his family and friends around him, but Raif knew his brother was simmering, ready to explode over Larkin's absence. Finally alone, Raif asked pointblank, "Why are you so surprised she's not here? You told her to get out when you woke up briefly the night before you woke up completely."

"No, I didn't."

"She says you asked her what the fuck she was doing there and then told her to get out. She thinks you blame her for almost getting killed."

"Oh, my God! I wasn't talking to her. LaFontaine was standing in the gap of the curtain. I was talking to him."

Raif inhaled sharply. "I *knew* something was wrong. You have to tell her."

"Drive me over there right now."

"Are you up to it?"

"Not, just yes, but hell, yes!"

Ray and Raif pulled up to Larkin's house which was aglow with festive Christmas decorations. Icicle lights dangled and twinkled in the gentle breeze. Garland with holly clusters wrapped around the porch columns and rails. Classic carols played softly from speakers mounted at each end of the porch. Ray leaned tediously on Raif's arm as they climbed the steps. Raif pulled the velvet cord, and the old chimes reverberated through the house. To Ray's consternation, Robert LaFontaine opened the door.

"Oh, to hell with it!" Ray muttered through clenched teeth. "Take me home now!"

The two limped down the steps with Raif supporting most of his brother's weight. Ray eased into the passenger's seat with a groan. Raif slowly left the driveway. Ray grumbled, "If you don't press that gas pedal, I will. Someday! I swear! Someday I'm gonna kill that bastard!"

"Ray!"

"Shut up and drive. And don't you dare say a damned thing to Larkin."

The car turned the bend in the road.

Larkin came to the foyer drying her hands on a dish towel. "Who was here?"

"Nobody." Robert smiled seductively. "Just a solicitor."

Ray's anger festered like an infected wound and spread like cancer as he gave new meaning to the phrase, "Bah, humbug." He made Ebenezer Scrooge look friendly as his gloom stretched to his family and friends.

If his parents had not stayed in Eau Bouease, Ray would not have even placed a wreath on his door to celebrate the holiday season. However, having missed Thanksgiving, Mrs. Reynolds would have her way and decked Ray's apartment to the hilt. A Douglas fir twinkled with lights and tinsel. Garland and holly boughs draped along the fireplace mantel, topped off by cinnamon and pine candles symmetrically placed on the mantel and wrapped with garland. Six stocking hangers adorned the edge of the protrusion, and from every doorway hung mistletoe, which the older couple used to their advantage every time one of them crossed a threshold.

Mrs. Reynolds planned Christmas Day to be a full celebration and the menu was written in stone. Raif and Chris, who had delayed her return to FBI headquarters again even if she had to pay for her own hotel room, were at the top of the guest list. Larkin, also, was invited; however, she forlornly declined citing a commitment to spend Christmas Day with Robert's family in Baton Rouge. Her absence did not stop Mrs. Reynolds from hanging a stocking for her on Ray's mantelpiece along with all the others and filling it with wondrous treasures.

Raif, on the other hand, dragged Chris and the Reynoldses into the woods on his property to chop his own tree. He decorated inside and out, even stringing lights on the Johnsons' house to Sheena's delight. His neighbors became close friends. Chris spent the week before Christmas baking with Mrs. Reynolds, reveling in experiencing a southern Christmas.

Christmas Eve, Mrs. Reynolds thumped Ray on the back of the head, ordering, "Get dressed. We're going to church."

"Mom," Ray quarreled, "I really have no desire to go to midnight mass." He rubbed the back of his head. "That hurt."

"We're not going to mass. Get dressed. You've lost enough weight that your jeans won't be tight. You don't have the 'they hurt my incision' excuse anymore. Move!"

Like a scolded child, Ray obeyed. He and his parents, with Mr. Reynolds driving the GT, drove to Charity Chapel, the nondenominational church Larkin attended. "Oh, no," Ray groaned. "Why are you torturing me?"

"Deal with it," his mother scolded again.

Inside, Raif and Chris had saved them a seat. "Were you behind this?" Ray growled in his brother's ear.

"Merry Christmas, Ray," was his reply.

Even Ray could not quell the Spirit during the service, and he had heart flutters when Larkin sang, "O, Holy Night," to dismiss the congregation.

After the benediction, Larkin came to speak to her friends. Ray refused to make eye contact with her. He asked, "Where's Robert?"

"He's not comfortable here." Her eyes searched his face as if she was looking for the answer to an unasked question. "Were you?"

"The service was quite nice. You sang just like an angel."

"Thanks."

"Well, Merry Christmas, Larkin."

"Merry Christmas, Ray."

Ray still moved gingerly with his hand pressed against his abdomen as he headed toward the exit. Larkin called after him, "Ray?"

"Yes?" He half turned.

"Sometime do you think we could talk about"—She breathed emotionally—"About Latrice? You're the only other person I know that…well, you know."

"It gets easier. You did the right thing."

"I know, but it's still hard. It hurts." She placed a fist over her heart.

"The department has a support group for us officers. Maybe you could come."

"Yeah, maybe. I need to heal."

"Me too." Ray rubbed his middle. "Good night, Larkin." He started out the door again.

To his back, she said, "Good night, Ray."

He turned around once more. "Do you have plans with Robert for New Year's Eve?"

"Yes, why?"

"Never mind. Larkin, it was him, not you." He went out the door.

Her face twisted in confusion, and she whispered to his retreating back, "All you had to do was say, 'Cancel them.

Spend New Year's Eve with me.' Why couldn't you?" She slowly shook her head.

New Year's Eve proved to be eventful in Eau Bouease. The night was unusually cool, but Raif had special plans for Chris. He picked her up and drove to the property he owned. Once there, he wadded the grungy jeans and sweatshirt he had worn through the worst ordeal of his life into a ball. He jammed them under a pile of twigs in the shape of a teepee, doused them with a liberal amount of lighter fluid, struck a match, and tossed it onto the bundle of rags, starting a bonfire. The flame made a loud swoosh. Raif grinned with satisfaction as the fire erupted, causing his dimples to deepen and showing the little scar on his cheek in almost exactly the same place as Ray's from a childhood accident. Then, he spread a picnic, including champagne.

Chris was overwhelmed. The expensive perfume he had given her at Christmas had been extravagant and flattering, but the quiet intimate picnic brought her to tears.

"Wait a minute," said Raif. "This isn't part of the plan. You're supposed to be having a good time."

"I am," she sniffled. "Can't you tell? This is the sweetest thing anyone has ever done for me."

He put his arms around her. "Dare I start the fireworks?"

"You have fireworks, too?"

"Yep." He lit a fuse, and over the next several minutes, he held her close as they watched their own private spectacle. They snacked and roasted marshmallows and laughed about actually burning the loathsome clothes and the fact that both he and Ray had said they wanted to burn them weeks before.

By unspoken agreement, they waited for midnight. At precisely twelve o'clock, Raif kissed Chris softly and gently and whispered, "Happy New Year." Afterward, they lay in each other's arms and counted the stars.

After a time, Chris could tell Raif had fallen asleep. She hoped a little piece of the shield over his heart had fallen away. But she also realized he was still guarded, almost as much as Ray, only without the anger. There was no animosity, no bitterness in this man beside her. The New Year would continue to be a healing balm for him. Chris just wondered what part she would play.

Robert LaFontaine acquiesced to Larkin's desire to be home by midnight. He enjoyed the parties and celebration, but he could pursue those pleasures after he had won Larkin.

When the clock struck twelve, he pushed his point. He kissed her hungrily. He tried to slip the sequined straps to her silver satin evening dress off her shoulders.

She pushed back from him. "Robert, stop it."

He pulled her to him again. "I want you. Make love to me."

She shoved him away more forcefully. "I said stop. You know this is *not* going to happen. Why can't you respect my choice?"

"Larkin, you're not a little girl. You're a very desirable woman. It's time to act like one."

"Robert, if I were pregnant and chose to have an abortion, would you support my choice?"

"Absolutely. It's your body."

"That's right. It is. And my choice is to respect my body and share it only with the man I plan to spend my life with. Support *that* choice."

"And who would that be—Reynolds?"

"It's time for you to go home." She pulled the thin silvery shawl that matched her dress over her shoulders.

"Larkin, the New Year just started." He regretted mentioning Ray. He realized too late that he had pushed too hard.

"And you will be starting it on that side of my door while I start it on this side of my door." She pointed sharply toward his car. "Good night."

Robert left reluctantly. *I'll call that little spitfire tomorrow and feign remorse. For now, I'll find a party in full swing. New Year's resolution: Conquer Larkin Sloan. If I have to put a ring on her finger to have her, okay.*

Larkin locked the door, turned off the light, and picked up her phone as she walked upstairs with Cyclops who hissed at Robert every time he came into the house. As if by reflex, she dialed Ray's number.

Ray, watching the celebration in Times Square on television, checked the caller ID. He allowed the call to go to voice mail and went to bed.

Raif had never been so happy, but he could not stand seeing his brother so miserable. He was determined to pull Ray out of his despair. After several weeks of convalescing, Ray was at last going into work half days. Raif showed up bright and early at his brother's apartment on January 13th, with a banana nut muffin sporting a candle. "Happy birthday!" he chirped.

"You, too," Ray replied in a manner that would have made Eeyore proud. "Thanks for the birthday cake. I didn't get you one."

"That's all right. I'll have something sweet tonight at dinner. Until then, I have a surprise for you—no work. We're going to meet our mother. Don't balk. I've already called ahead and pretended to be you. We get to see her privately, without barriers, since you're a cop." He grinned. "And I sort of hinted there might be new evidence in her case."

Ray could not help but admire his brother's ingenuity. "Why do I think we would've traded places to annoy our teachers if we had been raised together?"

"I don't know." Raif chuckled. "It would've been fun, wouldn't it?"

The twins drove to the Louisiana Correctional Institute for Women in St. Gabriel.

The prison guard found Audrey van Zandt in the prison library re-shelving books. "Audrey, you have visitors."

"Are you kidding?" she asked.

"It was a surprise to me too. In the ten years I've been here, you've never had a visitor."

"I never had one before you came either. Who's here?"

"A detective named Reynolds and I guess his partner. I didn't see them, but was just told to get you. This isn't regular visiting time." The guard shrugged. "Guess it must be official business. Maybe they're here to tell you something about your family."

"My family wouldn't let me know if something had happened," Audrey said bitterly.

"Well, come on. You won't find out here."

Ray sat on the end of the table in one of the prison interrogation rooms as Raif quasi-sat on the narrow ledge and stared out a small slit of a window reinforced with wire and watched blue-black clouds rush past a determined sun.

Audrey van Zandt entered the room warily. *What could a cop want with me after thirty-one years?*

When she entered, both men stood respectfully.

In dismay, Audrey exclaimed, "You look just like Jesse, except your eyes! You have my eyes. I would've known you anywhere. How did you find me? Oh, my God! It's your birthday."

Although a little worn by time, Audrey van Zandt was still attractive. She did have the same big blue eyes her sons had and wore her blonde hair pulled slicked back in a ponytail. She was slim, and despite her circumstances, carried herself well to stand five and a half feet tall, except when stressed, at which time she slouched. She slumped immediately upon seeing two men who could have been ghosts to her. Her eyes brimmed with tears. "Better yet— *why* did you find me?"

"We needed to meet our mother," Raif answered compassionately.

"Please sit down," Ray requested.

Audrey sat down tentatively. The brothers sat across from her. Ray explained a little. "I'm Raiford Reynolds, but everybody calls me Ray. I'm a detective. I used my position to track you down because I didn't know my brother existed at the time. He was having a little trouble, and a lot of people began to think it was me."

"Oh," said Audrey, hands clasped tightly in front of her. "They didn't keep you together."

"No, but we've found each other now, and all the trouble is over."

Raif said, "Believe it or not, I'm Raiford Gautier, but I'm called Raif."

"That's bizarre," said Audrey.

Ray and Raif agreed together, "Yes, a little."

"Audrey, will you please tell us what happened?" Ray asked. "From what you said when you came in, can I assume you meant Jesse Gatlin, one of the boys you shot?"

"Yes, Jesse Gatlin. I don't like to talk about it, but I've been going to the sexual trauma resolution group. You would be surprised how many of us in here were sexually abused in some way."

"No, I wouldn't," said Ray. "I've seen a lot."

"Of course you have. As a cop I mean."

"Yes." Ray nodded.

Raif asked, "Please tell us?"

"All right," she agreed. "I guess you deserve the truth. None of it was your fault, but at thirteen, having you was more than I could handle. Can you understand why I left you for someone else to love?"

"Yes, ma'am, and we've both been loved very much. You did the right thing for us, but we'd still like to know what happened," Raif assured tenderly.

Audrey nodded and relaxed a bit before two men who she sensed were worthy of knowing the truth about their beginning and her ending. "I had the biggest crush on Jesse. I'm glad to see that at least Jesse was your father because at first I really liked him, and I thought he liked me. My dad had forbidden me to see him. He told me that a nineteen-year-old man had only one thing on his mind when he hung out with a girl my age. I should've listened, but I thought I was in love, and the fraternity guys were having a summer bash on campus. Jesse invited my friend, Julia, and me to come. We lied, so our parents thought we were spending the night with each other."

A shake of her head accompanied, "Oh, I know we shouldn't have been drinking, but we were impressionable kids. We thought we were big, partying with the frat rats. That is, until they started passing us around."

Audrey tightened her clasped hands. "I tried to fight them, but I was too drunk to stand. But I wasn't drunk enough to forget how much it hurt, physically and emotionally, the way they laughed at my protests. I couldn't tell anybody what happened. After all, I was somewhere I wasn't supposed to be. I guess it was really my own fault."

Ray shook his head. "There is never a legitimate excuse for rape."

247

Someone did a good job as parents with these two men. She smiled slightly as she thought.

"He's right," said Raif. "Please finish your story."

"A week later, Julia slit her wrists," Audrey went on. "Then, I found out I was pregnant. My folks threw me out and haven't spoken to me since. I was an embarrassment to them. My father's political career was over all because of me. I wandered around the various shelters until I went into labor two months early. After I had you, nothing else mattered except making them pay. They killed Julia, just as sure as if they pulled the blade across her wrists; and me, too, I suppose. I felt dead inside. In my mind, I was exacting justice that never would've happened."

"Audrey, what are you doing sitting in prison?" asked Ray.

"Where else should I be?"

"Free is where you should be. Why didn't you tell your lawyer all of this? He could've argued diminished capacity. You were only thirteen. Even if you *had* consented, that still would have been statutory rape. We're living proof that something happened."

"I killed six men. I broke into my own home and stole my father's shotgun. I knew what I was doing."

"Still, you don't belong here. If I can get you out, will you let me help?"

"Where would I go? Nobody wants me." Tears she had never shed dripped silently down Audrey's cheeks.

"That's not completely true," said Raif. "Why don't you give your boys a chance to know you?"

Wiping tears away with the backs of her hands the woman barely whispered, "Do you really mean that?"

"Yes," the twins answered in unison.

Audrey was quiet for a time before she answered, "All right. Try. But if you can't, you know where to find me." Her trembling voice carried years of isolation and sadness. "A visit now and then would be nice."

Ray and Raif had a quiet birthday dinner with Chris. She brought Ray season tickets to the next football season of the Saints because she knew Ray was a die-hard fan and was always waiting for that miracle year. To Raif, she presented a golden retriever puppy, which he promptly named Sunbeam for all the light flooding his life.

Ray went home alone while Chris and Raif spent time with the puppy. The two of them discussed the search Chris had begun for her daughter. Raif encouraged her to find the child and set up a meeting. After meeting his mother, he told Chris, "I'm certain now that's it's the right thing for you. If nothing else, you'll get closure."

"Okay." She nodded as she scratched the puppy's ears. "I have a lead and should know something soon."

"Let me know what you find out." He kissed her tenderly. "I love Sunbeam. Thanks for my companion."

The next day found Raif poring over new blue prints and Ray driving to Baton Rouge to meet with the state attorney general. Ray had a new purpose: He was determined to get Audrey van Zandt out of prison.

30
Unsolicited Advice

Chris stayed in Eau Bouease until after she celebrated Ray and Raif's first birthday together with them. She checked her dwindling bank account since she had used all paid leave and knew she had to get back to work, but the last few weeks had been the best of her life. She had spent Christmas with her favorite twins and their family. It meant a great deal to her because it was the first Christmas she had actually felt wanted since her mother's death, though she knew in her heart how much her father loved her. The highlight of the holidays had been the New Year's kiss she received from Raif. Afterward, he had merely held her in the moonlight without words.

Chris also had a mission to close the hollow place in her heart. The weeks between Latrice's escape and the New Year, she had spent looking for the child she had given up for adoption. The day after the birthday celebration, she showed up at Raif's office with a file. "I think I found her," she announced. "I got this early this morning."

"Your daughter?" Raif stopped his drawing. "Really?"

"Yes. It appears she was adopted by Damian and Chelsea Kersh. They named her Lindsay. They live in upstate New York. It seems she's been well provided for and loved." She laid the file on the drawing board. "She's an honor student, plays tennis, and sings in both the full choir and the Madrigals. The only drawback I have is that she has been raised Jewish." She held up her hand, indicating for Raif to halt his comment as his mouth opened. "Not that I have anything against Jewish people, but I'm Christian. I can't help but want her to be Christian, too."

250

"Well, ma chère"—Raif took Chris's hand—"what are you going to do now?"

"Nothing. Pray." Chris sighed. "She's happy. I don't want to complicate her life."

"You sure?"

"No, but it's best for her."

"All right, if that's what you *really* want. Are we still on for dinner tonight before you fly out of my life?"

"Yes, sir."

"I'll pick you up at seven. Wear something slinky. I have reservations at a really swanky place."

Raif tapped lightly on the door to Chris's hotel suite. She opened the door quickly. "Wow!" she gasped. "You look as if you stepped from the pages of *GQ*. You wore the Armani." The navy blue double-breasted pin stripe with a starched white button-down shirt and a red silk tie was elegant.

He gulped at his own little surprise. Chris was decked in the definitive little black dress: satin, strapless, fitted, stopping at mid-thigh. High-heeled Roman sandals accentuated her muscular calves, and an onyx choker punctuated her long slender neck. Her short, dark blonde hair lay in perfect layers. Over her shoulder he saw a set table, complete with candles.

Raif nodded as his eyes roved over every inch of her body. His dimples deepened in appreciation. "I'm flexible. Dining in is good."

Chris slid her hands up his arms as she whispered, "It gives us time together."

Raif shook his head. "Not enough." He pulled Chris to him and kissed her as he had only fantasized before. He maneuvered her to her bed. Dinner was the last thing on either of their minds.

Raif woke as the sun streaked the sky. He reached over only to find an empty bed. He sat up and called, "Chris?"

Looking down, he saw a piece of paper in the shape of a heart with lip prints on it. A simple message read:

"Chris's heart. You hold it in your hands."

"Damn it!" muttered Raif as he realized Chris had left for the New Orleans airport without waking him. He dressed as quickly as possible. Knowing there was no way he could catch the FBI agent before she boarded her plane back to D.C., he did the next best thing. He tossed his jacket and tie into the back seat of his Nissan and broke every traffic law racing to his brother's office.

Raif burst into Ray's office since the detective had returned to work after his ordeal. Uncharacteristically, Raif rudely demanded, "I need your help! Get off the damned phone!"

"I'll call you back. My brother's here." Ray hung up the phone. "This had better be more important than speaking with the governor about Audrey."

Chris checked her bags. Since she had a couple of hours before her flight, she decided to grab breakfast when her stomach rumbled. *Seeing as how dinner was never touched last night, I'm starving.* As she sat down to hot beignets and coffee, her cell phone rang. Thinking happily that it was Raif, she did not look at the number.

"Hello."

"Hi," a young voice said. "You don't know me, but I think I'm your daughter."

Chris almost choked and literally spewed coffee across the table. "Lindsay?"

"You *do* know me."

"No, not exactly."

"Well, no matter. I'm Lindsay Kersh. I think you're my biological mother. I've been looking for you since October when my folks were killed in a car crash."

Chris's heart raced. "Killed? I didn't know. I didn't get that information." She pressed her chest with her hand. "I've been looking for you, too. I only discovered where you were a couple of days ago."

"Well, I would call that irony." Chris jerked her chin back and inhaled sharply at Lindsay's tone of voice.

The girl went on. "Now, I'm sure you had good reason to give me up for adoption, and the Kershes were good parents; so, I'm not mad or seeking revenge or anything like that. I'm sixteen and can be declared an emancipated minor. That's just it. I'm sixteen. I need a mother. I was hoping I could meet you. Maybe we could get to know each other."

"I would love that, more than you know." She squeezed her eyes shut to stop tears.

"Good." The boarding call for a flight could be heard in the background. "Where are you?"

Almost unable to breathe, Chris said, "Right now I'm making the second biggest mistake of my life. The first was giving you away." She checked the board for the status of her flight. "Now, I'm sitting in the airport in New Orleans waiting for the flight to take me to D.C. and away from the best man I've ever known."

"Why?"

"It's my job. I'm FBI. I have to get back to Quantico."

"Why?"

Sassy and impertinent.

"Can't you be a cop wherever this man is?"

"Well, I guess, I could, but…"

"Hey, I'm just a teenager, but what? Which is more important—the job or the man? I can get a flight to New Orleans just as easily as Washington, D.C. You decide, and

I'll book a flight. I'll call you and let you know when to pick me up. It makes no difference to me."

Chris turned her phone to look at it, trying to picture the girl who talked with such brazenness. "You seem a little bossy, young lady," she said, putting the phone back to her ear.

"Yeah, I know. My parents always said I must have gotten that from my biological parents, maybe you."

"Good heavens! If we get together, I think we'll have to set some rules."

"Fine with me. So, which is it—The Big Easy or the Big Sleazy?"

"You've helped me make my decision." *I don't think I can handle you alone.*

"What do you need, big brother?" Ray hung up the phone and eyed Raif curiously. "I've never seen you so disturbed or demanding."

Breathlessly, Raif poured out his needs. "I need you to keep Chris's plane from taking off. I need time to get to New Orleans. I have to stop her leaving. I can't let her go. I love her, and I was a fool not to tell her. What can you do?"

"Slow down, Raif." Ray held his hand up in a signal to tell his brother to halt. "Have you ever heard of a telephone? Why don't you just call her?"

"You don't tell a woman for the first time that you love her over the telephone. I'm old-fashioned. I have to look into her eyes. Please, Ray, help me."

"Hmm." Ray scratched his chin. "Well, I could call the airport and have her held as a possible terrorist."

"I don't want her hurt!"

"Still, that's one sure way of keeping her detained." He gave a short laugh. "Then, we can head out with sirens blaring all the way. I can do 100, 120, all the way there.

It'll give me a good reason to really let the GT out and see what she'll truly do." He shifted imaginary gears in the air.

"Do it." Although he had not had a migraine since high school Raif closed his eyes briefly and rubbed his forehead. He did not see the smirk on Ray's face. Nor, did he see Ray press the receiver button after dialing his own house phone. He only listened to a one-sided conversation.

"This is Detective Raiford Reynolds of the Eau Bouease Police Department...Yes, I need you to detain one Christine Milovich...She's booked on flight"—Ray looked at Raif questioningly.

"Delta 1201."

"She's booked on Delta flight 1201...She's posing as an FBI agent. She's a suspected terrorist...Yes, she's armed, and you should consider her *very* dangerous...Don't harm her. We need to question her...I'm leaving immediately...Thanks so much for your help." Ray hung up the receiver.

"Well?" demanded Raif. He thrust his hands out.

Shaking his head decisively, Ray said, "I can assure you Chris is *not* on that flight to D.C."

"No, she's not," came a feminine voice from the doorway. "But all you had to do was ask."

"Chris!" shouted Raif as he spun around. "How long have you been there?"

"Several minutes. Long enough to hear that you would let people think I was a terrorist. Long enough to hear you say, 'I love her.' Try saying it to my face."

"I love you." Raif pulled Chris to him. "Don't leave. Don't ever leave. Stay here. Marry me."

Chris giggled. *The shield over Raif's heart just evaporated.* "Not the most romantic proposal, but, yes," she responded. "I love you, too. I already emailed my resignation." She had a pleased smile on her face, as she rested both hands against his chest. "Ray, I hope you still have a place for another detective. You *are* lead detective now."

"As my first official act, I'll make one just for my sister-in-law."

"There's more." Chris took a steadying breath and patted her lover's chest with both her hands. "Raif, I hope you can handle a ready-made family. My daughter will be arriving day after tomorrow."

"Whoa!" He stepped back, eyes wide. "It works for me." His dimples stretch to their limit. "Is this a permanent move?"

"Yes. The Kershes were killed in October, the same day I first met you."

"Why do I sense you're hedging?"

Chris sighed. "Lindsay sounds a little headstrong. I might need your help with her."

"I'll do anything I can, but I refuse to wait forever to get married." He stepped back and lifted her chin. "How fast can you put this together?"

"How does February 13th sound?"

"Perfect." He pointed at his brother. "Ray, you'll be my best man."

"You know it."

Chris said, "You know who'll be my maid of honor, Ray. Can you handle that?"

"Just don't invite LaFontaine."

"Nope. Just family and close friends."

Raif and Chris met Lindsay at the airport two days later. She had obviously come prepared to stay. Dragging two large wheeled bags and a backpack strapped over her shoulders, she looked around to find the woman who had given her life.

Raif tapped Chris's shoulder as he pointed out a girl in ragged jeans, a Widespread Panic t-shirt, and dangling peace-sign earrings. "I'd have known her anywhere. She looks just like you." There could be no denying she was

Chris's daughter. She looked like her mother. She had the same soft brown eyes and dark blonde hair that she wore long and straight parted on the side. At sixteen, she was only an inch shorter than her mother.

Chris waved. A smile broke across the girl's face as she saw the man she had talked about with her mother had come to meet her as well. *Good sign. They want me here. And, damn! How could you want to leave that piece of eye candy, Chris?*

"Ground rule number one," Chris said upon meeting. "I'm in charge."

Lindsay laughed. "You said you'd have some rules. My first rule is: Don't *ever* search my things."

Chris arched an eyebrow. Behind his fiancée's back, Raif touched his index finger and thumb to his lips a couple of times and winked at his soon-to-be stepdaughter. The girl's smile got bigger. "I think this is going to work just fine, Chris."

They stowed Lindsay's things in Raif's Nissan. She said, "I have a few more things being shipped to the address you gave me."

"What address was that?" asked Raif.

"Yours," Chris confessed.

"Okay." Raif grinned and kissed her hand. "Sure of yourself, weren't you, lady?"

As they drove, Chris explained the circumstances surrounding the girl's birth. Lindsay accepted Chris had acted only with the child's best interests at heart even if her decision had been made under duress. Mother and child connected, and a bond formed easily, to Chris's relief.

The first night there, Chris invited Larkin and Ray to eat with her, Raif, and Lindsay. Ray and Larkin were cordial to each other. Lindsay eyed them and gave her mother a questioning look and received a wink. Lindsay said, "I think I'm gonna love my new family." Within days, she set about planning a wedding in a month.

Mother and daughter went together to pick up Chris's wedding dress and shop for shoes. As Chris tried on pair after pair, Lindsay brought a pair of flat peau de soie pumps with a strap around the ankle to her. The girl sighed. "Chris, were you ever a ballerina?"

Every time the child called her by name, the woman's heart ached to be called *Mom*, but that would take time. She answered, "Yes, until my mother died. Why?"

"The dress looks so much like a flowing tutu." She handed the shoes to her mother. "Try these. You wouldn't want to be taller than Raif, would you?" Her grin turned mischievous.

"Good point. What else is on your mind?"

"You're observant."

"Goes with both territories, mother and cop."

Matching brown eyes looked into Chris's. "Did you love my dad?"

A moment's pause elapsed before Chris replied, "As much as a fourteen-year-old can love, but I have always loved you. I did what I thought was best for you. I hope you truly understand."

"I do. The Kershes loved me lots." She sighed. "Just before they died, I had a pregnancy scare."

"What?"

"Don't worry. It was a false alarm."

Showing some agitation, Chris asserted, "As soon as I get back from my honeymoon, you and I have a doctor's appointment." She rubbed her face in anxiety. "Birth control is a better alternative than an unexpected pregnancy, but use condoms anyway."

Lindsay laughed. "I don't even have a boyfriend here yet. Relax."

"Any attractions?"

"A few. One in particular, but this is the South, so I'm not sure how it would fly."

Chris raised an eyebrow. "I'm not a native southerner. Who?"

258

Lindsay leaned in and whispered to her mother. Pulling back she asked, "So, what do you think, *Mom*? Tar and feathers or do you believe in love at first sight, at least first meet?"

Tears welled in Chris's eyes. "I believe you'll make wise choices." She stroked her daughter's hair. Lindsay rested a hand on top of her mother's. The bond sealed.

While the women put the wedding together, Raif supervised the laying of the foundation of his dream house. *I told you this would be the wedding gift to my wife. I really hope you like it.*

As he gave instructions to the contractor, Chris drove up. She came over and slipped an arm around her fiancé's waist. "I love my house."

The architect indicated the builder could get to work. "Really?"

"When I saw the blueprint, I told Ray I would give my right arm to live in this house."

Raif kissed her. "No need to sacrifice a limb, only give me your heart."

"Always and forever."

Lindsay met all her new family, and they loved her. She loved them, and Larkin no less than the others. As they talked during wedding plans, Lindsay discovered how much the two of them had in common. She related to "Aunt" Larkin on a deep level because Larkin had lost both her parents at a young age and could understand the feelings Lindsay had. Lindsay sensed her new aunt needed her assistance more than her new mother. *I'll fix you up, too, as soon as I get Mom situated.*

As the women planned the wedding and Raif worked on building his house, Ray continued negotiations with the state attorney general for Audrey's parole. The female attorney general was sympathetic to the case. She read the documents Ray presented and interviewed several witnesses in the original case. She tracked Audrey's family to Minnesota and received a cold reception. The comment made was, "Our daughter died in 1977." She left it at that and told Ray what was said.

"Fuck 'em," he muttered. "Can you present a case for Audrey's release? I'll personally guarantee her compliance with any conditions."

"I think I can," said Darlene Houston.

"In time for my brother's wedding?"

The state official puffed out air. "No promises. I'll call you."

A week before the wedding, Ray received a call. "You can meet Audrey van Zandt at the front gate of the prison in three hours," Houston's voice relayed in triumph.

"I'm on my way. I owe you big time."

After reviewing the case and hearing Audrey's story, the Louisiana Supreme Court heard arguments; and the judge's sentence of life without parole was commuted to twenty-five years to life. After thirty-one years, Audrey van Zandt was paroled and came home to Eau Bouease.

With only a navy blue polyester blend skirt and a simple white button-up blouse to wear and a few toiletries and under garments in a small valise, Audrey slid into the passenger seat of Ray's Mustang.

"What will I do out here, Ray?" She broke several miles of silence. "I have nowhere to live and no job."

"Well, actually, you do."

"Huh? How?"

"I was optimistic. I know you completed your high school requirements and got a degree in library science while in prison."

"Yes."

"Raif and I rented you an apartment in the same complex where I live, three doors down, and with my recommendation, you have a job in the library as an assistant."

She laughed, but it sounded more like a sob. "I need a few more clothes. Did you buy those too?"

He shook his head. "No. Raif did. He has good taste in women's clothes. I think you'll be pleased."

"I already am. My boys are awesome."

Audrey spent time getting to know her sons, but never usurped Dorothy Reynolds as Ray's mother or Raif's surrogate mother. She adored Chris and understood her on a deep, personal level. And the moment she met Larkin she turned to Ray and said, "Why aren't you having a double wedding? You're obviously head-over-heels for that woman. The harder you try to deny it, the more you both suffer."

"Not you, too, please," Ray whined.

So, on Raif's wedding day, Audrey celebrated the joy of one son but fretted the misery of the other.

Raif and Chris's wedding went off without a hitch. Raif had his actual mother filling the seat where the mother of the groom was supposed to sit.

All in all, February 13th, was the perfect day for the couple. The wedding was informal and held in the morning. The groom wore a simple, but elegantly cut tailored suit while Chris chose a cream-colored, street-length satin and silk dress that resembled a ballerina's costume with a soft, flowing, romantic tutu. She wore the shoes Lindsay had chosen, flats so she would not be taller than Raif. Before only family and their closest friends, among freshly sprung daffodils, beneath Japanese magnolia branches heavy with bloom, between rows of azaleas and under a brilliant azure sky, they were married at the Reynolds's beach-front home in Biloxi in the gazebo. Larkin caught the bouquet on a deliberate aim from the bride.

Lindsay sidled up to Ray. "Well, Uncle Ray, when are you gonna tell her you love her?"

"You don't know the whole story there, kid. Leave it alone," he responded.

She snorted. *No way, Uncle Ray.*

Raif and Chris flew to Tahiti for two weeks, leaving Lindsay, who was eaten up with curiosity, to investigate the whole story.

Lindsay settled into her new life. She made the decision to attend school where Larkin taught although she was by no means a discipline problem. She chose to go where she knew someone. In addition, she made it her business to get to know the whole story about Larkin and Ray.

During the two weeks she stayed with Larkin while Raif and Chris were on their honeymoon, Robert LaFontaine came around often. She watched him closely and with suspicion. *Too slick*, she assessed, but said nothing.

Cyclops hissed and arched his back before running up the stairs. *Smart cat*, Lindsay thought. *Animals sense things.*

Lindsay gagged as she listened to the prosecutor gloat about the way the Latrice case had feathered his nest. She was shocked when LaFontaine told Larkin, "The coven members seem to have had their spells broken now that the nut is dead. I'm negotiating deals for pleas. I can save the taxpayers lots of money."

Lindsay intruded, "They'll still go to prison, won't they? Mom told me about this case."

In a tone of condescension, Robert answered, "Yes, they'll go to prison, but without trials."

Lindsay plastered on a smile. "Excuse me. I'm going to call Dupree. We need to talk." Behind Robert's back, Lindsay flipped him the bird.

Larkin's mouth dropped.

"What?" demanded Robert.

"Nothing." She shook her head and acted as if nothing had happened.

Lindsay got to know Dupree Parks who had become a model student and had a huge role in the up-coming musical performance, a Broadway review. Larkin had discovered the young man's voice and was tutoring him so he could take his GED and get out of high school and the Eau Bouease ghetto. As soon as he passed his GED and took the ACT, Dupree was assured a place at a junior college near Larkin's hometown, thanks to her connections. He had latched on to her like a drowning man to a life preserver. He knew God had sent him an angel in Miss Sloan. He determined not to blow his last chance at salvation. He would not let his dream shrivel and die like a raisin in the sun.

While Larkin spent an extra ninety minutes after school with Dupree, Lindsay pestered her uncle Ray. Through her sneaky veiled questions, she determined *Ray is totally in love with Larkin but feels she chose LaFontaine over him. On the other hand, I know Larkin loves Ray, but thinks he rejected her and blames her for his close call with death.* By watching Larkin and Robert, Lindsay learned, *Aunt Larkin dates LaFontaine for companionship. She's not in love with him. She's basically said she doesn't really even like him very much.* The girl comprehended, *Aunt Larkin is guilty of using Robert to goad Uncle Ray.* Lindsay figured out *LaFontaine is obsessed with Larkin. She would make the perfect wife for someone with his ambitions.* Lindsay might have been only sixteen, but she did not equate obsession and love. She dug deeper and uncovered the long history between Raiford Reynolds and Robert LaFontaine.

Once she had all the information, she got busy. She confided everything to both her new parents who already knew much of the story and her new best friend, Dupree. At school as the two of them ate lunch together, she said, "We have to do something."

Dupree sighed. "Lindsay, your mind works overtime. What you want me to do to help Miss Sloan? I would do anything to protect her. She saved my life."

Plans were hatched to get Larkin and Ray together.

"I'll *talk* to them first," she said.

"Good luck." Dupree shook his head in doubt.

Plan one met with utter dismal failure. "They said I'm a little girl who 'doesn't have a clue about the nuances of a complicated matter,'" she complained to Dupree. "The only people who don't know Larkin and Ray are in love are Larkin and Ray. Even LaFontaine realizes it and goes out of his way to keep them from communicating."

"I don't like him," admitted Dupree. "He has no compassion in his soul. Let's talk to your family."

Lindsay thankfully knew all the other members of her new family would happily be complicit in any scheme she cooked up.

Consequently, Raif constantly badgered his brother to fight for Larkin while Chris nagged Larkin until Larkin finally told her that if she didn't leave her alone, she would marry Robert to spite them. However, Larkin merely poured herself into putting together the Broadway review.

Thinking she had met the two most stubborn people alive, Lindsay enlisted the help of the sanest member of her new family, Dorothy Reynolds, her new grandmother.

Mrs. Reynolds paid a visit to her son the first Friday in April, the morning of the Broadway review. She and Ray's father would be attending to show support for Larkin and Lindsay who was to sing a duet, "Somewhere" from *West Side Story,* with Dupree. Mrs. Reynolds marched into Ray's office. He was genuinely surprised to see her.

"Mom, what are you doing here?" He embraced her warmly.

"Dad and I are here to catch Larkin's Broadway review. He's gone shopping with Raif to get some things for the house. The three of them can't live in that townhouse much longer. I thought you needed your mother's advice more."

"Mom, don't start."

"Sit and listen," she commanded

The son obeyed. Dorothy sat across from him. "Ray, don't be a fool. Don't let your pride make you lose the perfect woman for you." Mrs. Reynolds reached into her bag. "I've brought you something. I didn't give it to you before because I knew you hadn't found the right woman. I vowed to give it to you when you found Miss Right." Ray's mother handed him the small, but perfect, diamond his father had given her when they became engaged. "Larkin is Miss Right.

"Your father gave this to me. We weren't rich in the beginning, and I knew he sacrificed tremendously to purchase it. The one I wear now came on our thirteenth anniversary after we both had successful careers. I want you to give this to Larkin. Do whatever it takes to get that girl back. Start by showing up at her big shindig tonight." Mrs. Reynolds stood. "Oh, and bring flowers."

Ray breathed an exasperated sigh. "Mom, she doesn't want me."

"Yes, she does. You have to make her know it."

As Dorothy spoke, Raif poked his head in. "You had better listen, little brother. I saw LaFontaine buying a diamond while I was out. The gig starts at seven. Be there."

Dorothy continued, "She'll say 'yes,' Ray. And when she does, Dad and I'll pay for any kind of wedding the two of you want." She kissed her son's cheek. "I'll see you tonight," Mrs. Reynolds prodded once more as she walked out the door with Raif.

Ray stared at the perfect stone in its black velvet box. It sparkled like Larkin's personality. It was only a quarter karat, but it was flawless. *Larkin's hands are small. Something large would look gaudy on her.*

He stood, put on his jacket, and stuffed the ring into his pocket. He had some things to do before seven.

♣♣♣

Ray arrived barely twenty minutes before the program. He glimpsed Larkin bustling around tending to last minute details. He wound his way to her and tapped her shoulder. She turned with a start.

"Ray!" She smiled brightly.

He presented her with a multitude of fresh-cut daffodils, the last of the season, which he had gathered from the nearby shady and still cool swamp. "Good luck. Will you please give me five minutes after the show?"

Larkin held the daffodils to her face and inhaled the sweet fragrance. "Yes, I'll give you five minutes."

Behind Ray, Robert LaFontaine cleared his throat and sniggered. "Oh, Reynolds, don't you know that roses are what you give the Prima Dona?"

"Larkin is not a Prima Dona. She's an angel. Take flight, my angel."

Before Robert could say anything else, Larkin pointed her finger sharply. "Not a word. Take a seat, both of you."

She accepted the dozen crimson roses Robert had brought and zipped backstage. She found a large container and placed the daffodils in water. Lindsay walked in as Larkin arranged the flowers.

She asked pertly, "Who brought you flowers?"

Larkin set the daffodils down with care and plopped the roses on a table. "Ray and Robert."

"Let me guess." She made a little clucking sound. "Ray picked the daffodils while Robert spent a fortune on the roses."

"Yep."

"Which do you like better?"

266

"Mind your own business. It's show time."

Ray found a seat with the rest of his family near the front of the auditorium. He was pleased to see the show was crisp and lively and admitted in a whisper to his brother, "I'm astonished at Dupree's talent."

Backstage after the show, rather than finding Larkin, Robert found the flowers, his roses half off the table and the daffodils resting in water. "Fuck this!" he raged. He flung the roses across the floor. Then, he got a wicked gleam in his eyes and gave a low sinister chuckle.

Ray pushed through the throng of patrons who were congratulating Larkin on another superb musical presentation. Parents and educators alike were once again amazed at the success of this young woman. She had a knack for finding something for these children to do that matched their skills and abilities and gave them confidence that they could become somebody other than a thug or a welfare mother. Dupree Parks's mother, Estelle Funchess, was among them. The joy in the woman's face said everything in Ray's mind.

Ray reached the two women and somewhat rudely interrupted them. "My five minutes?"

Larkin wagged her head. "Ray, stop being rude, and I'll give you more than five minutes."

"Sorry, but I need to say what I have to say now before the thorn in my flesh shows up."

"Why do you hate Robert so much?"

"He's a two-faced, back stabbing, social-climbing son-of-a-bitch, but I don't wanna talk about him. Please, just tell me you're not in love with him."

"We're *friends*, Ray. I've told him that over and over."

"That's all I needed to hear. I want you to know that the night I woke up in the hospital, I wasn't talking to you. He was standing in the opening in the curtain behind you. I was talking to him. I came to your house to tell you when I got out, but he answered the door."

267

Mouth gaped, eyes hooded as Larkin recalled the *solicitor* who had supposedly come to her house. "How dare he lie to me? He told me it was a solicitor."

"*Fooyay!* Forget him!" Ray snapped. "Larkin, I'm stubborn and short-tempered and sometimes arrogant and too proud. For these faults I apologize. But, damn it, woman, I love you. There. I said it." He punched the air.

Larkin brushed tears from her cheek. "Was it that hard?"

"For me? Yes, because it means I have to let myself be vulnerable again. That takes more courage from me than facing a thousand Latrices. Seeing you with Robert tears my heart out. He was supposed to be my best friend."

As the truth sank in, Larkin whispered, "Oh, now I understand."

Robert appeared in an unwelcome manner as he often did. "What have you done to make her cry this time, Reynolds?" he demanded as he finally found Larkin.

Ray clenched his fists inside his pockets and brushed the velvet ring box. A sly Mona Lisa smile crossed his face and his eyes glinted. Ignoring Robert completely, Ray dropped to one knee and pulled the ring out. "I'm asking her to marry me."

LaFontaine guffawed. "You're proposing to this magnificent lady with that little chip? Oh, my God! That really shows the esteem you have for her." He reached inside his coat and brought out a one karat solitaire with half a karat of chips on either side. "Please, Larkin, consider a much better offer."

"Stop it!" she hissed. "You're causing a scene."

"What do you expect from this buffoon?" By this time, the crowd, including Ray's family, had gathered. "Look. He even brought his joke of an entourage for back up. Oh, Ray, you are a pathetic loser. First, Mia. Now, Larkin."

That does it! The seething rage inside Ray finally boiled over. He closed the ring box in his fist, and with the same fist, punched Robert so hard he fell into the crowd behind him.

"Larkin!" Dr. Fairchild sounded authoritative as she pushed through the crowd. "What is going on?" The principal placed herself between the two men as if they were bickering children. "Backstage looks as if this fight started back there."

"What do you mean?" asked Larkin.

"Your roses are strewn all over the floor, and now these two are acting like children."

LaFontaine stood, rubbing his jaw. It was broken, as were Ray's knuckles, evidenced by immediate swelling. "What do you expect?" he said through clamped-together teeth. "Y'all see this man's temper. Of course, he pitched the roses I bought Larkin. I *will* be pressing assault charges." He added sarcastically, "*Detective.*"

"Go ahead," said Ray. "It was worth it to deck your sorry ass, but the only flowers I touched were the daffodils I picked for the woman I love. Roses might be the right thing socially, but daffodils are Larkin. They're the first flowers to bloom in the spring, indicating old things are passed away and all things have become new. You might know some form of etiquette, but you don't know Larkin."

Bracing his jaw to keep it from hurting, Robert said, "Oh, I do know her. She's First Lady material, exactly what I've been looking for."

"Is that all she is to you, Rob—a political pawn, a token on your arm? Do you love her—the woman—at all? I doubt it." Ray's voice took on a tone he might have used ten years before to reason with a friend, a fraternity brother.

In the back of the crowd, Dupree, out of makeup and costume, poked Lindsay. "What's happening?"

"Oh boy! What kind of family am I mixed up in?" Lindsay said jokingly.

"The best ever," responded Dupree, not getting the joke. "Now, tell me what's going on."

"Okay. Ray proposed. Then, Robert proposed." With each changing scenario, she dipped her head back and forth in a tick-tock motion. "Then, Robert said Ray was a loser and something about Ray's former fiancée. Then, Ray hit Robert. Robert says he's pressing charges. Dr. Fairchild said backstage was a mess. Robert said Ray destroyed the roses he had gotten for Larkin."

"Whoa! That's a lie." Dupree stepped up. "Miss Sloan, don't you trust that liar. Detective Reynolds didn't throw a fit back stage. Mr. LaFontaine did. I saw him. It scared me that you've been dating him 'cause he acted like my stepdaddy. I was afraid he might hurt you like Dwight used to hurt my momma. He's a low-down dog. I bet he's dirty, too. So what if Detective Reynolds hit him?" He gave a who-gives-a-damn shrug. "He probably deserved it. Detective Reynolds wouldn't've done it if he didn't deserve it. I remember Detective Reynolds now. He wudn't a detective when I first saw him, but he saved my life and got shot doing it. He's a hero, not a slime ball."

Larkin wanted to scream, but in spite of her frustration, she stayed calm. "Robert, I have told you many times I don't love you. No, I will *not* marry you." She turned her attention to the other man. "Ray…"

"Really?" said LaFontaine vindictively. "Well, do you want that whacko twin brother of Ray's to go to jail? The only reason I never charged him is because you refused to testify. I could subpoena you and hold you for contempt if you don't comply."

Oh! Dupree is so right about you. If I weren't a lady, I'd give you the bird just like Lindsay. "How dare you?" Larkin spat. "Do you really think you can blackmail me into marrying you? No charge you bring against Raif would ever stand. *Nobody* would testify against him, and you know it." She reared back, fists clenched as if she might also hit the man. "As a matter of fact, I don't recall seeing Ray hit you either. I think I saw you slip on a rose petal and bust your ass!"

270

The crowd burst into applause.

"Yeah." Ray nodded. "I saw that, too. In addition, I'm beginning to wonder how Latrice got out of those shackles she had on. The only person to see her that day was you. Did you slip her a key?"

"What? Are you crazy? I would never," protested LaFontaine. "You know they found a thin piece of wire."

"Yeah, yeah, yeah." Ray rubbed his injured hand with his good one. He continued, "Politicians associated with cop killers and serial killers don't look too good for the White House."

"Do you really want to go there, Ray?" Robert rumbled in a low tone.

"No, but I want you to go away. Why don't you resign and move to Baton Rouge? Go to the capital and run for office. Just get out of my life. *Please.*"

Robert narrowed his eyes to slits. "Well, my dear, I'm sure I can do better than a pitiful Mississippi orphan. Have a good life with Reynolds if that's what you really want, Larkin." LaFontaine shoved past Dupree and stalked off.

Larkin tugged Ray's arm as she called after LaFontaine, "Oh, I will, Robert. Ray, didn't you have something you wanted to give me?"

"I did." Ray pulled Larkin into his arms and kissed her soundly to loud applause from an exuberant audience.

He knelt again and presented the precious ring. "Will you marry me?"

"Absolutely, yes!"

He slipped the ring on her finger and kissed her hand. "When?"

"The next Friday the thirteenth. I think that's November."

"You wanna make me wait that long?"

"I'd like to date a bit." She lowered her voice. "I'll make it worth your while. I promise. I love you, Ray. I have always loved you, even before I knew you, and I always will."

"November thirteenth," he agreed. "That date is set in stone."

With the holiday season fast approaching, Larkin chose unconventional colors for her wedding. The primary color was candlelight white. Larkin's dress itself was a soft creamy color rather than stark white; the bodice, crushed velvet with a rounded neckline and long flowing angel sleeves. It tapered to a fitted waist and a simple A-line satin skirt, encircled by a satin sash. Larkin wore an uncomplicated wreath of baby's breath in her hair which was just as plainly pulled back from her face with ivory combs. Ivory peau de soie pumps completed the ensemble.

Chris, of course, was her matron of honor. Her dress was exactly like Larkin's except that the skirt was black and the sash was crimson, and the skirt was given a bit of elastic since Chris was pregnant. Lindsay Kersh and Audrey van Zandt were her two other bride's maids. Their dresses were the inverse of Chris's with black bodices and ecru skirts and green sashes. The ladies wore either ivory or black peau de soie pumps as their skirts demanded. Sheena Johnson served as Larkin's flower girl and wore an identical dress design as the adults except that it was all white with a shimmering gold sash, and she wore flat black patent leather shoes.

The bride carried a bouquet of crimson poinsettias and white rose buds with a long draping ribbon of gold satin streamers and English ivy. The attendants carried a single long-stemmed crimson rose while Sheena spread crimson and white rose petals in the aisle.

With the wedding being held at seven in the evening, the groom and his attendants wore formal tuxes with tails. Ray's was black with a white ascot and a white rosebud boutonnière. Raif was his brother's best man and wore a black tux with a crimson ascot and boutonnière while the other two groomsmen, Dupree Parks and Brian Baker, wore black tuxes with green ascots and crimson boutonnières. Brian Baker's five-year-old son, Trent, served as the ring bearer and wore a black tux with a black ascot without a boutonnière.

Ray's parents were dressed to the nines as well. Mr. Reynolds wore a simple black tuxedo without tails and a crimson boutonnière, and Mrs. Reynolds sported a crimson satin dress in the same design as the bride's except it was street-length accentuated by a corsage of white rosebuds.

Larkin asked Walter Bertram if he would escort her down the aisle and he wore a tuxedo to match the ring bearer, but he had a crimson rosebud boutonnière. In addition, since Dr. Rona Fairchild had once said that she loved Larkin as if she were her own daughter, Larkin asked if she would sit in her mother's place. Dr. Fairchild gladly accepted the honor and wore an outfit identical to Mrs. Reynolds in pine green.

Charity Chapel was also decorated, not only for the occasion, but also for the upcoming holiday season. Each golden stained-glass window held a hurricane lamp with a single lighted candle inside. The candles and holders alternated between white poinsettias and crimson rosebuds around the base with a crimson candle inside and deep crimson poinsettias and white rosebuds around the base with an ivory candle inside. Behind the pulpit where the pastor, who wore a black clerical robe, stood to perform the ceremony were two candelabra of ivory candles on either side of an ivory arch laced with English ivy and holly with berries. There was a single ivory unity candle for the bride and groom to light in a base of holly. The sanctuary did not contain pews, but the soft crimson velvet chairs against ivory carpet completed the picture.

The ceremony was traditional with tried and true vows being exchanged and I Corinthians 13, along with Ruth's plea to Naomi, being read. After the wedding vows, Ray made a simple statement to Larkin regarding his love for her, to her surprise. "Larkin Cherie Sloan, Reverend Paxton has just reminded us that when all things pass away, three things will remain: faith, hope, and love. Because of you, I have found a true and abiding faith. Because of that faith, I promise never to do anything to cause you to lose faith in me. I will be faithful to you as long as I draw breath. Before I met you, I felt lost and hopeless. You showed me that hope springs eternal. Because of that hope, I promise to always uphold and support you and to give you hope when you feel as if you can't go on. My angel, you are the very definition of love. Until you came into my life, I had no understanding of what love between a man and a woman really was though I had a wonderful example in my parents. You taught me the meaning of true love. Because of that love, I promise to love you unconditionally for all eternity."

Dupree stepped out from among the groomsmen to sing "The Wedding Song," and Lindsay graced the audience with Bette Midler's "The Rose." The only unusual offering of music was that Larkin sang to Ray using Don Francisco's "I Could Never Promise You," as her unique and special vow.

The pastor presented Mr. and Mrs. Raiford Michael Reynolds to a round of applause and the bride and groom's request that the entire congregation repeat "The Lord's Prayer." The reception that followed at the Hyatt Regency was a buffet with dancing and champagne. Once again, Dupree and Lindsay sang several times during the reception with Dupree making the first musical offering, an emotionally charged rendition of Stryper's "Together as One" as Ray and Larkin shared their first dance as husband and wife, a sensual ballroom offering that they had practiced several times to avoid embarrassment. Raif toasted his brother and his bride with glee, and the only unusual occurrence at all was that Audrey van Zandt caught the bouquet. Ray and Raif exchanged glances when recently divorced Walter Bertram put his arm around her.

Ray took Larkin to a secluded mountain resort with a fresh coat of snow on the ground for their honeymoon. As Larkin had promised, she made Ray's wait for their wedding night unforgettable as only a love that is pure and untainted can do.

31
The Truth about Thirteen

The principal introduced the commencement speaker, face aglow with pride. "Ladies and gentlemen, she's one of us, our 1999 valedictorian. She's a fellow educator. She's a published poet, and, now, the author of the bestselling novel, *Lucky Thirteen*. Please, welcome Dr. Larkin Sloan Reynolds."

An obviously pregnant Larkin Sloan Reynolds stepped to the podium to a round of applause. "Wow!" she said as she surveyed the rows of graduates and their supporters. "I cannot believe it has been thirteen years since I was right here in this very auditorium listening to my commencement speaker. Now, here it is May 13, 2012, a spectacular Sunday afternoon, and you are graduating. I am absolutely positive you couldn't care less that today is the thirteenth. You just feel lucky to be graduating. But that is what I want to talk about today—luck and thirteen.

"You have all heard how unlucky the number thirteen is. And, God forbid, should it coincide with a Friday. We have scores of movies telling us what an awful day that is. But why does thirteen have such a bad reputation?" She paused briefly for effect.

"First, Christians associate thirteen with the number present at the Last Supper. Tradition holds that Judas Iscariot was the last to sit at the table, and he is the pinnacle of evil as the man who betrayed Christ.

"In Norse mythology, Odin invited eleven of his friends to a party, which was crashed by Loki, the god of evil and turmoil and mischief. I am sure that party got *lively*." A ripple of laughter sounded from the audience. "Scandinavians believe the number thirteen unlucky due to the twelve mythological demigods being joined by a thirteenth evil one.

"Thirteen can never be divided equally to form groups. It's a prime number. There will always be one unlucky person left over, unloved and unwanted." Larkin put on a sad face.

"Another possibility for poor thirteen's bad name could be that there are thirteen full moons in a year. A woman typically has thirteen periods in a year, and in the past a woman who menstruated during a full moon was considered a witch. However, a woman living in a natural society tends to have her cycle correspond to moon cycles. Nonetheless, witches' covens are associated with having the perfect number of members, thirteen. I know that to be true because I met one once." The memory caused her to breathe deeply.

"In a Tarot deck, the number thirteen is reversed and can be interpreted to portend death. Thirteen reversed is thirty-one. I'm thirty-one. Should I be concerned?" Another ripple of laughter occurred, but slightly softer than before. Laughing about a mythical deity was one thing; death, another.

"As I said before, thirteen plus Friday spell disaster. But why? Well, during the Middle Ages, King Philip IV of France ordered the arrests of Jacques de Molay, the Grand Master of the Knights Templar, supposed guardians of the Holy Grail and other religious artifacts, and sixty of his senior knights on Friday, October 13, 1307. Most of them were tortured and executed, causing their sympathizers to condemn the date as evil. In the eighteenth century, the ship, the *HMS Friday,* was launched on Friday the thirteenth and never seen again.

"Christians and Europeans tend to view thirteen as unlucky, but that is not true for all civilizations. Some cultures revere the number. Even Christians once saw thirteen in a positive light as it was thought the Magi visited Jesus on the thirteenth day of His life, giving rise to the twelve days of Christmas. The Catholic Church still celebrates Epiphany twelve days after Christmas.

"We can thank the Egyptians for developing the first superstition about thirteen, but for them, it was lucky. They believed there were twelve steps on the ladder to eternal life and knowledge. The thirteenth step meant immortality, going through death to eternal life.

"The Sikhs believe that the Guru Navek De Ji gave out food for free. When he got to the thirteenth person, he stopped. The Hindi word for thirteen is Terah, which means yours. The Guru Navek kept saying, 'Yours, yours,' remembering God. And although he had been giving food away, when the money stores were checked, there was more money than before. Also, the Ik Onkar looks like thirteen and means one God. It is the symbol for the unity of God and a central tenet of Sikh religious philosophy.

"In Judaism, thirteen is the age at which a boy matures and celebrates his Bar Mitzvah. How many of you couldn't wait to become a teenager—thirteen?" She looked around the gathering with a knowing expression. "According to the Torah, the sacred writing of Judaism, God has thirteen attributes of mercy.

"In China, the number thirteen is considered lucky. The number one, when placed in the tens place, sounds like 'shi' and means definite in Mandarin. The number three sounds like living or life or birth. Hence, the number thirteen, which is pronounced 'shisan' in Mandarin, means assured growth or definitely vibrant.

"Even in American society, many famous sports figures have pushed their luck and worn number thirteen. In baseball Ozzie Guillen and, um"—She paused then whispered into the mike very fast—"*Alex Rodriguez* have worn it." Many chuckles sounded. "An NBA great who wore thirteen is Wilt Chamberlain. The International Basketball Federation, better known as FIBA, requires a player to wear thirteen. Some well-known basketball players who have worn thirteen in international competition, such as the Olympics, are Tim Duncan, Chris Mullen, and Shaquille O'Neal. In the NHL, Mats Sundin has tempted fate and worn number thirteen. In the world of soccer, my sport, Kristine Lilly and Michael Ballack, a Brit, have been number thirteen. NFL wide receiver for the New York Jets, Don Maynard, wore number thirteen; NFL quarterback, Kurt Warner donned the number thirteen for both the Rams and the Cardinals, and even got a Super Bowl victory with the Rams as number thirteen; but probably the most well known sports number thirteen was NFL Hall of Famer, quarterback, Dan Marino for the Miami Dolphins." She cocked an eyebrow and delivered as lopsided grin. "Well, maybe if he had worn twelve, he would have won that Super Bowl ring rather than breaking almost every record there ever was at the time." A smattering of applause greeted Larkin's reference to Dan Marino.

"Italians consider thirteen lucky, and old-school tattoo cultures regard it as lucky." She stuck her ankle into the open to display and intricate tattoo of the number thirteen.

"Colgate University epitomizes thirteen's good fortune. The college was founded in 1819—too bad it wasn't 1813—by thirteen men with thirteen dollars, thirteen prayers, and thirteen articles. As a matter of fact, the campus address is 13 Oak Drive, Hamilton, New York.

"In addition, the number thirteen must have had the utmost importance to our founding fathers. I mean, there were thirteen original colonies, and there are still thirteen stripes on our flag. The Great Seal of the United States is *covered* with the number thirteen. Some people say that is because so many of our founding fathers were Free Masons, and there are thirteen levels of Free Masonry. Very few achieve the thirteenth level of Grand Master, so that part could be true. They might have considered thirteen to be achieving the superlative.

"Let's look at the Great Seal to see how important thirteen is to it. If you have a dollar, take it out, and let's look at the Great Seal on the back." Larkin retrieved her purse from beneath the podium and took out a dollar bill, giving any who wanted to get a dollar out time to do so.

"Okay. If you don't have a dollar, but are sitting close enough to see one, look at this with me, and please check out a dollar closely when you leave. Let's first examine the right side with the eagle on it. Let's work from top to bottom. Count the stars above the eagle's head." She paused. "There are thirteen. Next, count the letters in *E Pluribus Unum.*" Larkin waited a moment before continuing. "Again, there are thirteen. Now, let's examine the shield. I think if you can see well enough to count the horizontal stripes, there are thirteen. I *know* there are thirteen vertical stripes. Now, count the leaves on the olive branch and the arrows in each talon. There are thirteen leaves and thirteen arrows.

"Now, let's look at the other side. *Annuit Coeptus* contains thirteen letters. Last, there are thirteen levels of the pyramid, the thirteenth being the top or the eye. This leads back to the Free Masons as the pyramid and the eye as the superlative being their symbols and the laying of the foundation of our country. This also takes us back to the Egyptians and the first superstition about thirteen with the highest level being immortality. Where are the Great Pyramids found?" Larkin laid down the dollar. "Egypt."

"So, I guess you have to draw your own conclusions about thirteen. There are too many conflicting opinions, but, hey, what cop do you know that would turn down a baker's dozen, thirteen, of doughnuts? Let me get a personal opinion. My husband is a cop. Ray, honey, which would you rather have, twelve or thirteen?"

From the back of the auditorium Ray shouted, "Thirteen, Angel. You know it." The audience roared with laughter.

After the humor, Larkin went on, "Just to let you know, Ray was thirty-one when we married. Don't you dare say marriage is equivalent to death!" She shook her head with